Death by
Chocolate Lab

Death by Chocolate Lab

Bethany Blake

KENSINGTON BOOKS

http://www.kensingtonbooks.com

KENSINGTON BOOKS are published by

Kensington Publishing Corp.
119 West 40th Street
New York, NY 10018

All Kensington titles, imprints, and distributed lines are available at special quantity discounts for bulk purchases for sales promotion, premiums, fund-raising, educational, or institutional use. Special book excerpts or customized printings can also be created to fit specific needs. For details, write or phone the office of the Kensington Special Sales Manager: Kensington Publishing Corp., 119 West 40th Street, New York, NY, 10018. Attn. Special Sales Department. Phone: 1-800-221-2647.

Kensington and the K logo Reg. U.S. Pat. & TM Off.

ISBN-13: 978-1-4967-0738-3
ISBN-10: 1-4967-0738-9
First Kensington Mass Market Edition: March 2017

eISBN-13: 978-1-4967-0739-0
eISBN-10: 1-4967-0739-7
First Kensington Electronic Edition: March 2017

10 9 8 7 6 5 4 3 2 1

Printed in the United States of America

Death by Chocolate Lab

Chapter 1

I was walking three powerful rottweilers, but I was pretty sure they weren't really to blame for my being pulled down the street like a drunken water-skier behind an erratic boat.

No, the dog at fault was a three-pound, one-eared Chihuahua with bulging eyes and a severe overbite—which he was applying, every few steps, to the bigger dogs' hind legs.

"Artie, enough," I chided him, awkwardly bending to scoop up the troublemaker. Immediately, the dogs ahead of me settled down. Straightening, I tucked Artie into a tote bag that advertised my business, Daphne Templeton's Lucky Paws Pet Sitting, and reminded him yet again, "Who's going to adopt you if you always misbehave in public?"

Artie, the most impudent dog I'd ever fostered, didn't respond. He merely poked his always trembling head out of the canvas tote, his brown eyes gleaming, like he'd been scheming for a ride all along.

"I hate to tell you, but *nobody* is going to adopt Artie," my sister, Piper, noted, catching up to us. She was walking with my basset hound sidekick, Socrates, who considered himself above group walks and never hurried. He shambled along at Piper's side, his droopy, solemn eyes fixed on something in the distance. He might've been interested in the dark clouds gathering ahead—a storm was definitely brewing—but I suspected that his real focus was inward. Socrates wasn't the type of dog who obsessed about where his next treat was coming from. I was convinced that he dealt with more profound issues.

"You have to admit, the Chihuahua is a mess," Piper added, glancing down at Artie, who had a long string of drool trailing from his mouth. His overbite was *really* bad. A shelf of tiny, crooked teeth completely obscured his weak chin. "A big, hot, steaming mess!"

"That's not exactly medical terminology, *Dr.* Templeton," I said. "I don't think they taught you that in veterinary school."

Piper, who wore her lab coat, because she needed to return to her practice after the walk, merely shrugged. "I just call 'em like I see them."

She was probably right, but I refused to give up on the prospect of a happy ending for Artie's so far sad story of abandonment by no fewer than three owners. Nobody could even say how he'd lost his ear. Shouldn't someone have known *that*?

I looked sideways at Piper. "We could . . ."

"Nope."

I'd known Piper wouldn't agree to let Artie stay with us. She—probably wisely—kept a strict limit on the number of strays and rescues I brought home at any given time, and allowed me to have only one permanent furry family member. Socrates. Since she let me live rent free in her beautifully restored 1860s farmhouse, I couldn't really argue.

I gave Artie an apologetic look, promising, "Somebody will give you a real home." Then I tightened my grip on the three leather leads in my hand. We were approaching a corner, and while traffic in the village of Sylvan Creek, Pennsylvania—a quaint lakeside community in the heart of the Pocono Mountains—wasn't exactly heavy this hot, sticky August evening, I needed to make sure the bigger dogs were returned safely to their owner, Virginia Lockhart. Virginia, a particularly aggressive attorney, would no doubt sue me for the few things I had and would shut down Lucky Paws if one of her prize animals got so much as a scratch. Macduff, Iago, and Hamlet were champion agility dogs, worth thousands of dollars each, and I carried minimal insurance.

Shaking off my concerns, I smiled down at Artie again. "He's so ugly, he's cute, don't you think?"

"I think he's adorable," someone said in a cheerful, heavily accented feminine voice.

Piper and Socrates stopped walking, and I reined in the rottweilers, putting them in a sit.

"Hey, Giulia," I said, turning to see Giulia Alberti watching us from the doorway of her shop, Espresso Pronto, the best place to get coffee in Sylvan Creek. Giulia was a native of La Spezia, Italy, and imported almost everything she sold in her Tuscan-inspired café.

I nearly started drooling, thinking about the almond-and-lemon, white chocolate–dipped biscotti she kept in a glass jar on the marble counter.

Giulia, meanwhile, was drawn to something—or someone—else.

"Who is this sweet little creature?" she asked, smiling

as she came out to join us on the sidewalk. She first bent over to set down a big bowl of water for the rottweilers, who gave her a grateful look before jostling to lap it up noisily. Then she allowed Artie to sniff her long, delicate fingers, one of which was conspicuously bare.

Would she and hotheaded banker Christian Clarke ever really tie the knot?

I couldn't ask, although everybody in Sylvan Creek wanted to know the answer to *that* question. Especially a waiting list of single guys.

Artie definitely seemed smitten with Giulia, too. He wriggled in delight just to be in her presence.

"You are quite the little man, aren't you?" Giulia teased, chuckling and tickling Artie's recessive chin. "Do you want a drink, too?"

Artie didn't seem parched. In fact, his drool problem worsened.

Typical man, little or not.

I glanced down at Socrates, who yawned and shook his large, wrinkled head, as if base attraction—like walking in dog packs—was also beneath him. And he certainly wasn't going to drink from a communal bowl.

Then I gave Piper a smug look that said, "See? Somebody already thinks Artie's cute!"

But my sister didn't meet my gaze. She was frowning at Giulia, who looked gorgeous, even though she was wearing a baker's apron over a basic black T-shirt and had her long dark hair pulled into a simple ponytail. Plain but large silver hoops dangled from her ears.

I had a sneaking suspicion that Piper was wondering if the rumors about her ex-boyfriend, egomaniacal dog trainer Steve Beamus, and Giulia were true. According to the town's gossip mill, Steve and Giulia had been linked romantically at one point. Maybe even while Steve had been seeing Piper.

As if realizing that she was being borderline rude, Piper finally spoke up. "Are you all set for tomorrow, Giulia? Do you need anything from me?"

"No, no," she assured my sister, shaking her head. She looked up from petting Artie. "I will set up tonight and will bring a generator for the truck. I do not even need your power." She cocked her head, so her earrings swung. "Do you think anyone will want hot drinks? I plan to serve freshly made lemonade with mint, iced coffee with sweet cream and sugar—and, of course, lots of cold, fresh water for the dogs."

"What's going on?" I asked, looking between the two women. "What am I missing?"

"Giulia, like some other local merchants, has agreed to be a vendor at this weekend's event," Piper said. "People and pets will need to eat and drink. Both days will be long and, most likely, hot."

My continued cluelessness must have been obvious. Piper lowered her wire-rimmed glasses, the better to look askance at me. "Did you really forget that we're hosting the agility trial at Winding Hill this weekend? It's a pretty big deal. Handlers are coming in from as far as Philadelphia!"

I *had* totally forgotten that Piper had offered a local agility club the use of her farm for a trial. "Um, of course I remembered that," I fibbed.

She clearly didn't believe me. She shook her head and sighed. "How do you run a business? Do you even have a calendar?"

"Yes, I have one of those!" I informed her.

I really did. It was dated 2011, and it was somewhere on the floor of the 1975 VW bus that served as my office, probably buried under a lot of burrito wrappers. I had a slight addiction to the vegetarian special at a cute little hole-in-the-wall shop called Burrito Casita.

"What is this *agility*, anyway?" Giulia asked, crossing her arms. "Something different from a dog show? Because I am looking forward to seeing puppies with fancy hairdos."

Artie seemed bereft over the loss of Giulia's attention, and the rottweilers were getting restless, so I piped up, the better to keep things short. My scientifically minded sister tended toward long-winded, technical explanations. "It's like an obstacle course competition for animals," I explained. "Handlers guide their dogs through tunnels, over fences, and across seesaws and high boards. Dogs that complete the courses quickly and without messing up win prizes. No fancy haircuts required, I'm afraid."

"It's not that simple," Piper said, correcting me. Of course, she knew quite a bit about the sport, having dated Steve, who taught classes in agility at his nationally known Blue Ribbon K9 Academy. "The courses are very complex, and the stakes can be surprisingly high. Dogs that advance to the national level can take home prizes of up to ten thousand dollars. And, of course, there are bragging rights for handlers whose animals win. Those are probably more important than ribbons, trophies, or even purses."

Giulia didn't seem to know what to make of that. Maybe dog sports and dog shows weren't such a big deal in Italy. Or, although her English was pretty good, maybe she didn't understand the dual meaning of *purses* and thought Piper was talking about handbags.

If she was skeptical about the value of competition itself on a metaphysical level, I had to agree. As the Chinese philosopher Lao Tzu once said, "When you are content to be simply yourself and don't compare or compete, everybody will respect you."

Amen to that.

Or maybe I was just too lazy for sports, dog or otherwise.

I glanced at my type A sibling, wondering yet again how sisters—even ones who were nearly six years apart—could be so different.

Piper and I were both doctors, but she made tons of money treating animals, while my Ph.D. in philosophy had paid off in enlightened thought, not cash. Which was fine with me.

Aside from both of us having slight frames, Piper and I looked different, too.

My older sister had aquiline features and stick-straight chestnut hair, which she usually pulled back in a tidy bun. Although she wasn't even forty, when not in her lab coat, she dressed like a schoolmarm in sweater sets and "slacks." And her intelligent brown eyes always seemed to be judging the world, which usually failed to meet her standards.

I, meanwhile, had long, thick, uncontrollably curly dirty-blond hair, which I preferred to let run wild. Sweater sets made me shudder. I liked to be comfortable in worn jeans and T-shirts that advertised a local rescue or my business. My eyes were a weird shade of greenish gray, and I was pretty sure if my sister had been blessed with the freckles scattered around my small, slightly upturned nose, she would've hired a plastic surgeon to arrange them in neater rows.

"Why are you staring at me?" Piper asked, so I realized I'd been studying her for too long. She nodded toward the rottweilers, who were lying down, post drink, but obviously restless. "Those guys are getting antsy, and I need to get back to my practice." The wind picked up, and she looked at the sky, her brow furrowing with concern. "We'd better keep moving."

"Yeah, I don't need *more* wet-dog smell in my van," I agreed, giving the rotties the go-ahead to stand up. I turned to Giulia. "I hope you bring biscotti tomorrow. And some of those Italian sodas!"

"Oh, I forgot to mention the sodas—which will be there," she said, grinning and offering Artie one last tickle. He nearly fell out of the tote, and I made a mental note to pester Giulia about adopting him. Nearly every business in the pet-friendly town of Sylvan Creek had a shop dog or cat, and Artie would make a great ambassador. Except for the drooling, of course. Then Giulia bent to pat Socrates on the head, but he gave her such a dead-level, discouraging stare that she thought the better of it and straightened, asking Piper and me, "Can I get you some espresso to go?" She glanced at the sky. "Or perhaps you would like to wait out the storm inside, over some gelato? I made dark chocolate today."

I really wanted some of Giulia's rich, authentic Italian version of ice cream, but I needed to return the rottweilers. "Some other time," I promised. "Thanks for the offer, though. And for the bowl of water." ·

Giulia smiled at my sister. "Piper?"

"No, I have to go, too," she said. Her tone was polite, but less than enthusiastic. "Thanks, though."

"Any time, *bellas*," Giulia said. She turned to go back into her little nook of a store, which looked very inviting, with its terra-cotta-colored walls and its dark wooden tables clustered on a rustic stone floor. Looking over her shoulder, she smiled and waggled her red-tipped fingers. "Ciao!"

"Ciao," Piper said glumly.

"You should never say that word again," I suggested

as our little party of pets and people resumed making its way down Market Street, the main thoroughfare through town. I was a small-town girl at heart, and I never got tired of looking at the historic architecture. Sylvan Creek was especially pretty at the height of summer. Nearly every storefront boasted planters and hanging baskets that overflowed with brightly colored flowers. As Piper, the dogs, and I strolled under the balcony of the Sylvan Creek Inn, which dated back to the early 1800s, the hotel's gas lamps flickered on. "'Ciao' just doesn't sound right coming from you," I added. "You're not a 'ciao' kind of girl."

Piper didn't reply. I suspected she knew that I was right.

All at once, Sylvan Creek's signature antique street-lamps flickered to life, too. It was getting that gloomy. Several shops also had their lights on, including two of my favorite haunts: a pet store called Fetch! which stocked locally made organic treats and unusual toys, and a tiny specialty bookstore called the Philosopher's Tome, which had lots of cozy nooks where a person who should have been drumming up clientele for a pet-sitting business could get lost reading about everything from Aristotle to Zeno.

The stores were owned by Tom and Tessie Flinch-baugh, a middle-aged married couple. Given that I was usually the only customer in Tom's bookshop, I was pretty sure Tessie's busy pet emporium kept her husband's store afloat.

As we passed by the Philosopher's Tome, I saw Tom sitting on a worn, overstuffed velvet-covered chair in a turret that was one of my favorite spots in the converted Victorian house. When he saw us passing by, he rose, shoved up one of the windows with effort, and leaned out. "I got a new . . . meaning old . . . copy of

Seneca's *Letters from a Stoic*," he informed me. The wind rumpled his graying hair and made his rosy cheeks even pinker. "Stop by when you want to check it out."

I loved that Tom never made me *buy* anything. When he said "check it out," he wasn't suggesting that I just look at the volume. He frequently let me borrow books, like he was running a library. In return, I always volunteered to watch his and Tessie's ancient poodle, Marzipan, for free. But the truth was, the Flinch-baughs didn't go out much and had never vacationed, that I knew of.

"Thanks, Tom," I said. "I'll be in."

"Don't forget that Marzipan has an appointment with me Monday," Piper added.

Tom didn't reply. He just nodded, hurrying to close the window against the coming storm. In the distance, the first streak of lightning crossed the sky. Socrates and Artie seemed unconcerned—well, Artie shivered constantly, so it was hard to tell if he was nervous—but big, supposedly tough Macduff, Hamlet, and Iago flinched.

If any of the trio—especially the pack leader, Macduff—ever really bolted, I'd be in serious trouble, so I forced myself to stay calm. Animals always fed on human emotions. And there really was no reason to panic. My van was half a block away. At least, I was pretty sure I'd parked my distinctive, flower power–pink VW in a space obscured by a huge, shiny green pickup truck.

"Will Tessie be selling dog stuff at the trial?" I asked, waving to the proprietor of Fetch! who was kneeling in the display window, tying a cheerful summery bandanna around the neck of the shop's mascot, a life-size plush Irish wolfhound called Shamrock. Although I didn't think Tessie Flinchbaugh was more than fifty, like her husband, she appeared older. She was stout, with silver-streaked hair, and had a penchant for wearing shirts that featured seasonal embroidery. She had sunflowers on that day. I saw them when she waved back at us. As Piper and I moved past the store, I returned my attention to my sister. "You said there are other vendors coming. And it seems like dog people would like her high-end merchandise."

"Yes, Tessie'll have a tent," Piper said. She gave me a rare look of approval. "I'm impressed by your business acumen." Then she arched her eyebrows. "I'm assuming you plan to market Lucky Paws, too? Perhaps even had some promotional materials made? Such as tennis balls with your logo on them? Frisbees? Something like that?"

I hadn't even remembered the event, so obviously I hadn't done that. Nevertheless, I said, "Oh, I'll be promoting. Don't you worry about that."

"Good," Piper said, stopping in front of her office, which was located in one of Sylvan Creek's oldest buildings. Of course, my sister had turned the once eyesore into the prettiest structure on the street. Templeton Animal Hospital's ancient wooden siding was painted a lovely shade of pale blue-green, which contrasted nicely with the crisp white trim. Each window featured a box filled with pink, red, and purple flowers, which I was incapable of identifying by name. The door was a welcoming sunny shade of yellow. "Maybe someday you'll be able to pay me rent for the room you've squatted in at the farm," Piper added.

Like I needed *that* reminder again. I knew I was a freeloader, but I didn't see how it was such a bad thing. Piper could never use all the space she had, and who had kept her company since Steve Beamus had ended things in his cold, callous, obnoxious way?

I didn't bother pointing those things out. Arguing with Piper was usually futile. Instead, I assured her, "Business is about to take off. Just you watch!"

As if on cue, lightning struck again, and business really did "take off"—in the form of three rottweilers who tore free of my grasp, sending me sprawling on my butt as they ran pell-mell down the street.

Poor Artie didn't even yelp when the tote went flying, too.

How bad had his life been if he just rolled with punishment like that?

"I've got Artie," Piper promised. Out of the corner of my eye, I saw her and Socrates move to aid the Chihuahua. "You get the runaways."

I scrambled to my feet, fighting the urge to run after the dogs. I knew that chasing scared animals would only make matters worse. And I was pretty sure Virginia Lockhart would not only sue me, but would also *kill* me if anything happened to *all three* of her prizewinners. She was that kind of lady. I believed that she was fond of the rotties but *really* loved the glory they brought her.

"Come!" I called to Macduff, Hamlet, and Iago. "Come!"

Before the dogs even had a chance to respond, though, someone appeared seemingly out of nowhere.

A tall, imposing, *despicable* guy, who somehow managed to block all three dogs' retreat, then stop them in their tracks with an ear-piercing wolf whistle and the strange guttural command "Hold, enough!"

Chapter 2

"You really shouldn't be walking dogs you can't control," Steve Beamus informed me in his know-it-all way. He was escorting Macduff into my van with a hearty pat to the dog's rump, but he managed to look me up and down. I didn't like the way he smiled crookedly when he added, "You can't weigh more than ninety pounds soaking wet."

Ugh.

Had he just leered at me?

What had Piper ever seen in him?

I mean, Steve was handsome enough, if your taste ran toward Sears catalog models. He had even features and thick fair hair that was somehow remaining under control even in the developing gale, while my curls were repeatedly smacking me in the face, like I was in a Three Stooges routine gone horribly awry.

"I normally don't have any trouble with these dogs," I said, guiding first Hamlet, then Iago into the VW, too. Giving them each a scratch on their oversize, silky black-and-tan heads, I dared to release their leads. "They just got spooked by the storm."

Of course, thunder had to rumble right then, and

Hamlet nearly jumped back out of the VW bus. I caught his thick leather collar just in time, but he weighed well over one hundred pounds and practically bowled me over. "Easy, Hammie," I urged, pushing him back into the van and getting slobber on my T-shirt when he butted his big skull against my chest. "It's just a little storm!"

"No offense, but maybe you're just too petite to handle these big boys," Steve said.

The comment was offensive and yet borderline flirtatious, too. I turned to see that Steve's lips—which my sister had kissed—were twisted up in a smirk.

Yuck. I'd rather be covered in dog saliva than touch his mouth.

And speaking of Piper . . . The moment I got Hamlet settled down, I glanced around.

Where the heck were she, Socrates, and Artie? They had certainly beaten a hasty retreat.

Then again, I couldn't really blame Piper for avoiding her ex. *I* wanted to be free of him, and I'd never even dated him.

Still, he had helped me, and I wanted to be gracious. As he closed the van's side door, giving it a self-satisfied pat—like he was Superman and had saved all of Metropolis—I said, "Thanks for the assist."

Steve shrugged with mock humility. "It was just fortunate timing. I was about to leave, after hanging around for a half hour. If you and Piper hadn't *finally* shown up, I would've been gone." He nodded, gesturing past me, over my shoulder. "Axis doesn't like sitting in the truck for too long. He gets restless."

Turning around, I finally realized that the big forest-green pickup that was parked next to my vehicle was Steve's. I hadn't even noticed the professionally applied gold seal on the door, which advertised Blue Ribbon K9 Academy.

Not that I was ashamed of my ride, but I couldn't help comparing Steve's logo to the one on my van. My friend Moxie Bloom had insisted she could paint a cute puppy and do the lettering, but while Moxie was artistic, she'd obviously overestimated her talents when it came to painting large scale on metal. The misshapen dog was often mistaken for an equally misshapen pony, and the airbrushed, bulbous letters looked like they belonged on a subway car or highway underpass.

Lightning flashed again, even closer, momentarily illuminating a face that was peering at me from the window behind the truck's driver's seat. I recognized Steve's prized agility *and* breed champion, a pedigreed chocolate Labrador retriever with the long-winded name Colebrook's Axis Hero-of-the-Day.

When Piper had dated Steve, I'd enjoyed annoying him by referring to the sweet-faced, good-tempered dog as Cookie Puss.

"Hey, Cookie!" I said, going up on tippy toes, the better to peer through the glass. I assumed the Lab, who had stood up on the seat, his tail wagging, would be competing at the upcoming trial and said, "See you tomorrow, I guess!"

Just then, the rain, which had been barely holding off, started to come down, and I turned back around to find Steve scowling at me for using the nickname. And someone else had joined us, too. A much more welcome person, who was accompanied by Socrates and had the tote bag containing Artie slung over his shoulder.

I looked between the two guys, and it suddenly struck me that neither one of them really should've been standing in front of my sister's clinic on a stormy evening, after the hospital was technically closed. And although we were all starting to get soaked, I couldn't help frowning and asking a question aimed at both men.

"What in the world are you *doing here*, exactly?"

Chapter 3

"I guess Piper didn't want to see Steve, huh?" I ventured after Socrates, Artie, and the guy I sometimes dated, Dylan Taggart, had all taken refuge in the VW, out of the rain, which was hammering the roof of the van. Fortunately, the rottweilers had settled down now that they were out of the wind and lightning, because there was no way my faulty windshield wipers could handle the buckets coming down. We were stuck in the parking spot for at least a few minutes. I turned to Dylan, who was sharing the front seat with a clearly displeased Socrates. Actually, Dylan didn't look too happy, either, to have a wet basset hound right under his nose. "Is that why she sent you out with the dogs?" I asked. "To avoid Steve?"

Dylan, who was a vet tech with my sister's practice, shrugged in his mellow fashion. "I don't know, Daph. I probably shouldn't gossip about my boss."

I raised a skeptical eyebrow. "Since when?"

Dylan laughed, revealing even white teeth. He was handsome in a hippie-surfer way, with a lanky, lean but muscular build, a blond ponytail, and a slight tan, which managed to outlast the worst Pennsylvania winters, probably because he'd soaked up a lot of sun during three years of wandering in Hawaii. Piper was forever threatening to fire him for wearing board shorts under his lab coat.

"Seriously, Dylan," I said. "Was Piper avoiding Steve? And why was he—obviously—here to see her?" Less than two months before, Steve Beamus had shattered my sister's heart by unceremoniously dumping her via *text message.* She had never made an outward show of being upset—Piper didn't like to exhibit weakness— but I knew she'd been really hurt. I stared hard into Dylan's light blue eyes, pressing him for answers. "What did that jerk want?"

Dylan merely grinned. "I don't know, Daph! Piper doesn't talk about her love life with me. She *directs* me." He made a stern Piper-esque face, and although he might not have approved of gossiping about his boss, he wasn't above mimicking her. "Run that urine test, Dylan! Vaccinate the cat in room three! Look for worms in that specimen!"

Socrates and I both reared back, and I made a face. "*You* have to do that? Look for worms?"

Dylan kept smiling. "Did you really think Piper handles those duties? I do all the dirty work."

"I guess I thought somebody anonymous in a distant lab tested the specimens," I said, studying Dylan. It might take me a while to get some unpleasant images out of my brain. Then again, I was a pet sitter. I might not get my hands *that* dirty, but I'd scooped my share of poop. "Getting back to Steve . . ."

"He probably just came to apologize," Dylan said, shifting on the seat. Socrates, I noted, was somehow managing to take up more than his share of worn fabric and sprung springs, so the human was practically pressed against the window. "I don't know why you're making such a big deal out of this."

I felt my eyes grow wide. "What do you mean, Steve needed to apologize? Are you telling me they had a fight? Because I didn't know they even talked anymore."

Dylan opened his mouth, but he didn't say anything. He'd clearly already said more than he'd intended.

I narrowed my eyes, demanding answers. "When? What did they argue about?"

Dylan sighed. "That is my cue to go." The rain had let up, and he reached for the door handle, which might or might not work. Then he hesitated. "I almost forgot why I *volunteered* to bring the dogs out to you. . . ." He craned his neck to look past Socrates to the backseat, where Artie was waiting patiently in the tote, his eyes bulging extra large. "That *is* a dog, right?"

Socrates made a snuffling noise that sounded suspiciously like laughter.

"Yes, that's a dog, and you know it!" I said, defending Artie. "And what did you want?"

I wasn't sure how I felt about Dylan "volunteering" to see me. We had an unusual relationship, because we liked each other, but we disliked commitment and prized our freedom. If I were the kind of person who posted about my relationships on social media, I definitely would list our status as "complicated." I was not that kind of person, though.

"I'm playing a set at the Lakeside next week," he said. "I thought you might want to come. I wrote some new stuff."

It wasn't clear if he was asking me on a date or just trying to fill seats at Sylvan Creek's only "pub," which was really just a wooden shack, barely balanced on a rickety pier that looked like it was about to sink into

Lake Wallapawakee. Regardless, on Fridays, Saturdays, and Open Mic Mondays, locals and tourists alike jockeyed for prime spots around tables made from old wooden barrels, to sit under the twinkle lights, eat beer-battered fish or crabs delivered daily from Baltimore, and enjoy the water views. I probably would have made an appearance even if Dylan hadn't invited me.

"I'll see if Moxie wants to come," I said. Dylan might've been suggesting a date, but I didn't want to sit alone while he was onstage, playing guitar. "She hates folk music, but she likes to crack crabs."

Dylan grinned again. "Sounds good."

The rain had dwindled to a drizzle, and I really needed to deposit the dozing rottweiler triplets at Virginia Lockhart's McMansion before returning to Winding Hill, so I dropped a hint by turning the key in the ignition and resuscitating the VW. It was always a happy surprise when the engine sputtered to life. "See you then."

"I'll be at the agility trial tomorrow, too," Dylan said, opening the door. Immediately, Socrates seemed to spread out even wider on the seat, forcing Dylan to put one foot on the pavement. "In case there's an animal emergency, you know?" he added, leaning back into the van. "It's supposed to get really hot."

I turned on the windshield wipers and was pleased to discover that they were also working that night. And when they cleared the glass, so I could see outside, I sucked in a sharp breath, because walking right past me was quite possibly the most handsome man I'd ever seen, not counting guys on movie screens.

I glimpsed him for only a second, but he looked right at me, too, and there was something about how his dark hair fell over his forehead, and the set of his jaw, and the way he carried himself. . . .

Easy, there, Daphne!

The whole thing was over in an instant, and I turned back to discover that Dylan was still halfway inside the van—leaning closer, right past a disgruntled Socrates, as if the guy I dated now and then might want a *kiss good night.*

Chapter 4

The worst of the storm might have passed quickly, but a light rain lingered on until nearly 11:00 p.m. As I stood at my bedroom's open window, enjoying a cool breeze while I called my friend Moxie, I could still see lightning flickering far off to the east.

When the faint sound of thunder faded away, I was surprised to hear a different rumbling noise, caused by tires on gravel. Leaning out the second-story window, I looked down the unpaved road that gave Winding Hill Farm its name and saw headlights headed in our direction.

I glanced down at Socrates, who was ostensibly asleep on his dog bed—yet managing with one of his big paws to ward off Artie's repeated stealthy attempts to join him. The Chihuahua was quiet, though, and not reacting to the sound of the approaching car. I made a mental note to let Giulia know that Artie didn't get yappy about noises at night.

"Are you there?" Moxie asked, interrupting my thoughts. "Hello? Daph?" She sounded impatient. "Did you butt dial me or something?"

"Oh, sorry," I said, apologizing, my eyes trained

again on the approaching vehicle. "I was just watching this car that's coming up the road—which, as you know, dead-ends at the farm."

"Do you think Piper invited somebody over?" Moxie asked, clearly intrigued. "Because I've never known her to stay up past ten thirty!"

My sensible sibling was a stickler about her own bedtime. She liked to get a solid eight hours of slumber, while I slept and usually woke when the mood struck.

"I'm pretty sure Piper's not having a party," I said. "She's hosting this dog club's agility trial tomorrow, and it starts early. Now that the rain has finally ended, one of the vendors is probably coming to set up. Or maybe somebody's delivering the obstacles and equipment."

I was just wondering who might be in charge of creating the actual courses when the vehicle drew close enough for me to identify it as a truck. A familiar pickup, with gold lettering that glittered on the front door when the driver parked under a light near the barn.

I kind of forgot about Moxie again and grumbled, "Really? Steve Beamus? *Again?*"

"What did you just say?" Moxie was really interested at that point. I could picture her in the turret of her tiny attic apartment above the Philosopher's Tome, her green eyes wide as she gnawed on a brightly painted fingernail, waiting for the gossip. Moxie, owner of Sylvan Creek's unique hair salon, Spa and Paw—which served humans *and* had a cute room where pets could get prettied up, too—was a key cog in the local rumor mill. "Steve Beamus is there?"

"Yes," I confirmed, somewhat distracted. Steve was unloading a large, red retractable tunnel from a trailer hitched to the back of his pickup. The truck bed was also filled with gear. He had a big job ahead of him, if he was working alone, as it appeared. "I should've known nobody else around here would have the equipment to create an AKC-standard course," I noted absently. "It probably had to be Steve."

"I have no idea what you're talking about," Moxie said. "Just tell me, are he and Piper back together or not?"

"No!" I said that firmly, then added, with less certainty, "At least, I don't think so. . . ."

I changed my tune because as I watched, Piper—who'd silently slipped out of the house—walked across the lawn that separated the farmhouse from the barn and handed Steve a thermos.

Coffee? For that creep?

The moon had emerged from behind the clouds, and Steve's white teeth gleamed as he smiled and accepted the drink.

Piper's back was to me, so I couldn't see her expression.

"What's going on?" Moxie asked. "What's happening?"

"Piper and Steve are talking," I said quietly, although they were well out of earshot. "Steve was unloading stuff from his truck for the dog thing, and Piper brought him something to drink. Now they're chatting away."

"He's so conceited and thoughtless," Moxie said. Of course, thanks to me—and lots of other people in town—she knew all about the Steve and Piper breakup saga. It had been pretty big news in Sylvan Creek for a while. "I hope she's not falling for him again."

"I don't think so," I said, frowning. In less than a minute, Piper's and Steve's body language had changed. Steve's hands were in his pockets, and he shrugged, then turned his face away, like he was dismissing my sister, while she crossed her arms defensively. They exchanged a few more words, then Piper tossed up her hands, turned on her heel, and stormed away.

"Nope," I told Moxie, with relief. Downstairs, the door slammed, so I knew my sister was inside again. "I would say Piper looked closer to killing than kissing Steve."

"I'm surprised *somebody* didn't kill him a long time ago," Moxie noted. "He has a way of rubbing people the wrong way." There was a pause; then she added, "Yet he never lacks for girlfriends. Ever."

I'd known Moxie since kindergarten, and I thought she sounded funny—like maybe *she'd* been involved with Steve at some point.

But I would've known about that, right?

"Anyway," Moxie continued, sounding like her usual self again, "Piper's cool, for somebody who wears matchy sweaters. She can do way better."

"Yeah, she can," I agreed, pulling a curtain across the window so I could focus on my conversation. I didn't need to watch Steve finish his task.

"Um, what did you call about?" Moxie prompted.

"Jeez, I've kind of forgotten," I admitted. In fact, it took me a second to remember why I was on the phone. Then I recalled how Dylan and I had parted— awkwardly—and said, "I wanted to know what you're doing Monday night."

"That depends on what you're about to suggest," Moxie said. "I may be busy . . . or I may not."

I had a feeling she would opt for busy when I extended my invitation, but I tried, anyhow. "Dylan's playing at the Lakeside," I said. "Do you want to go?"

I could practically hear Moxie making a face. "You

know I hate acoustic folk music! When's he going to start riding the European avant-garde wave?"

"Um . . . given that he's not European or very avant-garde, probably never," I said. "And his music is good. You know it."

Dylan really was a talented musician. If he had more ambition, he probably could make a decent living as a songwriter or a performer, even. He had charisma. I would've ended up kissing him that evening if a certain basset hound, now snoring but still managing to force Artie to sleep on a pair of soft flannel pajamas I'd left on the floor, hadn't stuck his big muzzle in between us. . . .

I shook off the memory of Dylan's lips nearly brushing mine.

"Are you coming or not?" I asked Moxie. Before she could say no, I added, "I'm buying the beers."

That was all you could get at the Lakeside. American brewed beers, like Budweiser, or the house wine, which came out of big boxes that the owner, Harry Popple, didn't even bother hiding behind the bar.

The deal was enough to tempt Moxie, though. "Okay," she agreed, but with clear reluctance. "I'll meet you there." There was another brief silence. "Are you and Dylan . . . ?"

"Good night," I said quickly, before I had to explain a relationship that I didn't fully understand. "See you Monday. Around eight."

I signed off without waiting for her to reply. Then, stepping over a small pile of snoring dogs, I found a clean pair of pajamas and got ready for bed. Soon I was on the floor, on an antique Persian rug, twisting myself into the lotus position for my evening meditation. But I couldn't focus on my mantra and settle my brain.

Outside, I could hear Steve continuing to work. And other people were arriving, too. I heard more cars and the muffled sound of greetings and conversations.

Giving up on my pursuit of a Zen state, I untwisted myself and headed to the window again. Pushing aside the curtain, I saw that Giulia Alberti had arrived and was setting up her mobile coffee stand.

Christian Clarke's distinctive red BMW was parked there, too, and I soon located Giulia's handsome boyfriend standing in the shadows, looking decidedly unhelpful. He had his arms crossed over his chest, standing just like Piper had done not too long before. I couldn't see Christian very well, but I was pretty sure he was staring in the direction of Steve Beamus's truck.

Had Giulia and Steve ever really had a relationship?

Were they *still* together, secretly?

And where was Steve, who had a lot of work ahead of him? In spite of the noise I'd heard earlier, it didn't look like he'd made a lot of progress unloading since Piper had left.

The sound of a loud, but mild curse ended my speculation, and I shifted to watch Tom and Tessie Flinchbaugh struggling to erect a white tent by moonlight. So far, they had only two poles laid out on the ground, and Tom was already injured. He was alternately sucking and shaking out his thumb while Tessie fussed over him.

It crossed my mind to go help them, but I was not exactly handy and would probably just make matters worse. I'd bought a chair from IKEA once and, after a fruitless two-hour struggle, ended up giving the pieces to a thrift store.

"Sorry, guys," I mumbled.

Then I peered harder into the darkness. There was another car parked farther away, on the gravel road. Although a large oak tree cast the vehicle in shadows, I was pretty sure it was attorney Virginia Lockhart's big Lincoln Navigator.

I often saw that SUV when I picked up Macduff, Hamlet, and Iago at Virginia's huge house, in an exclusive development called Foxview Heights, just outside Sylvan Creek. The Navigator was also frequently at Winding Hill. At Piper's invitation, Virginia sometimes brought the rottweilers to the farm to train them off leash on trails that ran through the wooded part of the property. It was a safe place to practice recall and teach them not to chase squirrels and rabbits. But surely Virginia wasn't working with the dogs so late at night, right? And while she would attend the trial, that didn't start for hours.

So why was she there?

Yawning, I checked my clock and realized just how late it was. Before I knew it, the sun would rise, and I would need to get up and find a way to promote my pet-sitting services, like I'd told Piper I planned to do.

Pulling the curtains shut again, I went over to Socrates's bed, knelt down, and gave him a kiss good night. He would tolerate such displays of affection only when he was asleep, and even then, he grunted and wriggled his bulky body.

"Good night, Artie," I added, stroking the Chihuahua, too. He'd edged closer to Socrates, and I had a feeling he'd make several more—probably unsuccessful—attempts to share the bed over the course of the night. At my touch, Artie snorted and snuffled, too, but happily, like he was enjoying a good doggy dream.

I hoped so.

After rising, I went to my bed, pulled down a color-ful comforter I'd picked up in India—long story—and lay down. But my sleep, when it finally came, was fitful, interrupted by the sounds of voices and vehicles out-side. I had a weird dream, too, about a dark-haired man in a rainstorm. A guy who might have literally been the man of my dreams—or my worst nightmare.

I woke up at 3:00 a.m., feeling unsettled. And that sensation worsened when I heard yet another car start up outside.

I tossed off my covers, which were way too hot, anyway, and went back to the window just in time to see a Jeep—the vintage, stripped-down army kind that young guys liked—driving off.

I'd expected to see Steve leaving, but his truck was still there.

What was he *doing*?

All at once, I had this terrible thought.

Was he *in the house* with Piper? Making up? Or, worse yet, making *out*?

Oh, yuck.

I hopped back into bed, almost wanting to pull the covers over my head. The night was getting warm and sticky, though, and I didn't want to suffocate, so I took a few deep, calming breaths, reminded myself that Piper's love life was none of my business, and let my thoughts drift away.

As I'd predicted, the sun came up way too soon.

And when I opened my eyes, someone was *in my bed*, staring at me, with his face right on my pillow.

Chapter 5

"Artie, how did you even get up here?" I asked the eight-inch-tall dog, who had somehow managed to get onto my bed, which had a very high antique pine frame topped with a thick, soft mattress. *I* had to climb to get into it. Lifting Artie off the pillow, I saw a puddle where his mouth had been, and I made a face. "Oh, and you drooled, too."

Artie didn't appear apologetic. In fact, his overbite made it look like he was smiling with self-satisfaction.

I swung my legs over the side of the bed, then hopped down, with the little dog cradled in my arm like a football, and scolded him mildly as I set him on the floor. "Don't do that again, Artie. Dogs have their own beds."

Socrates, who was stretched out on his overstuffed purple-velvet pillow, opened one eye to give Artie an "I told you so," disapproving look. Then he promptly went back to sleep, while I checked the clock and was surprised to realize it wasn't even 6:00 a.m. Since I was already up, though, I decided to take advantage of the quiet, because surely vendors, dogs, and handlers would start arriving within the next hour. I was pretty sure the trial officially kicked off at eight.

After pulling on jeans and a T-shirt that advertised Lucky Paws—my promised, if unoriginal, promotional effort—I brushed my teeth and ran my fingers through my curls, then headed downstairs to make some tea and feed the dogs.

"Piper?" I asked softly, padding into the kitchen barefoot. Moments later, I heard the click of toenails on wide, gleaming pine planks as both Socrates and Artie joined me. But for once, Piper wasn't up before me, making her daily bowl of steel-cut oatmeal with cranberries.

Putting the kettle on the stove, I next headed to the fridge and pulled out a glass container that held Bone Appetit Ham-and-Cheese Muffins, which I'd made for Socrates and Artie. Socrates waited patiently for his muffin, which he liked delivered on a china plate meant for humans, while Artie pawed impatiently at my knees, licking his protruding chops.

"Here you go," I told him, setting his treat made of bacon, rolled oats, cheddar cheese, and honey—my own recipe—right on the floor. Knowing they would both need more for breakfast, I added some rice-and-turkey mixture to their waiting bowls, too.

While Socrates ate with decorum, and Artie snuffled away, I finished brewing my raspberry leaf tea and sat down in the sunny breakfast nook to relax and daydream for a few minutes, fully expecting Piper to show up at any second.

But she still hadn't come downstairs by the time my tea and the dogs' meals were gone. As I slipped on some flip-flops waiting by the back door, I hoped she wasn't upset and brooding about the argument she'd had with Steve. That didn't sound like typical Piper behavior, but even a strong woman might crumple a little when her heart was broken, right?

"Come on, boys," I said, summoning the dogs, who followed me outside—where I stopped short, hoping even more fervently that Steve wasn't the reason Piper was lingering in bed, for a different reason.

Because Steve Beamus's truck was *still* parked by the barn.

Chapter 6

It turned out that Piper wasn't sleeping late. As I should've expected, she was already up and busy, working in the barn with Winding Hill's elderly caretaker, Mr. Peachy, who was always an early riser, too. When I stepped through the big sliding red door, which was open on its iron track, they were both inside, standing close together and puzzling over a piece of paper that Piper held. Her hair was uncharacteristically mussed, and she had bags under her eyes, as if she hadn't slept well.

"What's up?" I asked them both. "What are you looking at?"

"It's the plan for how obstacles should be laid out in the ring Steve *didn't* finish setting up before he took off," Piper said. She was clearly aggravated. "We're trying to figure out where things go, since he's not answering his cell phone, either."

"That's weird," I said, wondering if Steve's short spat with Piper had been bad enough to make him abandon the whole event. I didn't want to mention the fight in front of Mr. Peachy, though, so I didn't speculate out loud.

"It's weird—and rude," Piper said. "There's only about an hour left before dogs and handlers start arriving, and all the obstacles for the jumping class are still in the trailer behind his truck."

"Nothin' to do but set up ourselves," Mr. Peachy said, taking the paper from Piper's fingers and squinting at it. He must've been seventy-five, with a permanently curved spine and bowed legs. But his appearance was deceptive. He was a wiry, leathery man who got up every morning at the crack of dawn, first tended to his small cottage—an outbuilding on the Winding Hill property—then walked a half mile through a small patch of woods to take care of whatever needed attention at the main farm. He was the reason every beam was straight, there wasn't a hint of peeling paint anywhere, and the flower beds were always free of weeds. "No use worryin' about Steve Beamus when there's work to be done," he added in his can-do way.

"You're right," Piper agreed. She leaned against Mr. Peachy's old red truck, which he usually parked in the barn. He liked to keep the classic vehicle, which was so ancient that it had wooden slats around the cargo area, out of the weather. Plus, there were no roads to the cottage. Piper rubbed her eyes. "But this shouldn't be your problem," she reminded Mr. Peachy. "I invited the agility club here."

Mr. Peachy smiled crookedly at both of us, and in spite of the fact that he was resigned to working, I thought he looked uncharacteristically tired, too. Or maybe age was finally catching up to him. "You girls are like family," he said, bending to scratch behind Artie's remaining ear. "I can start carrying the equipment to the second ring, if you like."

Piper smiled, but weakly. "Thanks, Mr. Peachy."

Although he was a grandfatherly presence at the

farm, we always addressed him as Mr. Peachy. It was just habit at this point. I wasn't even sure what his first name was.

"It's no problem," Mr. Peachy promised, tipping his worn baseball cap to us.

When he was out of earshot, I asked Piper, "Umm . . . not to pry, but did Steve take off because you fought?"

My sister's cheeks flushed. "How do you know about that?"

"I saw you guys last night, out my window," I admitted. Seeing that Piper was getting even redder with irritation, I added, "I wasn't spying! I just wanted some fresh air, and I couldn't help seeing you offer Steve something to drink. Then you were obviously arguing." I really hadn't meant to spy, but I wasn't above prying. "What was that all about?"

"Nothing," Piper mumbled, avoiding my gaze.

I took a moment to study my sister. "What's going on with you two? Are you getting back together?"

"Nothing's going on!" she repeated.

"Well, I heard a car drive away from here pretty late. Maybe Steve got a ride with that person, and he'll be back soon."

"Probably," Piper agreed. But she had a pained expression on her face, and I realized that she was likely imagining Steve driving off with some woman. A new conquest.

And she was probably right.

What did my smart, accomplished sister see in that guy?

What did *so many women* see?

I knew that asking those questions, again, would be futile, so I didn't bother. Plus, I could hear vehicles starting to arrive for the trial. I assumed the early people were folks from the kennel club and vendors, but some handlers were probably starting to show up, too, to get their dogs settled into crates in prime shady spots.

"We'll offer the barn for dogs that mind the heat," Piper said, as if reading my mind about the rising temperature. "It's pretty cool in here. And can I count on you to help me and Mr. Peachy set up the second course? The jumps aren't really heavy. It will only take a few minutes if three of us do it."

"Sure. I'll be right there," I promised. "Just let me get some extra water bowls ready for the agility dogs who come in here."

I intended to help Piper and Mr. Peachy, but as it always seemed to happen, one simple task turned into many more, including setting up some fans to make the barn even cooler and taking a phone call from somebody who wanted me to watch two slightly neurotic greyhounds. The next thing I knew, I'd been busy for a half hour.

"In spite of the fans, Piper's gonna kill me," I told Artie and Socrates, leading them toward the door.

Socrates clearly agreed. He hung his head, and a low grumble echoed in his white-streaked chest, as if he was trying to tell me, "Yes, you are in trouble."

Resigning myself to a scolding—which wouldn't really be fair, since I was helping in my own way and taking care of my business, as Piper was always advising me to do—I stepped into the sunlight.

As I'd worked, I'd heard cars, conversations, and some barking outside the barn, but I was still surprised by how many people and dogs had arrived. Most of the handlers had established what looked like small campsites, with crates and blankets and portable fans for both dogs and owners. The trial was all set up, too. Two rings, defined by low white plastic fences, were

filled with obstacles, including the tunnel I'd seen
Steve take out of his truck and a colorful hoop through
which dogs would jump, as well as lines of poles that
the dogs would slalom through, like canine skiers.

Searching for familiar faces, I saw Giulia manning
her already busy coffee stand. While she handed out
cold drinks and accepted cash, her boyfriend, Christian, lounged in a nylon folding chair he'd set up in a
shadow cast by the cart. He was reading the *Wall Street
Journal* and seemed oblivious to how busy Giulia was.
As I watched, she maintained her smile but wiped
sweat from her brow with the back of her hand.

I started to walk over, thinking *I* could offer to
help, and buy an Italian soda, only to bump, literally,
into Virginia Lockhart, who had Hamlet, Iago, and
Macduff on their leather leads.

"Sorry," I said, stepping back and petting the pack
leader, Macduff, who was nuzzling my hand. I smiled
at Virginia, who somehow managed to look cool and
comfortable in what was definitely an expensive white
linen, sleeveless top, khaki-colored shorts, and sporty,
but feminine flats. Most handlers wore tees or polos
and old sneakers. Her dark hair, secured by a water-
color-print scarf, was sleekly polished, too, while my
curls were going insane, thanks to the humidity. "I
guess I was really distracted," I added. "I didn't even
see you." I glanced at the dogs, whose panting mouths
all seemed to be grinning. "Or my three favorite rottweilers, who are hard to miss."

The dogs might've been happy, but Virginia did not
seem amused by our human fender bender. She
crossed her arms over her ample chest and scowled.
"You should be apologizing for nearly losing my dogs
last night! Why didn't you tell me they got loose?"

"Because nothing really happened," I informed her.

I didn't remind her that she hadn't given me much chance to say anything when I'd dropped off Hamlet, Iago, and Macduff at her house in Foxview Heights. She'd hurried the dogs into the gorgeous home she shared with her state senator husband, Mitch, and left me standing on the stoop in the drizzle while she wrote out a check. The next thing I'd known, a massive door was being shut in my face. Honestly, the huge brass knocker had nearly bumped my nose. Feeling muzzles poking at my hand, I stroked Iago and Hammie, too. "They just got a little spooked by the storm."

Virginia jutted out her pointed chin. "The next time an incident happens, I am to be informed," she warned me.

At least, it felt like a warning.

If I was ever in court, I would want Virginia Lockhart defending me. But outside a courtroom, she could be a tad abrasive, to put it nicely. I wondered, briefly, if she bossed around Mitch or if he was as strong-willed as his wife. I'd met him only once, and he'd been jovial in a fake way, like he was angling for a vote—which was probably the case.

"I will call you about watching the dogs next week," Virginia added, so at least I knew I hadn't been fired. Then she gave the leads a quick tug, made a *ch-ch* sound, and said, "Lay on, Macduff!"

I watched them all walk away, with Macduff in the lead, and wondered why she and Steve both spoke to the rotties like they were actual characters in a play by Shakespeare.

Why not talk to them like normal American dogs?

I also suddenly wondered how Virginia even knew that Hammie, Macduff, and Iago had been loose.

Had Steve told her?

And speaking of Steve . . .

I looked around again, but I didn't see him or my sister. I did find Tessie and Tom Flinchbaugh, who were working at their mobile pet shop. Like Giulia, they had lots of customers. Tom was under the tent, which they'd apparently figured out how to erect, ringing up a customer. He had a big bandage on his hand, and I thought that was probably overkill. I was pretty sure he hadn't even been bleeding when I'd seen him wincing the night before. Tessie, meanwhile, was showing a potential customer the features of a pet puzzle that would dispense treats if a dog could figure out how to open tricky little flaps.

"You are insulted by that, aren't you?" I asked Socrates, who did *not* like dog toys. Especially ones that assumed he would be challenged by simple tasks.

Two droopy, but wise brown eyes blinked up at me, so I knew he agreed that the toy was beneath him.

"I bet you'd like playing with the puzzle, though," I added, smiling down at Artie.

Only Artie wasn't next to me.

Following the sound of laughter—which often trailed in Artie's wake—I found him and groaned out loud. "Artie! No!"

Chapter 7

I seriously doubted that a thrice abandoned Chihuahua had ever been offered formal agility training, but what Artie lacked in experience he made up for in exuberance.

As I climbed over the low white fence that defined one of the two courses, he gleefully navigated one obstacle after another, first launching himself through the colorful hanging hoop, like a lion at a circus, then climbing the A-frame, where he stood tall, his tail wagging with excitement.

"Artie, get down from there," I said, catching a glimpse of Piper, who stood outside the ring, shaking her head with disapproval.

I wasn't sure why she was so unhappy. The event hadn't officially started yet, and Artie wasn't hurting anything. In fact, some people seemed to find him quite entertaining. A small crowd was gathering.

Still, I didn't want to make Piper mad, so I called to Artie again. "Come!"

No one knew much about why Artie had been given up several times, but I suspected that it had something to do with his lawless, free spirit, which I admired.

Although, at that moment, I would've preferred that he listen to me, as opposed to dart down the A-frame and duck into the long red tunnel. I waited for a moment, but apparently, Artie thought he'd found a pretty nifty hiding place, because he didn't emerge from the other side.

"Daphne . . ." I heard a warning in Piper's voice, and more laughter from the people who'd gathered around the ring.

"I'm getting him," I promised, with a glance down at Socrates, who'd joined me on the course, too. "Do you want to bring him out?"

Socrates looked genuinely offended by the suggestion that he debase himself by walking into a tunnel. In fact, he lay down and yawned.

"Daphne!" Piper's voice was sharper, and I looked over to see her scowling at me and pointing to her wrist, although she wasn't wearing a watch. "The trial starts in five minutes!"

"Okay, okay!"

Apparently, I would have to debase myself. Getting down on all fours, I crawled until I could poke my head inside the tunnel.

"Artie, come over here."

I started to summon him again, but suddenly my throat got very tight, making it difficult to talk, because Artie wasn't alone inside that obstacle.

I froze in place for a second, then backtracked slowly on my hands and knees. Forcing myself to stay calm, in spite of just having seen a *body*, I stood up and called to Piper, telling her in a shaky voice, "I . . . I found Steve Beamus."

Chapter 8

"I can't believe he's really dead," I muttered to Piper. We stood with the rest of the crowd just outside the ring while the local coroner, Vonda Shakes; some uniformed police officers; and an ambulance crew bustled around the tunnel, doing official-looking things. I stroked Artie, who was cradled in my arms and shaking more than usual, as if he understood what he'd just seen. Socrates, sitting at my feet, was his usual composed self. I looked down to see him observing the goings-on as keenly as any human. Then I turned to Piper. "Are you okay?"

She was pale, but she nodded. "Yes. I'm fine."

She was lying, in her stoic way. Of course she wasn't "fine." A guy she'd cared about—at some point, at least—had almost certainly been murdered, and she'd been the one to confirm that he was really deceased. Although I'd tried to assure her that it was too late to save Steve—I'd seen his blank, wide-open eyes and a dark and nearly dried bloodstain on his head—she'd insisted on crawling in to check his pulse.

Once again, the reality of what had happened at

Piper's peaceful farm struck me, and I looked around at the gathered crowd. Christian Clarke had a comforting, or possessive, arm draped around Giulia, who was gnawing her fingernails, her brow furrowed. She seemed stiff in her boyfriend's embrace.

On the other side of the ring, Tom and Tessie Flinchbaugh were standing slightly apart from everyone. They were deep in a conversation that looked almost like an argument. Their mouths were drawn down, and their hand gestures were small, but frequent and rapid. I couldn't imagine the mild-mannered couple bickering about anything, but Tom was definitely agitated. He kept wiping his balding head with a limp handkerchief.

Then I searched for Virginia Lockhart, but she was gone. The shady spot under a willow tree at the edge of the property, where she'd set up her crates, was empty, so I assumed she'd packed up Macduff, Hamlet, and Iago and gone home. That made sense to me. Obviously, the trial was canceled.

All at once, I remembered how I thought I'd seen Virginia's SUV parked near that same tree the night before.

Had she been scoping out a good spot to set up for the day?

Or had I been wrong, and had she not been there at all?

"He didn't deserve this," Piper said softly, interrupting my thoughts. "He wasn't always the nicest person, but this . . ."

My sister rarely got emotional, and I turned to discover that her eyes were glistening. It was unnerving to see Piper close to crying, and I didn't mean to make things worse, but I had to discuss something with my rule-following, hyper-honest sibling, and I had to do it quickly, because more sirens were approaching.

"Piper," I whispered over Artie's shaky little head. "This is your farm, and the police are going to question us. I promise I won't mention that you and Steve argued last night, and you shouldn't say anything, either. It'll just complicate things."

Piper's eyes widened with disbelief, and she opened her mouth, like she was about to disagree.

But before she could say a word, someone interrupted our conversation, telling us in a deep, commanding voice, "Don't either of you go anywhere. I may want to hear about that argument later."

I didn't recognize the speaker until I turned and realized that, while I'd never talked with the stranger who'd walked up behind us, I'd seen him twice before.

Once on the street, walking past my van.

And once in my dreams.

Chapter 9

"Who are you?" I asked, although I was afraid I knew who'd overheard me urging Piper to withhold information. The man's dark gray tailored suit, so out of place on a farm during a dog trial, was kind of a giveaway.

"I'm Detective Jonathan Black," he informed me, confirming my suspicion. As my stomach twisted, his gaze darted between me and Piper. "And you two are . . . ?"

"I'm Piper Templeton," my sister said. "I own Winding Hill Farm."

Piper looked at me, as if I should go next. "I'm her sister, Daphne," I said. I nodded to the dogs. "These guys are Socrates and Artie. I live here . . . rent free. I have a pet-sitting business."

I wasn't sure why I added the extra stuff. I supposed I was nervous. Not only had I just gotten caught trying to obstruct justice, but also Jonathan Black was even more handsome up close than I'd thought when he'd walked past my van. He had thick, nearly black hair that fell over his forehead in an appealing way; a strong jaw that was marked by a small, intriguing scar;

and very dark blue eyes that reminded me of the sky the previous evening, right before the storm had hit. Those eyes were intimidating, as was his attitude. He was tall and stood with a relaxed sort of confidence, so he looked like he owned the farm, and we were the visitors. And not very welcome ones.

Before I could blurt out more random things— and I was on the verge of doing it—Detective Black returned his attention to Piper. "Did you argue with the dead man last night? Did I hear correctly?"

Piper was fair to begin with, and she'd been more pale than usual since seeing Steve's body. But she got ashen then. Still, she nodded and answered without hesitation. "Yes. We did have a fight."

Piper didn't elaborate. I thought that was probably smart. She might want to get a lawyer before answering more questions.

Detective Black frowned at me, and although *I* hadn't quarreled with Steve Beamus, I got the sense that I was in worse trouble than my sister. The thunderclouds in Jonathan Black's eyes would've sent Macduff, Hamlet, and Iago racing for the hills. Artie, sensitive to human emotions, like all dogs, wriggled until I set him down next to imperturbable Socrates.

Luckily, before I could get a lecture about the *possibly* bad counsel I'd just offered Piper, we were interrupted by the coroner, Vonda Shakes, who approached us, pulling latex gloves off her hands. The rubber fingers made very official snapping sounds as she removed them. "Piper, Daphne," she said, offering my sister and me a sympathetic frown. "I'm so sorry."

Needless to say, we knew Vonda. I often sat for her perky little King Charles spaniel, Maximilian, and Piper was Max's vet. Plus, we lived in Sylvan Creek. Everybody knew everybody.

I stole a glance at Detective Black.

How did we not know him?

He kind of stood out.

Apparently, Vonda was acquainted with the new-comer. "Of course, we'll need to do an autopsy," she told Detective Black. "But I'd say you can safely proceed on the assumption that this is a homicide."

He nodded. "Okay." Then he glanced between Piper and me again. "Don't. Go. Anywhere."

"Of course not," Piper agreed for both of us. She must've seen the doubtful way Detective Black looked at me, because she added, "I'll keep an eye on Daphne. I promise."

How did *I* become the one who needed to be watched?

"I don't even have enough gas in the VW to go five miles—and that includes the half mile I'd coast down the hill," I informed everybody. "Plus, my passport got stolen in Istanbul two years ago. I'm hardly a flight risk."

Detective Black studied me for a long, long time. I had no idea what he was thinking, but after a while, I felt my cheeks getting warm.

Then he broke our gaze and lightly touched Vonda's arm, indicating that she should accompany him over the fence and into the ring. Once inside, he immediately began to direct the scene. "I want every piece of evidence bagged," he told the uniformed officers. "Photos from every angle." He pointed to the tunnel. "That's a bloodstain. Don't miss any of those, because the fabric is red. . . ."

I was preoccupied with observing Detective Black and trying to pretend that Piper wasn't glaring at me when someone rested strong, reassuring hands on my shoulders, and I caught a familiar whiff of coconut sunblock, which apparently didn't work that well.

"Daph, are you okay?" Dylan asked as I shifted to face him. "I came as soon as I heard about Steve—and you finding him."

"You were supposed to be here an hour ago," Piper noted through gritted teeth. Dylan's unconventional relationship with time was a constant source of irritation for her, like the board shorts. And she was having a pretty bad day.

"Sorry," he said, but absently. He really didn't understand Piper's obsession with punctuality. He subscribed to Einstein's theory about time being a river. A lazy river, in Dylan's view. He was also busy folding me close to himself in a comforting embrace.

Right before I leaned against him—I really did need a hug, enough to overlook our uncertain relationship status—I caught a glimpse of Detective Black, who was no longer directing the other officers.

No, he was standing stock-still, watching *me.*

Chapter 10

The day of Steve Beamus's murder turned out to be incredibly long, and by late evening, I was really glad to sink into the confines of a dimly lit booth at a small restaurant called Franco's to share a glass of wine with Moxie and Piper while we waited for our dinners to arrive.

Poor Piper looked wan and exhausted, but Moxie was full of energy and questions. I felt drained, like Piper, and wished I had a dimmer switch for my best friend, so I could tone her down a bit.

At least we'd already told Moxie everything about finding Steve's body and getting questioned by police.

Unfortunately, she'd latched onto a new, related subject: Dylan's arrival on the scene, and the fact that the hug he'd offered me had ended up stretching on for quite a while, until I'd gotten too warm and wriggled out of his embrace. At which point, he'd tried to pull me close again.

"It sounds like he was being protective," Moxie noted, digging deep into an overflowing bread basket to get one of the warmest, softest rolls on the bottom.

Franco's had the best bread, made in-house from a secret recipe that dated back to the restaurant's founding in the 1920s. In fact, little had changed since that era. The place still felt like a speakeasy, with dark paneled walls, flickering candles on all the tables, and a hushed atmosphere, conducive to sharing secrets. "He was being romantic, don't you think?"

"It was more weird than romantic," I said, grabbing a roll. Tearing it open to release the yeasty steam, I dipped my knife into a waiting plate of softened butter, which I slathered over the bread. "I felt almost suffocated, which is not Dylan's style. I don't know what got into him."

"Really?" Piper asked skeptically. She was sitting next to me and pulled back so she could see me better. Candlelight reflected off the lenses of her glasses, so I couldn't see her eyes, but her tone was clearly disbelieving. "Honestly, Daphne? You have no idea what might've gotten into Dylan?"

I shook my head. "No. I don't."

Piper sighed and addressed Moxie. "Daphne and the detective we talked about, Black, had a certain *chemistry*. If *I* picked up on it in the few moments I saw them together, Dylan surely did, too. Assuming he saw them together, which he almost certainly did. And even a *ridiculously* laid-back guy can get jealous."

"Hey!" I cried out too loudly for the very subdued dining room. But I had to object to everything Piper had just said. "First of all, Dylan is not 'ridiculously' laid back," I told my sister. "He's just got an admirably relaxed attitude toward life."

Piper rolled her eyes. "One time, there was a payroll glitch, and he didn't get paid for *three weeks*," she informed us. "He didn't even notice! *I* found the error!"

That seemed like a situation that would benefit Piper, so I wasn't sure why she seemed so aghast.

"Dylan doesn't need much money," I reminded her. "Guitar strings cost, what? A couple dollars? And he gets his flip-flops at the Dollar Store."

Piper snorted a wry laugh. "Yes, his quality footwear 'blew out'—to use his own phrasing—at the clinic the other day, during a procedure—"

"We all know Dylan's *usually* a mellow hippie throwback," Moxie interrupted before Piper and I could start arguing. She popped some bread into her mouth and talked while chewing. "I wanna hear about the detective and the 'chemistry.'"

"There *was* no 'chemistry,'" I informed her. Moxie's eyes were gleaming with far too much interest. She'd dyed her spiky hair bright red, and that was glowing by the light of our table's candle, too, so overall, she looked like she was about to combust. Before she could get too excited, I repeated, "No. Chemistry."

Piper and Moxie shared a skeptical look over their wineglasses, so I added, "Seriously, Jonathan Black is kind of terrifying. And he has no interest in dogs. I tried to introduce him to Artie and Socrates, and he didn't so much as greet them."

"In Detective Black's defense, he was there to investigate a murder," Piper reminded me. "One committed by someone who used a *tool*, which indicates that the individual had at least one opposable thumb."

Shrugging, I took a sip of my wine. "I think how people treat animals says a lot about them."

"Yet you really disliked Steve," Piper said softly. She fidgeted with the stem of her glass. "And he loved—in fact, built his whole life around—animals."

Part of me wanted to tell Piper that "building a life around" and "loving" animals were two different things.

In fact, I'd often thought Steve mainly liked *controlling* animals—and showing lesser humans how easily he could exert power over dogs. I believed in having well-behaved pets, but Steve had always seemed like a bit of a showman to me—as evidenced by the odd, dramatically delivered Shakespearean command he'd used to stop the running rottweilers.

"Hold, enough!"

Why not just "Come"?

All at once, I was struck by a strange thought.

How did the dogs understand that unusual command?

I studied my sister for a moment.

And why had Dylan indicated that Piper and Steve had fought *prior* to last night?

"Piper?" I ventured tentatively. "Did you still care about Steve?" I leaned forward so I could watch her expression. "Were you guys back together?"

I was seated across the table from Moxie, but I could tell she tensed up, waiting for Piper's answer. And given that Moxie loved a good, twisty-turny romance, she was probably disappointed when my sister said, "No. We weren't." Then Piper hesitated before adding in a whisper, "Not really."

"What does that mean?" I asked. "And is that what you argued about last night? Your relationship?"

I'd pushed reticent, private Piper too far. She didn't answer me, and I didn't force the issue.

"I'm sorry I didn't like Steve," I said quietly. "It was mainly because he hurt you."

"No," she countered, eyes downcast. "You didn't like him before that."

I wasn't sure what to say, and I was grateful when Moxie tried to explain, albeit in terms my sister probably didn't really understand. "I think Steve and Daphne just have . . . had . . . different auras. Sometimes opposites attract, but sometimes they're just . . . opposite."

I thought about a certain tall, intimidating, very serious detective. A guy who basically lived to enforce law and order, while I loved chaos. He also really hadn't seemed to care about dogs, which were a huge part of my life.

Could there ever really be chemistry?

No . . .

"I know you didn't like Steve, either, Moxie," Piper said, interrupting my thoughts. She kept staring at the table. "Maybe nobody in this town did." She finally looked up at Moxie and me, confessing, "*I* wasn't exactly fond of him sometimes. He could be argumentative and bullheaded. But he certainly didn't deserve to die."

"No, he didn't, Piper," I agreed. "Of course, nobody believes that."

"Somebody believed it," she reminded me. "Somebody believed it strongly enough to *bludgeon* him."

There was a long silence, and that very grim word *bludgeon* seemed to hang in the air.

Then Moxie asked, "Did they find the weapon?"

"I don't think so," Piper said. "At least, the police didn't tell us anything about finding it."

I wondered if, like me, Piper was suddenly having slight misgivings about going home late tonight, after dinner. I hadn't thought much about my own safety, or hers, up to that point. I'd assumed that whoever'd killed Steve had targeted him for a reason. But to think about the weapon still being out there, along with the killer who'd wielded it . . . It was kind of creepy.

Fortunately, before I could get too worried about things beyond my control, the waitress arrived with our meals, cutting short the discussion. Both Moxie and Piper had ordered Franco's signature pork medallions in a sour cherry sauce with wild rice pilaf, which almost made me regret being a vegetarian, until a plate heaped high with pasta and garlicky house-made marinara—another secret recipe dating back to the Roaring Twenties—was slipped under my very grateful nose. As we all adjusted our napkins on our laps and prepared to dig in, I found myself recalling how Detective Black and his partner, Detective Fred Doebler, had questioned me about the day's and the previous night's events.

Detective Doebler was older, but Jonathan Black had clearly been in charge, just like he'd taken the lead at the crime scene. He'd asked all the questions, and I'd ended up saying more than I'd wanted under the pressure of his intense gaze.

I'd felt like I was betraying Tom and Tessie Flinchbaugh when I mentioned their presence at Winding Hill right before Steve's death, but I was pretty sure they'd never be seriously considered as suspects. They were two of the most mild-tempered people I'd ever met, and they had no reason to hate Steve. At least, not that I knew about.

I'd felt guilty for admitting that Giulia and her boyfriend, Christian Clarke, had been there late, too. But I wasn't the only person who'd seen them at Winding Hill. Surely the truth would've come out sometime.

And then there was the car that looked like Virginia Lockhart's, and the Jeep I'd never seen before.

All at once, I pictured Steve and Piper arguing

when she'd brought him the thermos. And I recalled seeing Steve at his truck, unloading the retractable vinyl tunnel that would become his temporary resting place. The trailer had still held a lot of equipment the next day.

Something wasn't adding up. . . .

I tried to focus, but my brain, which was not used to thinking so hard since I'd finished my doctoral dissertation, started to hurt, and I was actually glad when Moxie changed the subject back to one of her favorite topics. Men.

"So, tell me," she said, leaning forward, toward me. She was more subdued, but there was still a small gleam in her eyes, and a slight smile played on her bright red lips. "What's this Detective Black look like, anyhow? Just out of curiosity."

I didn't want to answer that question. Detective Black was undeniably gorgeous. That was a fact. But if I started using terms like *athletic build*, *deep blue eyes*, and *strong jaw*, Moxie and Piper would definitely get the wrong impression.

Luckily, as I tried to figure out how to avoid answering, I suddenly didn't have to bother. Fate was providing a three-dimensional response to Moxie's inquiry.

I jerked my thumb toward the restaurant's front door, which had just opened and then closed behind a new customer, and told my friend, "He looks exactly like *that*."

Moxie spun around to get a not very subtle glimpse of Detective Black, and she offered a low whistle of approval.

I, meanwhile, nearly choked on my pasta, because the detective was not dining alone.

He was accompanied by a woman I certainly hadn't expected—or hoped—to see that night.

Chapter 11

"Mom, what are you doing here?" I groaned as Maeve Templeton swept toward our table, tossing a chiffony floral scarf over her shoulder like it was a mink stole. Her wide-legged, Lauren Bacall–inspired pants billowed out like sails. I leaned to look past her, to where Detective Black was settling into a booth and accepting a menu from a waitress. "And why are you with *him?*"

My mother ignored my questions. She frowned in an exaggerated way, although I knew she wouldn't hold the expression for very long. She prided herself on having incredibly smooth skin for her age—which even Piper and I weren't allowed to know.

"I am so sorry, girls," she said, bending down to squeeze Piper's and my wrists. Then she patted Moxie's arm, too, presumably to make her feel included. "I was out showing homes all day and just heard about everything that happened at Winding Hill. You must be so shaken! And poor Steve . . ."

My mother's voice trailed off, because while she was obviously shocked by the murder, she hadn't liked Steve, either, after he'd dumped her daughter. I also noted that my mother had made the tragedy more about the property than about the victim. She was no doubt worried that the value of Piper's investment had just dropped precipitously.

"I tried to call you both," Mom added in a slightly accusing tone. "But I couldn't get through."

"We turned off our cell phones about an hour ago so we could relax," Piper explained. "Sorry if you were worried, but it was a long day."

"Actually, my battery's dead," I noted. It seemed like I couldn't keep myself from saying things that would agitate my mother. "And the phone hardly works, anyhow. I ran over it with a wheelbarrow once, and it's never been the same."

Mom opened her perfectly lined lips, no doubt in preparation for a lecture about my lack of responsibility, which would inevitably touch upon how she could help me get a Realtor's license if I would just *apply myself* and take the exam. But she stopped herself, apparently realizing that diving into that bottomless pit of a topic would leave her dinner companion waiting far too long.

I glanced across the room to see Detective Black studying the menu like he would be tested on *that*. Even off duty and slightly slouched in the booth, he was a commanding presence. He wore a black polo shirt and jeans, and his legs were stretched out far under the table. He definitely had a way of claiming space.

"Seriously, Mom," I said, returning my attention to our little party. "What are you doing here with him?"

Mom turned to waggle her fingers at her companion. He did not waggle back—I wouldn't have expected that—but he did look over and nod to all of us.

Apparently, he had no interest in wandering across the room to mingle with witnesses.

Or were Piper and I both *suspects*?

I hadn't been disrespectful when discussing Steve during my earlier questioning, but honesty had kept me from going overboard and singing his praises.

Mom turned back around. "Jonathan is new in town, and he doesn't know many people yet," she explained. "The maternal side of me couldn't bear to think of him eating alone every night."

I took a few moments to digest all that.

First, she'd confirmed my suspicions that Detective Black was new to Sylvan Creek. And she'd used his first name, which I had *not* been invited to do. Last but not least, Maeve Templeton had a "maternal side"? Why hadn't she ever shown it to *me*?

Of course, my mother was also working a business angle by wining and dining *Jonathan*.

"Although he is *single*," she continued, emphasizing the last word and shooting Piper a meaningful look, "he is interested in purchasing property. Which I think is very sensible. Renting is such a terrible investment!"

That was a mantra we'd grown up with, and I couldn't believe Mom still tried to hammer that message home, given that I'd completely ignored that advice for my entire adult life.

And no wonder Mom was trying to set up Piper and Detective Black.

What could be more romantic than two sensible property owners discussing their mortgage rates on a first date? It would be a match made, if not in heaven, at least in the Recorder of Deeds office.

"I like renting," Moxie said, piping up, with a shrug.

"My landlord—you know, Mr. Flinchbaugh—does everything!"

My mother did not dignify that comment with a response. Maybe she couldn't even understand what Moxie had just said. Maybe it sounded like Greek to her.

"I must return to Jonathan now," Mom said. Then she leaned close to Piper and practically winked as she whispered, "He's considering a *four*-bedroom, which means he *must* be ready to settle down."

Of course, my mother didn't fully wink. Facial movements of any type caused wrinkles and were to be avoided when possible. That was another Maeve Templeton axiom.

She spun around dramatically—what she lacked in expressions, she made up for in sweeping gestures—but looked back, adding, "Given what has occurred at Winding Hill, I want you girls to stay with me tonight." It was my turn to get a pointed look. "Sans animals, of course!"

She sailed away before Piper and I could both refuse her offer. My sister might've been the unquestioned favorite, to the extent that none of us even bothered pretending otherwise, but Piper couldn't last one night at Mom's house, either. It was never clear which towels were only "for show," and woe to the person who dried her hands on the wrong one.

"That is not happening," Piper grumbled, digging her fork into her rice pilaf, which had to be getting cold, like my pasta. "Not happening."

"Definitely not," I agreed, setting down my fork. I really hated cool marinara. Sitting back in the booth, I decided I'd just ask for a doggy bag the next time the waitress stopped by.

She seemed quite busy at the moment, smiling

incandescently as she took Detective Black's order. He handed her the menu, and for a second I thought she might hand it back and ask for an autograph. She looked that starstruck.

Did we have such a dearth of good-looking men in Sylvan Creek that when one arrived, women pounced on him?

"Stop staring at him," Moxie whispered, nudging me with her foot. "Although it's definitely hard not to!"

"I wasn't staring," I said, without taking my eyes off the exchange that was happening across the room.

I honestly wasn't fixated on Detective Black and his interaction with an extremely flirtatious server.

My mind had wandered elsewhere, from doggy bags to *dogs*.

Specifically, one *missing* dog.

All at once, I sat bolt upright and blurted to Moxie and Piper, "I've gotta go! Now!"

Chapter 12

Given that I had already been caught trying to "tweak" justice—I liked that word better than the one Detective Black had used, "obstruct"—I probably shouldn't have set out to explore Steve Beamus's property after telling Moxie and Piper that I needed to leave dinner early to catch a new PBS special on the Dalai Lama.

Fortunately, Piper'd been preoccupied enough to forget that I didn't own a TV.

Heck, I wasn't even sure PBS still existed.

I'd had to make up some excuse, though. I couldn't have told my sister or Moxie that I needed to break into Steve's house to check on Axis. Not only would Piper, especially, have objected, but I hadn't wanted Detective Black, who probably had super-keen hearing to match his piercing laser stares, to overhear my plans. Although, in retrospect, he hadn't even looked up from his discussion with my mother as I'd sneaked out of Franco's.

"Where do you think Cookie Puss is?" I asked Socrates and Artie, whom I'd picked up before heading out to investigate. The dogs, in safety harnesses, were sharing the front seat, although Socrates kept surreptitiously squishing the Chihuahua against the door every time we rounded a curve.

Artie cheerfully held his ground. He seemed to think it was a game.

I took my eyes off the dark, twisting country road for just a second to glance at both dogs.

Axis always used to go everywhere with Steve, just like Socrates usually accompanied me. But I couldn't recall seeing the Lab at Winding Hill the night before. Axis might've been in the truck, though.

Had someone harmed Cookie Puss, too?

Or *stolen* him?

Or was he home alone, terrified and confused by Steve's failure to return?

"We're not really going to 'break in,'" I told Socrates, who I swore understood our mission. He was giving me disapproving looks. "It's not a crime if you don't plan to take anything—and you use a key."

Not that I had a key. Yet.

But, no offense to him, Steve hadn't been a very original guy. I was pretty sure he'd have one of those fake hollow rocks near his porch or a key stashed under his doormat.

All at once, my van lurched in a strange, somewhat alarming way. It was too late to turn back, though. Leaning forward, the better to see the lonely rural road, I patted the steering wheel and urged, "Keep going! You can do it!" We were almost to Steve's house but were approaching an intimidating rise, steep enough possibly to overwhelm an engine that sometimes failed while we were going *downhill*. "Come on!"

Someone else was coming over the hill, too, from the other side. I could see headlights starting to glow in the humid, misty air.

Then, as the VW began to wheeze upward, the other car came roaring past, moving way too quickly for the narrow road.

I saw the vehicle for only a moment, but I was pretty sure it wasn't technically a car. It was a Jeep. Kind of like the one that I'd seen at the farm the night of Steve's murder.

Was that a coincidence?

I didn't have time to wonder right then.

The VW thankfully crested the rise, and I saw the sign for Blue Ribbon K9 Academy just in time to make the turn onto the long driveway that led to Steve's house and his adjacent warehouse-like training facility.

Unfortunately, as I'd feared, the van's cobbled-together engine chose that exact moment to give up the ghost.

Chapter 13

I really regretted baiting my mother with my comments about my worthless cell phone, because clearly karma was at work. I was stuck in the forest with no way to call for help.

Could my mother sense that I was suffering payback from the universe?

Was she laughing over dessert with Detective Black as she reeled him in to buy a *five*-bedroom and marry Piper as part of the deal?

"Come on, guys," I said, urging Socrates and Artie to move faster down the long path that connected the main road to Steve's house. It was pitch black, and the property was heavily wooded. I swore I heard stuff rustling in the underbrush with every step we took.

"*We are to learn about fear, not escape from it,*" I reminded myself and the dogs softly, quoting Jiddhu Krishnamurti.

I believed, in theory, that the Indian philosopher was correct. We shouldn't run away from fear.

But as something that sounded *bear sized* moved in the trees, and I recalled how Steve had looked lying lifeless in the tunnel, I might've picked up the pace just a little.

Okay, I yelled, "Run, guys!" Then I tore off like a bat out of heck, sprinting as fast as I could in my flip-flops until I stumbled right up onto the porch of Steve's dark log-cabin home.

Breathing hard, I lifted the doormat with shaking fingers.

The dogs joined me, their toenails tapping the wooden floor. Socrates hadn't hurried at all. He was the last to arrive.

"Don't laugh at me!" I told him, feeling under the mat. "Something is out there!"

Unfortunately, while I was convinced that the woods were filled with dangerous creatures, my hunch about the doormat was proven wrong. There was nothing beneath it except dirt. A lot of dirt.

Straightening and swiping my fingers on my jeans, I spied a suspicious-looking flowerpot. I couldn't imagine Steve planting flowers.

I lifted it, and a few moments later, Artie, Socrates, and I were *in*.

And I was screaming way too loudly for someone on an investigative mission.

Chapter 14

"What type of person puts a nine-foot-tall taxidermied grizzly bear smack in the middle of a dark foyer?" I asked the dogs once I could breathe again. I rested one hand against my still heaving chest. "Who *does* that?"

Socrates made a sound that was very reminiscent of a snorted laugh. He hadn't for a moment believed the bear was alive, like I had. He trotted past me and Artie, who had also gotten spun up at the sight of a huge predator looming over all of us, with its front legs outstretched and its jaws gaping.

As my eyes adjusted to the gloomy interior of Steve's house, I got even madder when I realized that Steve had hung a jacket on one of the bear's paws. It was bad enough that he had probably killed the majestic creature, then mounted it as a trophy. He didn't have to diminish the animal, too, by treating it like furniture.

"Really, Steve?" I muttered, snatching away the jacket and tossing it onto a bench.

I knew that Piper was more pragmatic about animals than me. She saw the circle of life and death every day at her hospital, and she had no problem with people hunting if they ate the meat. But had she really approved of Steve's use of a bear as a coatrack?

I took another deep breath and reminded myself that there was nothing I could do for the grizzly. I was there to help a dog.

Yet, even as I called softly for Axis, I knew that the retriever wasn't there. He would've already come running to greet me, Socrates, and Artie. And once the sound of my screams and Artie's barking had subsided, it was obvious that no one living—human or animal—was inside the house.

The place had that too-still, oppressively hushed feeling.

So where was Axis?

Had the police or some friend of Steve's taken him?

Or was the dog really missing?

I started fumbling along the wall for a light switch, then recalled the Jeep that had passed me on the road.

I knew it was unlikely, but if that vehicle belonged to the killer, maybe he or she had been here—and might return. And so I decided that, although I wasn't particularly fond of spooking around in the dark, it was a better choice than lighting up the house and signaling that someone was inside.

As my eyes adjusted, the dogs and I moved farther into the room, which was actually fairly well lit by moonlight streaming through two massive triangular windows at the top of the ski lodge–like, A-frame structure.

"There's gotta be a landline here," I whispered, walking around a huge sectional that dominated the open, soaring great room. From what I could tell, everything in the place screamed "single guy," from the bear to the big couch to the ginormous TV and a tacky, nearly life-size painting of a regal elk, which Steve probably would've liked to have killed and mounted, too.

Had my sister's ex been trying to compensate for something small with all the oversize furniture?

For a second, I almost laughed; then I recalled that Steve had been murdered, and that shouldn't happen to anyone. Not to a bear, an elk, or a person, no matter how dislikable. "Sorry," I said out loud to Steve and the whole universe, so I wouldn't suffer from more bad karma.

I really needed the universe to give me a break, in the form of a telephone, so I could call . . .

All at once, just as I found a phone and answering-machine combo on an end table with legs made of antlers, I stopped short.

Who, exactly, did I intend to contact?

Rule-following Piper would seriously disapprove of my sneaking into Steve's house, especially since I'd achieved nothing. She might even refuse to come get me.

Moxie didn't have a car, and her Vespa scooter was worthless in any situation more than two miles from town.

My mother would answer her cell, but what if she was still with Detective Black? She'd blab everything, and I'd probably get arrested.

Or, worse yet, she'd rush over here and come bursting through the door in her high heels and matchy outfit from Talbots to haul my butt home. I'd definitely get that lecture on responsibility I'd avoided earlier, and it would be delivered while I was trapped in her Lexus sedan.

No. I was *not* calling Maeve Templeton.

I picked up the receiver and started to dial Dylan, then hung up before his phone could ring. I'd already leaned on him once that day, and I didn't need him to start thinking I was some sort of damsel in distress.

"Why didn't I get AAA, like Piper is always nagging about?" I muttered to Socrates, who had jumped up onto the couch, the better to watch me grapple with my dilemma. Artie had disappeared into the kitchen, probably in search of food. I could hear him snuffling, like maybe he'd found something. I put the phone back into its cradle. "Why don't I ever listen to my sister?"

Socrates cocked his wrinkly head, as if to say, "Really? AAA? You are not the kind of girl who plans ahead like that."

Obviously, he was right.

I certainly hadn't planned for what happened next: I heard footsteps on the porch, and a second later the front door opened to let somebody else inside the big, dark, isolated house with me.

Chapter 15

"You can stand up, Ms. Templeton," a familiar voice informed me as I crouched, only half concealed, by the antler table. My effort to hide was also hampered by the fact that Socrates was still sitting in plain view and Artie was dancing around me, yipping and licking my face. "In fact, please get up," the person added. "Now."

Was I relieved or dismayed to realize that I'd been joined by Detective Jonathan Black, who switched on the small light in the foyer?

I wasn't sure. Part of me would've preferred to face a murderer, especially when I rose up, dusted myself off, and saw the grim expression on his face.

"What are you doing here?" I asked him, hoping he couldn't see the faint flush of embarrassment on my cheeks. "Shouldn't you be touring a five-bedroom colonial with my mother about now?"

Detective Black checked his wristwatch. "It's nearly eleven p.m. And I don't like colonials."

I had no idea if he was joking about that last part.

He frowned at the grizzly, as if he also thought it

was in poor taste, then moved farther into the room. There was a lot of space between us in the big, open floor plan, but I stepped back, nearly tripping over Artie.

"Shouldn't I be asking what *you're* doing here . . . in the dark?" he noted, glancing at Artie, then Socrates. "And do you *always* have dogs with you?"

"Generally, yes," I informed him. I crossed my arms over my chest. "Why wouldn't I?"

My response seemed to puzzle him, as usual. I'd seen that look on his face—the furrowed brow and the frown—a lot when he'd questioned me about the murder.

Then I suddenly recalled how he'd addressed me by name before he'd even seen me, and I wondered if I'd been *followed*, which would've been uncalled for. I didn't really think I was a suspect. At least, not one worth tracking at all hours of the night. And he was clearly off duty, still wearing his jeans and polo shirt.

"How did you know I was here before you turned on the light?" I asked him suspiciously. He was walking farther into the house. Closer to me. He switched on another lamp, on an end table that matched the one I'd just hidden behind. I took a few steps back. Just because he was a police officer didn't mean he couldn't be a stalker—or a killer. "Detective" would actually be a pretty good cover for a murderer. "Seriously, I think you need to explain how you knew it was me."

The corners of his mouth finally twitched with amusement—at my expense, of course. "Even by moonlight, I recognized your basset hound, and the Chihuahua's also distinctive, to put it mildly," he said. "Not to mention the fact that your old VW is blocking the road to the house. The horse and the graffiti make it pretty memorable. And your name is right on the side."

"Oh." I guessed I had left a few clues to indicate I was there. "It's not a horse," I advised him, jutting out my chin. "It's a dog—like Artie. They are both slightly misshapen but totally lovable dogs."

Oh, gosh, did Detective Black grin when I said that. It transformed his whole face, and if he hadn't been laughing *at* me, I probably would have smiled, too.

Instead, I reminded him, "You still haven't explained why *you're* here."

He gave me another funny look. "I'm investigating a murder. Remember?"

"It's awfully late for investigating," I noted. "You pointed out the time."

He began to walk around the room, studying everything from the rafters to the rugs. "Something is bothering me," he said, seeming distracted. Socrates tracked the detective's progress with his intelligent eyes, while Artie trotted right on his heels. "I wanted to check out the house one more time." He returned his attention to me. "I really think *you* need to explain yourself now. Why you're here, and why you parked so far away, which seems odd."

"I didn't so much park as drift to an unexpected stop," I said. "And I'm here because I'm worried about Steve's dog, Axis."

Detective Black's eyebrows arched. "There's *another* dog?"

"Yes," I said. "A prizewinning chocolate Lab named Axis, sometimes known as Cookie Puss."

Detective Black reared back slightly. "*Cookie Puss?*"

"Yes, I call him that. Because he has such a sweet face. Which is brown, like a cookie."

"Okay." Detective Black stretched that one word out for about a mile.

"Anyway, I think it's odd that Axis is missing," I continued. "He usually went everywhere with Steve. But I'm not sure he was at Winding Hill, Piper's farm, last night. And if he was there when Steve was killed, he never would've left the body willingly. He would've stood guard."

I got even more concerned for Axis when I realized that if he'd been at the farm when Steve was murdered, he definitely would've stayed near the tunnel and barked to alert someone that Steve was in trouble. Unless someone had taken him—or silenced him.

"That *is* curious," Detective Black agreed. He resumed walking around, then paused in front of an ostentatious wood-and-glass case that was filled with books and trophies. Each trophy was topped with a golden dog. The books all looked like spy and thriller paperbacks, with the exception of one beautifully bound work. I was too far away to read the gold-embossed title on the leather spine, but the volume was thick. "Very interesting."

He might've been referring to my observations about Axis or the contents of the case.

"So, are you going to help me look for Cookie Puss?" I asked. "I'm really worried about him."

Detective Black finally faced me again. "I'm a homicide detective, not a dogcatcher."

"I really think it might have something to do with the crime," I argued. "It's a weird coincidence, Axis going missing and Steve getting killed. Plus, what if Cookie Puss—"

"Please call the dog Axis," Detective Black interrupted. "Retrievers are working dogs, and some of them are warriors. They deserve respect."

The comment caused *me* to rear back with surprise. Did he perhaps like dogs, at least a little?

"All right," I agreed. I'd never meant to insult Axis's dignity, the way I felt Steve had degraded the bear in his foyer. I just loved the dog's sweet face. My shoulders slumped a little. And, let's face it, I'd liked bothering Steve, too. But in the future, I would refer to Axis by his proper name. "What if *Axis* is in trouble?" I asked again.

"I'm afraid Steve Beamus's pet can't be my priority right now," Detective Black said. His mouth set in a grim line. I wasn't sure why he had suddenly gotten so serious. "I'll keep what you told me in mind, but there's a good chance the dog is fine. He's probably staying with one of Mr. Beamus's friends or relatives. Who knows?"

I knew. I could sense that something was odd. But I could also tell that I wasn't going to get anywhere by arguing with a stubborn police officer.

"Is your ride or a mechanic or a tow truck coming soon?" he added. "Because you are free to go at any time."

"I, um . . . I don't have a ride or a tow," I admitted. "I wasn't sure how the dogs and I were getting home, before you came along."

He looked askance at me. "Before *I* . . . ?"

"You *are* going to take us back to town, right?" I asked. "We can't walk!"

Detective Black didn't seem convinced of that.

"I'm wearing flip-flops," I said, pointing at my feet. "And look at Socrates's legs in proportion to his head. He's built for thinking, not walking. Then there's poor Artie. . . ."

As I spoke, I realized that the one-eared Chihuahua would probably make it through the journey, while

Socrates and I would get eaten by the *live* bear that I was certain lurked outside. Artie was a survivor.

"Why not call your boyfriend?" Detective Black asked, interrupting my thoughts. He'd been examining a taxidermied squirrel—what clues might *that* hold?—but he met my gaze for a moment. His eyes were impossibly dark blue. "Can't he come get you?"

"I don't have a boyfriend," I said, confused.

Was he making that assumption based on one hug I'd shared with Dylan?

"Are you sure?" Detective Black asked. "Because Dylan Taggart seems awfully concerned about you. Enough that he approached me on the street and spent quite a bit of time trying to convince me that you wouldn't hurt a flea." He looked at the dogs. "Which isn't exactly accurate, given that your pets are wearing flea collars."

The observation was funny, but my heart sank. "Dylan did *what?*" I groaned, digging my hand into my curls. "Please tell me you're joking."

"I seldom joke," Detective Black said, although his eyes were gleaming with ill-concealed amusement right then. He set down the squirrel, which he'd been holding the whole time, and a shadow crossed his face. "I am going to assume that his offer to buy me an organic chai latte while he pleaded your case was not a bribe on your behalf."

Once again, I couldn't tell if he was being serious.

"I really don't want to call Dylan right now," I grumbled. I was at once furious with Dylan, but grateful for his support. Our already complicated relationship had just gotten a little more complex. "His car is less reliable than mine," I added. In fact, Dylan was living in Sylvan Creek only because his Subaru had broken down while he was en route to a beach in New Jersey.

He'd taken a job with Piper to earn enough money to fix it and ended up sticking around for a while. "We'd probably wind up with two stranded vehicles blocking the road."

Detective Black hadn't been in Sylvan Creek long, but he already knew my associates. "I don't suppose your sister or your friend with the bright hair or your mother could help."

I kept shaking my head the whole time he was talking. "Nope, nope, and *nope.*"

Detective Black sighed heavily and resumed pacing around. "Just find someplace to wait *quietly*, please. I won't be too long. Then we can at least try to figure out what's wrong with your van."

I didn't tell him that everything was probably wrong. I had a feeling I should just be grateful for the prospect of a ride. "Thanks," I said, wandering over to the kitchen. I was starting to get hungry, since I hadn't finished my pasta. The open floor plan allowed me to continue watching Detective Black as he walked about. He returned to the trophy case and stood before it again, head cocked and one hand rubbing his jaw, while Artie sat at his feet, looking up hopefully.

It's never happening, Artie, I thought as I absently opened Steve's refrigerator, just to check it out.

Not surprisingly, he had a lot of meat.

I stood there for a long time, inventorying a plastic bag of pepperoni slices, a big blob of ground beef, something called a Wonder Chicken, which was obviously roasted at the grocery store, and . . .

All at once, I spied an item that didn't belong there—because *I* would've actually eaten it without feeling morally reprehensible.

Then I closed the fridge and scanned the counter, first noticing a big pill bottle on top of a piece of paper. I recognized the letterhead, which featured silhouettes of a dog and a cat sitting together in a crescent moon.

All the documents that came from Templeton Animal Hospital were printed on that stationery.

Moving closer, I picked up the bottle and read the label.

Lysodren. 500 mg.

Setting down the medication, I checked the printout from Piper's practice.

"Administer daily to Axis for treatment of Cushing's disease. . . ."

I'd heard of that disorder before. It was chronic and could make a dog lethargic, thirsty, and prone to infections.

"Oh, no," I muttered.

If Axis was alive, as I insisted on believing, he would need to take Lysodren every day. I hoped whoever had him knew that.

I was worried, but also distracted by something else on the counter. An item that was out of place at Steve's, just like the unexpected food I'd found in the fridge.

Forgetting, in my excitement, that Detective Black probably wouldn't take orders from me, I nevertheless summoned him.

"Hey, you have *got* to come look at what I found!"

Chapter 16

"*Tofu?*" Detective Black said. "Really? *Tofu?*"

He wasn't asking me to confirm his identification of the white cubes I'd found pressed between paper towels on a plate in the refrigerator. He was unhappy that I'd interrupted his trophy-case cogitation to show him a pile of coagulated, draining soy milk.

I wanted to rap him on his handsome head.

"Don't you get it?" I asked as Socrates and Artie joined us in the kitchen. "Steve would never eat tofu. Look at everything else in his refrigerator. It's a monument to meat!"

"Maybe he was trying to get healthy," Detective Black suggested, with a shrug. Using his foot, he subtly edged Artie away from his ankle, against which Artie'd been leaning, still with a hopeful, almost adoring look on his face. Even I had to admit that the little dog was getting pretty clingy—and to what end? Detective Black clearly had no interest in him. "Maybe Beamus wanted to kick the meat habit," Detective Black added. "Lower his cholesterol?"

"Are you serious?" I gestured to the whole house. "Look around this place! Steve likely ate the bear and the squirrel, too. Not to mention whatever poor animals probably gave their lives so he could have a set of hideous end tables. Guys like Steve don't give up meat, even to save their lives."

Detective Black leaned against the counter and smiled in what I thought was an indulgent way. "You're sure of this?"

I had a hunch that the man who stood before me wasn't a vegetarian—he did not have the same vibe as Dylan, who ate a plant-based diet, like me—and I held out the plate to him. "Would *you* eat this? Give up a cheeseburger and eat *curds*?"

"No," he conceded, wrinkling his nose. "I would not."

At least he was honest.

"And look," I added, pointing to a carton that was right next to Detective Black's elbow. "Almond milk! It's vegan food!"

"Don't tell me," he said. "You are a . . ."

"Vegetarian," I informed him. "I don't think there's anything wrong with eating dairy and eggs, if they're produced humanely. In fact, I kind of *need* cheese."

"I see."

I saw another glimmer of amusement in his eyes. He observed me closely, like I'd just provided him with clues to who I was, while I really wanted him to focus on the strange things I'd just found that might help him solve a crime. Or maybe he was multitasking, because as he watched me, he reached over and rested the back of his hand against the carton of almond milk.

I didn't know what he was doing until he said, "I'm not sure if vegan products will help to find Steve Beamus's killer, but I will give you this, Ms. Templeton . . . Someone was just here, because this 'milk' is still cold."

Chapter 17

"Will you please admit that I helped you?" I requested as Socrates, Artie, and I walked with Detective Black back down the lane to our cars. As he had pointed out several times, my van was blocking the road, so he'd been forced to hike, too. "I showed you the milk!"

"Yes, you've mentioned that quite a few times," he said, like *I* was the one who kept repeating things. "But I don't know if it's even important." He looked over at me, but it was hard to see his face. The moonlight was blocked by the trees, which seemed less threatening now that I had another human with me. In fact, I hadn't even thought about bears since giving Steve's grizzly a sympathetic pat farewell. "It's likely that Beamus's family has arrived to plan the funeral. Somebody might be staying at the house."

"So where was that person?" I asked, scooping up Artie, who seemed to be getting tired, probably because he'd tried so hard to impress a man who refused to succumb to a one-eared Chihuahua's charms. "It's awfully late."

"Perhaps he or she is drowning his or her sorrows at the bar everyone talks about. The one your boyfriend's playing at this Monday, according to flyers posted in every store window in town."

I saw a flash of white teeth and suspected he was grinning.

I almost protested again that Dylan wasn't really my boyfriend, but I decided not to bother. Besides, I'd recalled something else that might be important. "Remember how I told you that I saw a Jeep last night? Late?"

He seemed confused by the sudden, seemingly random comment. "Yes?"

We continued walking, but Detective Black motioned for me to hand over Artie, and for a moment I forgot what we were talking about. I stopped in my tracks.

"Do you really want to carry him?"

"No. I just want to spare you the burden of doing it," he said. "I'm trying to be a gentleman."

"He's not very big. . . ." Why was I fighting this chance for Artie to bond with someone he'd been dying to meet all evening? "Well, okay. Thanks," I said, passing Detective Black a very excited, wriggling dog.

I was almost hurt by how eager Artie was to abandon me.

"Don't lick me," Detective Black warned Artie when the little dog lunged for his face, tongue flapping. He got Artie under control and returned his attention to me. "About the Jeep . . . ?"

"One passed me when I was driving here. It was headed in the other direction. I wondered if it was the same one that I saw at Winding Hill."

"Jeeps are pretty common," Detective Black noted.

I disagreed. "I don't see a lot of them around here. Not the classic army kind."

"You and your mother are authorities on Sylvan Creek, aren't you, Ms. Templeton?"

That didn't sound like a compliment.

"It's a small town, and I've lived here my whole life—except for college. And traveling," I said. "And can you please call me Daphne? I'm not exactly British royalty. You don't need to use a title."

"All right, Daphne," he agreed.

I noticed that he didn't suggest that I use his first name.

"Um, can I call you Jon or Jonathan?"

I saw another flash of white teeth. "I think you just did."

I would take that as permission to be on a first-name basis.

"You know, Jonathan . . ." I opted for the more formal name, since I felt like I was already pushing the boundaries of familiarity with him. "I really could help you solve this murder. I know stuff about people around here that you don't. Like the fact that Steve would never eat tofu."

We'd reached our cars, and Jonathan handed back Artie, who tried to cling to his shirt.

Really, Artie? After all I've done for you?

"Thanks, Daphne," he said. "But I have a partner. One who actually attended the police academy."

I glanced at Socrates, who didn't find that amusing, either. "Ha. Ha," I said sarcastically, speaking for Socrates, too.

My van and Jonathan's off-duty pickup truck were close to the road, and there were fewer trees there, so I could see his face better in the moonlight. He appeared serious. "Why do you want to solve this murder? It doesn't seem like you liked Beamus very much."

"I didn't," I agreed. "But I want to make sure my sister isn't wrongly accused—"

"Yes, I know you want to protect her."

He was referring to my "tweak" of justice. I overlooked the comment.

"And I really think something has happened to Axis," I said. "I want to find him, and soon, because he needs medication I found in Steve's kitchen."

Jonathan took a moment to consider my comments. Crickets and cicadas chirped and buzzed around us, and the air had that pungent, sweet smell of woods in summer. We stood close enough that I could also smell, just faintly, Jonathan's cologne. It was a fresh, masculine scent.

I wondered what he was noticing about me.

Probably the way the humidity was making my long curls into tight, crazy spirals, or the spot on my jeans, where I'd wiped the dirt off my fingers.

"Give me your keys," he finally said, breaking our silence.

"What?" For a second, I didn't know why he wanted them.

"Your keys," he repeated. "So I can try to figure out what's wrong with your van." He shot the VW a dubious look. "Aside from that *pony* on the side."

"I told you, it's not a . . . Oh, never mind," I grumbled, digging into my pocket and retrieving a beaded key ring shaped like Africa that I'd tried to buy at a fair-trade shop in Nairobi, only to be accused of shoplifting and nearly detained for trial. "Here."

Jonathan held up the ring for inspection, dangling it in front of his face. "Given your stolen-passport anecdote, I suppose there's a story behind this."

"Yeah, but it's a long one," I said, not wanting to

give him more reason to think I was a lawbreaker. "For some other time."

"Oh, I look forward to that." He didn't sound like he really did.

Going around to the driver's side, he climbed behind the wheel and tried to start the engine. It wouldn't turn over, but the electrical system buzzed to life. A moment later, he got out and returned the keys to me, dropping them into my palm.

"Well?" I asked.

"I know what's wrong," he said.

I was impressed. "Really?"

"You are out of gas," he said drily.

"Oh." I cringed. "Oops."

"You didn't fill the tank after mentioning today that it was almost empty, did you?"

What did he have? A photographic memory?

"No, I did not," I admitted. "I had other things on my mind!"

Jonathan sighed. For a second, I thought he was going to drive off and leave me standing alone in the woods again. Then he grudgingly said, "Come on. I'm sure you can lead me to a convenience store that's open all night, and we can bring back a gas can."

I didn't tell him that the nearest open market, QuikSave, was a twenty-minute drive away. "Thanks," I said, following him to his pristine black Ford F-150. He got in the driver's side, while I opened the front passenger door and started to set Artie on the seat.

"Dogs ride in the back," Jonathan advised me. "No exceptions."

"Oh, fine," I agreed, noting a distinct shortage of junk on the floor, a dearth of half-empty cups in the cup holders, and a lack of unusual smells, which were all commonplace in my van. "Your truck, your rules."

But as I opened the back door, I quietly apologized to Socrates, who really preferred riding up front. I was pretty sure he would've liked to *drive*, if given the chance. "Sorry," I whispered, boosting him into the high truck. He didn't like accepting assistance, either. "It's not up to me."

Socrates turned his head away from me, like I'd betrayed him, while Artie, who'd managed to hop in by himself, made a move to jump up front.

"Sit," Jonathan ordered quietly but without room for negotiation.

For once, Artie listened.

I got into the front seat, and Jonathan put the truck in gear. Although I had a million questions for him—such as "Where did you come from?" and "Why are you here?"—we didn't talk for a while. I got the impression that he wanted to be quiet. Yet after about three miles, I couldn't help turning and asking him, "What if whoever is staying at Steve's house didn't arrive to plan the funeral? What if he or she was here *before* the murder?"

Chapter 18

When I woke up early the next morning, it was hard to believe anything bad had ever happened at Winding Hill. Sunlight streamed through the tall kitchen windows, which were open to let in a soft breeze that smelled of the lilacs and honeysuckle that were in bloom just outside the door.

As the water boiled for my morning tea, I assembled the flour, milk, eggs, and fruit I would need to make Socrates's favorite breakfast, Banana-Apple Pupcakes.

"Just be patient," I told the dogs, who watched from a bed near the door as I mixed the batter for the pet-friendly pancakes. I didn't make a big deal out of the fact that Artie was actually on the cushion with Socrates, who didn't seem to be making any effort to push off the smaller dog. I just nonchalantly went to the fridge and took out a bowl of staple food I always kept on hand. "I'll give you some rice, chicken, and veggies to tide you over."

Both dogs licked their chops as I scooped out their breakfasts. Then, while they ate, I heated a griddle and finished the pupcakes, which I stacked on two pretty robin's egg–blue plates I found in the china closet. I didn't think Piper would mind my effort to make the meal a little more special.

"Let's eat outside," I suggested, setting their breakfast, along with my tea and a bowl of yogurt and fresh blueberries, on a tray.

Holding open the door, I allowed Socrates and Artie to trot past me onto the patio, which had a sweeping view of the valley. In the distance, I could see Sylvan Creek's distinctive three church spires poking up through the trees that lined the town's streets.

"Hey, good morning."

The sound of an unexpected greeting nearly caused me to drop the tray.

"Piper, what are you doing here?" I asked, surprised to find my sister relaxing on a wicker rocking chair, sipping her usual cup of strong black coffee. I placed the tray on a long antique wooden table. "Why aren't you at work?"

"It's Sunday," she reminded me. "The office is closed, except for emergencies."

I set Artie's and Socrates's plates in a shady spot on the brick floor, next to a bowl of water that Piper had already freshened in anticipation of the hot day. Both dogs dug right in.

"You usually go to work, anyway," I said, taking a seat at the table. "There's always an 'emergency'—even if it's only paperwork."

Piper shrugged. Her face was drawn, and her eyes looked tired, like she hadn't slept much the night before. Even her hair didn't look as shiny as usual. "I just didn't feel like going today."

"How are you doing?" I asked quietly. "And be honest."

"I don't know," Piper said, staring into the distance. I followed her gaze and saw that Mr. Peachy was at work painting the barn's white trim. That was a never-ending task, and like Piper, he rarely took a day off. I had a feeling he got lonely in his small cottage. "One minute I tell myself that I'm okay," Piper continued, so I returned my attention to her. "Because Steve and I weren't really back together."

I was about to eat a delicious-looking bite of creamy yogurt and sweet-tart berries, but my hand froze in place halfway to my mouth. "What do you mean by 'really back together'? That's twice you've said that."

Piper finally met my gaze again, and she looked guilty, because she'd been keeping secrets from me. "We might've gone out a few times lately," she admitted, quickly adding, "But it was no big deal." She fidgeted with her mug, picking at an imaginary chip on the rim, and grew quieter. "At least, not to him . . ."

I didn't want to be angry with a dead man, but it sounded to me like Steve Beamus had been stringing Piper along.

"Is that what you two fought about before he got killed?" I asked. "Your relationship, or lack thereof?"

"In a way," Piper said, looking up at me. "When I brought him the coffee, he told me he was going to be busy for a week or two, so I shouldn't expect him to contact me."

I rolled my eyes. "Really? He couldn't even call? Or send a text?"

"That's what I thought," Piper said. "But at first I acted like I didn't care, because I didn't want to seem clingy. I am *not* clingy or weak!"

"That's true," I agreed. "You are the strongest person I know."

I was being honest, but my sister had suffered from a small Achilles' heel. One named Steve Beamus.

Setting down her mug, she groaned, rubbed her

face with her hands, then confessed, "I started to leave, but I couldn't seem to bite my tongue. I turned back and blurted, 'Seriously? You can't even *call* me? And you're not going to tell me what's keeping you so busy? I don't even deserve that courtesy?' That's when the fight started."

"Good for you," I said, raising a spoon to Piper. "You did the right thing by confronting him."

She didn't agree and slumped in her chair. "No. I sounded pathetic."

I wasn't sure what to say. In my opinion, Piper's outburst had been warranted. I wasn't even officially seeing Dylan, but I couldn't imagine him disappearing without telling me what he was up to. And, while we didn't call or text every day, he would never tell me that he was too busy even to be in touch. That sounded kind of cruel, to me.

Yet I could also understand why Piper was upset with herself. She could've acted like she didn't care what Steve did. That would've given her the upper hand.

But who wanted to play games like that?

Wasn't it better to admit she was hurt?

"I still think you did the right thing," I told her. "I don't think you should feel badly."

Piper merely slumped lower. Then she narrowed her eyes at me and changed the subject. "By the way . . . where were you last night? And don't tell me some crazy story about a documentary. I know you don't have a TV or any other way to watch PBS that I know of."

I should've been ready for that question, but I wasn't. Fortunately, before I had to admit that I'd broken into Steve Beamus's house, been surprised there by Jonathan Black, then spent two hours with the detective, who'd been *very* unhappy when he'd found out just how far away the nearest open gas station was, a car came up the road.

"Visitors!" I said, pretending I'd forgotten about Piper's inquiry.

But when the vehicle emerged from a canopy of trees, I realized my relief was probably premature.

The dark sedan approaching Winding Hill had the "trying too hard to blend in" air of an unmarked police car. And sure enough, a few moments later, Detective Jonathan Black and his partner, Detective Doebler, got out of the car.

Judging by the suits and the expression on Jonathan's face, I had a feeling they weren't making a social call.

Chapter 19

"Hey, good morning," I chirped too cheerfully as Jonathan and his partner approached the patio. Artie raced to Jonathan, who didn't bend down to pick up the dog, in spite of the two having bonded a teeny bit the night before. He had a very grim and purposeful look on his face. I knew we were in for bad news, but I kept acting happy, for some reason. I supposed I needed to compensate for the shadow the two men were casting on the day. "Can I get you two something?" I offered. "Coffee? Tea? I have a great hibiscus blend!"

Before they could answer, Piper stood up, looking pretty grim herself. And a little nervous. Her gaze darted between Jonathan and Detective Doebler, and she swiped her hands down the sides of her khaki pants. "Detectives . . . What brings you here?"

As had happened before, Detective Doebler, fidgeting and hot in an ill-fitting seersucker suit, deferred to his partner.

"The coroner ran a routine toxicology test as part of the autopsy," Jonathan informed us. "We got the results back this morning."

Apparently, we weren't even going to exchange polite greetings or share a laugh about how I'd spilled the iced tea I'd insisted on buying at the mini-market all over the front seat of his previously pristine truck. I was sure that was funny by now.

But, no, Jonathan was all business.

He did finally look at me, though, if only to ask a question that at first made no sense to me, until I linked it to the "toxicology report" comment.

"You did say that you observed your sister giving Steve Beamus a *thermos of coffee*, correct?"

Chapter 20

"I don't have any idea where that thermos went," Piper said, leading me, Detective Doebler, and Jonathan to the barn. "I haven't seen it since the night before . . . the night . . ." Frowning, she addressed Jonathan. "Did the coroner set a time . . . ?"

Although Piper couldn't seem to finish that question, Jonathan understood what she was asking. He nodded in a very official, almost curt way. "Yes," he said. "The time of death has been established."

He'd answered Piper's direct question but withheld the information she really wanted. Apparently, he was going to play everything close to the vest, which made me nervous for my sister. She was definitely being treated like a genuine suspect. One who might accidentally slip up and reference something that wasn't public knowledge yet, like the time of death.

I was also unhappy with Jonathan—or should I call him Detective Black again? Any small rapport we'd established the night before had vanished in the light of day. A part of me understood that he needed to act professionally, but a part of me wouldn't have minded a joking reference to tofu or even the artwork on my van. Artie, popping along beside Jonathan in hopes of another ride, also seemed disappointed to be shunned, while Socrates kept shaking his droopy head. I knew he was thinking that both Artie and I were fools for having believed we could be pals with a man who might try to put Piper in jail.

Last but not least, I was angry at myself for mentioning the stupid coffee when I'd been questioned.

Why couldn't I ever keep my mouth shut?

Why was I about to talk right then, when I knew I should just stay quiet?

Yet I heard myself telling the detectives, "Piper was trying to be *nice* to Steve by giving him coffee! She didn't poison him!"

Jonathan stopped and gave me a dead-level stare. "I didn't say she did."

Piper also shot me a look. A warning one that matched her tone of voice. "Daphne . . ."

I wasn't quite finished yet. "He was hit on the head. I saw the wound!"

"Perhaps the poison didn't do its work quickly enough," Detective Doebler ventured, only to earn a silencing look from Jonathan.

Yup, Jonathan really wanted to keep tight control over any and all information.

As we reached the barn, Mr. Peachy put down his paintbrush, lifted off his cap, and scratched his head, clearly confused by the arrival of so much company. He took a few steps toward us while Piper hauled open the big door.

"What's happening here?" he asked, with concern. He looked among all of us, his gray eyes clouding over as he no doubt recognized the detectives. Then he turned to my sister. "Anything I can help with, Piper?"

Detective Doebler spoke before Piper could respond. "We're looking for a silver thermos," he said. "Have you seen one?"

Mr. Peachy shook his head. "No . . . I don't think so. . . ."

"It was Steve's," Piper said. "I filled it for him two nights ago, while he was working here. And since the police didn't find it in his truck, I thought he might've set it down in the barn. Have you seen it around?"

Mr. Peachy didn't answer right away. I was pretty sure he was putting puzzle pieces together in his mind and trying to figure out why the thermos might be important. Then he set his cap back on his head and tugged it down to his ears. "I think I have seen that." Waving his leathery hand, indicating that we should follow him, he shuffled into the barn. "Come with me."

We all followed him into the building, which was cool and quiet.

I should've been searching for the thermos, but I found myself watching Jonathan. He didn't seem bothered by the heat, although he again wore a dark suit, which was paired with a subdued, but classic gray tie.

For some reason, I tried to imagine Dylan in those clothes, but every time I pictured him wearing the suit, he was cracking up, like he would don a tie only as a joke.

Jonathan was not laughing. He seemed to sense me watching him and finally met my gaze. But I couldn't read his eyes. It was almost hard to picture *him* grinning, like he'd done the night before, when he had also been working but hadn't exactly been on duty.

Or had I imagined the smiles and the glimmers of mischief in his eyes?

We kept staring at each other, me feeling strangely disappointed, like Artie clearly was. Obviously, the Chihuahua and I couldn't switch between personal and professional modes quite as easily as Jonathan.

Heck, I didn't really have a professional mode.

"Hey, partner?" Detective Doebler interrupted the weird moment by calling to Jonathan, who, let's face it, was more of a boss than a partner.

"What?" Jonathan asked, jolting a little, like he'd been daydreaming, too.

We both turned to face Detective Doebler, who was holding aloft a silver mug, the handle smothered by a handkerchief, presumably to preserve any fingerprints.

"Got it."

Chapter 21

Although she'd initially planned to stay home all day, Piper dealt with stress the way she always did: by going to work.

We both knew that she hadn't poisoned Steve, but we were also learning to brace for unpleasant surprises.

I probably could've found something productive to do, too, such as balance the books I was supposed to keep for tax purposes. But it had been so long since I'd even opened the computer program Piper had installed for me that I couldn't quite bring myself to do it.

Not sure how to occupy myself, I puttered around the kitchen, where two leftover Banana-Apple Pupcakes were still on the griddle. They smelled good enough for human consumption, and I knew that if I sampled one, it would taste pretty good, too.

Reaching out, I tore off a tiny bite, only to be stopped by a deep and accusing "Woof!"

Socrates seldom spoke, but when he did, I listened.

"Sorry," I said, pulling back my hand and cringing with shame.

Artie looked disappointed in me, too. His little brow was furrowed, as if to say, "You would really steal our treat? You have a whole refrigerator full of human food!"

"Sorry," I repeated, holding up my hands in a gesture of surrender. "It won't happen again!"

After shooting me one last disapproving look, Socrates shambled out of the kitchen, his head hanging low and swaying back and forth in a tsk-tsk manner. Artie followed, his recessed chin high and haughty, since he was finally *not* the one in trouble.

I watched them wander off.

Were those two becoming unlikely friends?

Would somber Socrates ever really accept the smaller, affectionate dog's overtures?

Turning slowly, I noticed that Piper's laptop was open on the counter.

And speaking of friends who weren't always friendly . . .

"I'll just Google him quickly," I said to no one in particular. "I'll look at, like, *one* result—which probably won't even relate to him. It's a very common name."

I promised myself all that, but as I typed "Detective Jonathan Black" into the search engine, I knew I was kidding myself. And sure enough, two hours later, I was still sitting at the counter, delving deeper and deeper into the life of a man who turned out to be fairly easy to track down in cyberspace.

I couldn't stop myself from snooping, because the story was pretty compelling.

Not to mention scary in spots.

I was so absorbed in my research that I initially ignored the phone I'd finally recharged when it boinged to let me know I had a message. At the third notice, though, I reached into my back pocket and pulled out a cell that was probably also worse for wear because I repeatedly sat on it.

I was mildly irritated to be disturbed, until I read the message, which was from Piper, typed in her very formal way, without abbreviations or, heaven forbid, emojis.

> I may be late tonight. I've been taken in for official questioning.

Chapter 22

"Please, Virginia," I begged, resting my hand on Virginia Lockhart's house's huge crimson front door, which I feared she was about to slam in my face. She hadn't invited me inside and wasn't even coming out onto her porch to talk with me. Her face was half hidden in the shadows of her foyer, which was dark, although the day was sunny. "Can't you please help me . . . and Piper?"

"I told you, I'm not a criminal lawyer." Virginia repeated what she had, indeed, told me several times in the past few minutes. "I specialize in divorce and family law."

I hadn't known that. I'd always pictured Virginia stalking around courtrooms, raising objections and bullying witnesses like the lawyers on *Law & Order*. Still, she must've learned about criminal law in school, and I believed she'd protect Piper, who was looking more and more like a real suspect in Steve's death. Plus, I didn't know any other lawyers, and we needed one. Quickly.

"I don't know who else to turn to, especially on a

Sunday," I told Virginia. "Piper has been taken in for questioning!"

Virginia hesitated, and while she considered my request, a big head nudged the door open wider.

"Hey, Macduff," I said, greeting the leader of the Lockhart dog pack. He stuck his head out farther, and I scratched behind his ear.

Virginia grabbed the dog's collar and pulled him back inside, ordering him sharply, "Macduff, retreat!"

Once again, I thought her choice of a command word was strange. And I didn't know why she was in such a terrible mood, when I had the sister who was potentially in big trouble after *traces of poison* had been found in a thermos she'd handed to a man who was later bludgeoned.

"I'll give you free pet-sitting services for a year if you'll help us," I said, sounding a little desperate. She didn't look convinced, so I upped the ante. "Two years!"

"I would bill you for my services," she reminded me. "I don't do pro bono work. At least not for veterinarians who can well afford to pay for representation. Piper doesn't treat my dogs for free."

That was true, but she didn't have to put it so bluntly. I froze for a moment, like she'd smacked me. As I struggled to form a reply, I heard a car door shut behind me. Turning, I saw that Virginia's husband, state senator Mitch, had arrived and was headed toward me.

He was a ray of sunshine, smiling like he was at a casting call for a toothpaste commercial. He had his hand extended when he was still ten feet away, and in true politician fashion, he remembered my name, although we'd met only once. Virginia was my only liaison with the dogs.

"Daphne Templeton!" Mitch said, giving my hand a few hearty pumps that left my shoulder hurting. His bleached white teeth glittered, and his fair hair gleamed, too. He wasn't exactly handsome—his nose was slightly bulbous, and he was leaning toward a middle-aged paunch—but he would look okay on a campaign poster. Releasing my hand, he added, "What brings you here to rottweiler central?"

His smile never changed when he mentioned the dogs, but his eyes clouded over just a tiny bit.

Did he not like the sweet rotties?

All at once, I recalled some of the things I'd learned about Jonathan while snooping online.

Or was I misreading Mitch, like I'd recently misjudged another man's opinion of dogs? At least, I was pretty sure I'd done that. . . .

"Daphne was just leaving," Virginia interrupted before I could tell her husband why I was standing on their front porch.

"With the dogs, I hope? Permanently this time?" Mitch asked, still grinning ear to ear, like he was joking.

But he wasn't. I was fairly certain of that, too.

Virginia obviously agreed. "Not funny, Mitch."

She finally stepped outside and shut the door behind herself, like she didn't want her husband to cross the threshold, either. She crossed her arms over her chest, and her mouth was set in a firm line. When I saw her in the sunlight, she appeared older and less polished than usual. I tried to figure out why and realized that she wasn't wearing makeup. I didn't think I'd ever seen her without lipstick, eyeliner, and mascara.

I was also surprised to discover that she was wearing a shapeless gray sweatsuit.

No wonder she'd tried to hide inside. This was a

side of Virginia Lockhart that I'd never seen and one that she probably preferred to keep hidden.

I'd been so busy pondering Virginia's appearance that it took me a moment to grasp that I was in the middle of some kind of marital standoff. Virginia still had her arms crossed, and Mitch's smile had finally vanished. The day was warm, but there was a chill in the air on that porch.

Their spat wasn't my chief problem, though.

"Virginia," I said, drawing her attention to me. I spoke more calmly, but still earnestly. "Won't you please consider helping Piper, at least until we can hire another lawyer? I think she's in serious trouble. Steve was killed at her farm, after an argument, and now the police found traces of some chemical in a thermos she handed him."

Oh, gosh, that sounded awful, and I wished I hadn't explained everything in front of Mitch. If he blabbed, that news would be all over town. Some people might actually believe Piper was a killer. But what could I do? I needed to plead my sister's case to Virginia, and Mitch didn't seem inclined to step past the barrier that was his wife's body to enter his own house.

"Please, Virginia?" I repeated. "Of course, we'll pay for your services." I didn't feel like complimenting her right then, but I added honestly, "I've always thought that if I was in trouble, I'd want you as my attorney."

Virginia opened her mouth, and I could tell that she was about to turn me down again. But before that could happen, Mitch said softly and seriously, "Virginia, I think you should help Daphne and her sister. It really seems like the *least* you can do at this point."

Mitch had totally shed his political false front, and

there was a lot of unspoken backstory related to his comments.

I was curious, but more than that, I was happy when Virginia grudgingly agreed through gritted teeth. "Fine." She turned to me. "I will go get dressed."

"Thank you," I said, addressing both Mitch and Virginia.

Neither one of them replied. Mitch followed his wife into the house, and although he'd been so quick to welcome me, I ended up waiting on the porch, worrying about Piper and wondering why Mitch believed Virginia should be obligated to do anything.

And what the heck did he mean by "at this point?"

Chapter 23

I leaped up off the couch when Piper finally arrived home at about seven o'clock. Artie rushed to greet my sister, and for once, even Socrates appeared sympathetic. His eyes were droopier than usual, and I was pretty sure I heard him whine, briefly and very softly, when Piper crashed down onto a chair, rubbing her face with her hands.

"Are you okay?" I asked, sitting down again, too, right next to her. The dogs drew close, and I rested one hand on her knee. "What can I get you? Tea? Something to eat?" While I'd waited for her return, I'd picked some raspberries off the bushes near the barn and made her favorite dessert. "How about some cobbler, with a big scoop of vanilla ice cream?"

"No, thanks," Piper said glumly. She let her hands drop, and I saw that she was exhausted. Her cheeks were hollow, and her eyes were rimmed with red. "I think I'll just go to bed."

I didn't mention how early it was. She definitely needed some sleep.

Still, I had to ask, "What happened? Why were you gone so long?"

"I made the mistake of trying to convince them that I didn't kill Steve, when I should've just forced them either to arrest me or let me go," Piper said. "I just kept thinking that they would have to believe me, because I *am* innocent. I don't know how the poison got in the thermos or how Steve ended up in the tunnel. . . . I'm sure I don't know. . . ."

I drew back, confused, because Piper almost sounded like she doubted herself.

Had Jonathan and his partner grilled her so intensely that she'd begun to question herself?

"Of course you're innocent," I assured her. "You are!"

Piper didn't rush to agree with me. She just stared blankly ahead, her hands limp at her sides.

"Did Virginia help you? What did she say?"

My sister shrugged. "I don't know. Maybe. She didn't say very much."

I'd thought that Virginia's legal training and sharklike nature would kick in when she actually started working for Piper. But apparently, I'd been wrong. It sounded like Virginia had literally done "the least she could do."

I really couldn't understand that. Virginia was never overly nice to me, but I'd never thought of her as completely heartless. And if she planned to bill Piper, shouldn't she have protected my sister's interests?

"What is wrong with her?" I muttered.

Piper sighed and closed her eyes. "I'm sure she tried."

I exchanged concerned glances with Socrates and Artie, who both appeared worried. Socrates even deigned to rest a big paw on Piper's foot in a very uncharacteristic gesture of support, and I patted her knee again, not sure what else to do.

Under most circumstances, my sister was a fighter—and usually a winner.

Okay, she was almost always a winner. I couldn't recall ever beating her at a board game, even the ones that were 90 percent luck, like *Sorry!* I used to think she could control the dice with her mind.

But she was mourning right then, and that was stealing away her fight.

It probably didn't help that I had trouble understanding the depth of her grief. I was still angry about the way Steve had treated her. I felt sorry that he was dead, but I couldn't bring myself to *like* him, and I knew that added to Piper's misery.

I wished I could cry, so maybe she'd cry, too, and let out some of the pain I was sure she was hiding.

"I'm going to bed," Piper finally said, standing up. She tried to smile. "Maybe things will look better tomorrow."

"I'm sure they will," I promised as she went upstairs. "This will all be cleared up soon."

Her silence told me that she wasn't reassured.

The dogs and I sat quietly for a long time, just listening to Piper get ready for bed—before eight o'clock. She moved slowly, like she was completely beaten down.

Knowing what I did about Jonathan at that point, I could imagine that he was a tough interrogator. What sort of ordeal had he put my sister through to make her doubt her own innocence, even for a moment?

I needed to know, and when I heard Piper's bedroom door shut, I found my cell phone, hit it against my palm to get the loose wires connected, and punched in the four on my speed dial.

The person on the other end answered immediately. Of course.

"Hey, Mom," I said. "Where is Jonathan Black living right now? I *really* need to see him."

Chapter 24

"There is no such thing as Realtor-client privilege," I grumbled, tearing apart a particularly gooey cheese stick. The mozzarella refused to break, even though my arms were stretched nearly as wide as possible. "I know my mother made that up."

Moxie made a face as she struggled to crack open a crab. We were at the Lakeside, sitting at one of the old barrels that served as tables and enjoying the bar's signature messy food and the sunset over Lake Walla-pawakee. As I'd expected on a warm August night, the place was crowded, and I wondered, like I always did, how the old pier could stand up under the weight of so many people. I swore I felt the whole clapboard building sway sometimes.

"Not to side with your mother, but I kind of understand why she wouldn't give you Detective Black's address," Moxie said, reaching for a mallet. As a vegetarian, I found the whole process of cracking crabs a little barbaric, but obviously, I was in the minority. Most folks at the Lakeside had bushel baskets at their tables. "Especially since you were upset with him."

I finally got the cheese—the glorious cheese—to snap apart. "But—"

"Think about it," Moxie interrupted, licking her butter-covered fingers before wiping them on what was left of a napkin. "Your mom could've lost a sale. And what could you have really accomplished by confronting him? You might've made things worse for Piper."

"That's possible," I grudgingly admitted. "But if you'd seen Piper when she got home, you would've been mad, too. She was *crushed*—and I know whose fault that was!"

"I hate that Piper is possibly in trouble," Moxie agreed. "But it sounds like Detective Black was just doing his job."

"No." I shook my head. "Piper will hardly talk about what happened, but she says she was questioned for *three hours.* Isn't that torture? And it sounds like Jonathan basically bullied her to the point that even she's not sure she's innocent!"

Moxie stopped digging white meat out of a claw long enough to meet my gaze. Then she bit her crimson lip and ventured hesitantly, "Are you sure you didn't want an excuse to see *Jonathan?*"

"No!" I answered quickly and vehemently. I jammed the broken cheese stick into a dish of warm marinara, which splashed on my shirt. "Definitely not!"

Moxie watched me skeptically, no doubt in part because she didn't believe me, but also because I was cramming a really big glob of seasoned bread crumbs, mozzarella, and spicy tomato sauce into my mouth. As I savored the delicious treat, I thought about Jonathan's past. And when I could talk again, I nearly opened my mouth to tell Moxie what I'd learned by researching him online. Then something made me stay quiet, for once. I just had this sense that Jonathan wouldn't appreciate being the subject of gossip, and if I shared his history with Moxie, the whole town would soon know everything.

Maybe a person like Jonathan Black would like to maintain his privacy.

I looked down at my shirt, which sported not just a new stain but also a peace sign, and felt conflicted.

Or did he deserve privacy?

I was reconsidering my decision and was about to blab everything to Moxie when someone said, "Excuse me, but did you know that you have *cheese* in your hair, Daphne?"

I turned slowly on my stool, which wobbled beneath me, to discover that the man I'd just been thinking about had materialized.

I'd recently been determined to talk with Jonathan, but suddenly I wasn't so certain that was a good idea. Maybe Moxie was right about me possibly causing more trouble for Piper, because I could already feel myself getting aggravated with him.

Did he always have to find fault with me?

So I had a little cheese in my curls. *Big deal.*

I was about to thank him, in a tone frostier than my mug of Budweiser, then turn my back on him, when Moxie took it upon herself to suggest in a chirpy voice, "Hey, Detective! Why don't you join us?"

Chapter 25

"No, thanks. That's all right," Jonathan said in response to Moxie's invitation. He smiled at her, and I thought she might melt away, like the clarified butter she was again licking off her fingers. I also had to admit that Jonathan looked pretty good in a gray V-neck T-shirt and jeans. He turned to me and grew more serious, like he could tell I wasn't happy with him. "I don't want to interfere with your night out."

I wanted to thank him for understanding that three would be a crowd, but suddenly Moxie popped up off her stool and said, "No, please. I was just leaving—"

"What?" I asked, dumbstruck. "Since when?"

Moxie bent to pick up her purse, which was shaped like an oversize red Chinese take-out container. "I want to get out of here before the folk music starts," she informed me. "You know I love Dylan, but simple chord progressions played on a beat-up guitar, accompanied by lyrics about the plight of the workingman . . ." She mock shuddered. "I just can't take it!"

"But . . . but . . ."

"Here. Have a seat," she told Jonathan, gesturing to

her empty stool. "You can finish the crabs, if you want. There are two left."

Jonathan warily eyed the seat and the unappetizing pile of shells Moxie was offering him. If there was even a single unpicked crab in that mess, I couldn't see it. Then he looked at me, as if seeking permission. He must've seen that it was about to be denied. "Thanks, but . . ."

For some reason known only to her—at least until I called her later and demanded that she explain herself—Moxie would not leave well enough alone. "Where else are you going to sit?" she asked Jonathan. "The place is packed." She gestured to me. "And Daphne's going to be all alone. It will look weird if you're standing somewhere by yourself, and she's sitting here with no one to talk to." She patted the stool, smiling. "Just sit down."

Jonathan looked at me and arched an eyebrow, again asking unspoken authorization to join me.

I stared back at him for a long time, not sure why in the world he'd want to hang out with me. Then I realized he probably wanted a seat more than a dinner companion. I sighed and rolled my eyes. "Oh, fine. Sit down."

"Thanks," he said, taking Moxie's place. He pushed aside the soggy newsprint that held the disgusting pile of shells, then wiped his hand on a none too clean napkin. "So nice of you to let me join you."

I caught the sarcasm.

"Did I have a choice?" I asked, spinning around, because I couldn't find Moxie to say good-bye and to warn her that we would talk later.

How had she disappeared so quickly?

And had she just stuck me with both a detective *and* the bill for her meal?

It seemed that way.

Feeling decidedly unhappy with my friend, I turned back around to find Jonathan watching me.

I took a moment to remind myself that I shouldn't get into a confrontation with him. At least not one that could land Piper in more trouble.

Yet not two seconds later I heard myself ask in an aggravated tone, "Why in the world are you here? And what did you *do* to my sister?"

Chapter 26

"I'm here because, as I told you, I saw your boyfriend's flyers all over town," Jonathan explained, after placing an order with the waitress, who'd interrupted *my* attempt to conduct an interrogation. "I like folk music. I thought I'd stop by."

I didn't believe for a second that he appreciated folk music any more than Moxie did. I barely knew him, but I would've guessed that his tastes ran to dark and thunderous symphonies, like Beethoven's Fifth. I could practically hear the ominous opening notes— "dun, dun, dun, *dun!*"—whenever he walked into a room. I was pretty sure he'd "stopped by" to see if any suspects in the Steve Beamus murder were lurking around, drinking beer, and loosening up their tongues. I didn't dispute his assertion about his musical tastes, though, or correct him again regarding Dylan's and my relationship. I just folded my arms across my chest and let him keep talking.

"As for your sister," he continued, "I understand that you're upset because I questioned her so thoroughly. But *you* need to understand that I'm solving a murder, not throwing a tea party. I'm not worried about whether the conversation is polite or people are comfortable. I have to ask tough questions, sometimes repeatedly, to get to the truth."

I uncrossed my arms and rested them on the table, leaning closer to challenge him. "You can't really believe that Piper is guilty—"

He raised a hand, stopping me. "I don't want to—correction, I *can't*—discuss my thoughts on that. Surely you understand that, too."

I supposed I did get why he couldn't speculate about Piper's guilt or innocence. At least, not with me. And I also grasped on some level that he did need to ask difficult questions in his pursuit of justice for Steve. Yet I remained irritated with him.

Sitting back, to the extent that I could on a wobbly three-legged stool, I traced the condensation on my mug of beer. Then I raised my eyes to meet his gaze, and I spoke more calmly, too. "I'm also mad because when you *stormed* Winding Hill, you acted like we'd never met. I know we aren't best friends, but we spent an hour in your truck together. You could've at least smiled at me."

Jonathan leaned back, too, so our waitress could slide a frosty mug of beer and a plate of the Lakeside's jumbo lump crab cakes in front of him. It was pretty dark by then, so she lit the old-fashioned netting-covered candle that was on our table, too. Jonathan thanked her; then he turned back to me, his face lit by the flickering flame. "Yes, didn't you promise to pay to have my vehicle detailed? To remove the iced tea stain from the upholstery?"

Had I offered to do that?

Perhaps, but that wasn't the point.

"I just don't get how you can be joking with me

now. . . ." I hesitated. "You are joking about me paying to clean your truck, right?"

"Not re—"

Of course, he hadn't been serious, so I continued, talking right over him. "I don't get how you can be friendly now, and at Steve's house, but act totally aloof when you put on your suit and tie."

He poured a neat circle of ketchup next to his fries. I liked to smother mine. Then he frowned. "I have to separate the personal and the professional, Daphne. It's the nature of my work."

"I could never do that," I said. "I think Cicero was right when he said, 'A friend is, as it were, a second self.' I couldn't ignore a second self!"

Jonathan had been about to pop a fry into his mouth, but he hesitated. "You quote Cicero and have a dog named Socrates. . . ."

"I've got a Ph.D. in philosophy," I told him. Before he could make some cutting remark, I added, "Please don't make fun of how impractical the degree is. Believe me, I hear that enough from my mother."

"I wasn't going to say anything," Jonathan said. "I'm actually quite impressed."

Did I care?

Not enough to offer him my dinner, like Moxie had done with her leftover crabs. I pulled the basket, which still held a half dozen mozzarella sticks, closer to myself, then circled it protectively with my arms.

"I guess you weren't kidding about liking cheese," Jonathan noted, with a nod to the basket. "Is that all you're eating? Cheese?"

"Yes." I paused, still not overly eager to share, since the appetizer did constitute my entire meal. Then, my shoulders slumping, I pushed the basket toward him. "I *suppose* you can have some, if you want."

He gave me an inquiring look. "I doubt you eat crab—"

"Nope," I informed him, although even I had to admit that the Lakeside's crab cakes were tempting. They consisted almost entirely of chunks of white crab meat, were broiled to a golden brown, and were accompanied by a dish of house-made, tangy tartar sauce and fresh lemon wedges.

"How about french fries?" he inquired as my mouth began to water traitorously. "Do you eat those?"

"Yes," I said. "Probably too often."

Jonathan smiled in that way that transformed his face.

Had the woman in his past—the gorgeous blonde I'd seen with him in a photograph on the Internet—sparked that smile a lot? Or was she the reason it so seldom appeared now?

It was probably the latter. Along with a lot of other stuff that had happened to him . . .

"Daphne?" he prompted. "Do we have a deal?"

I nodded. "Sure."

I pushed my basket even closer toward the center of the table, and he turned his plate so the potatoes were within easy reach, and for the next few minutes, we ate in a companionable silence, me pretty much depleting his pile of fries while he focused on the crab cakes.

The night was warm, but there was a comfortable breeze on the lake, which lapped at the pier just below our feet, and the sound was soothing, too. But the evening was also energized by quiet conversations punctuated by bursts of laughter at the tables scattered around us, beneath long strands of twinkle lights. When the wind picked up slightly, the candle on our table flickered and the old buoys that were hung on fishing nets draped around the shack—rustic decorations that attested to the building's age—rattled against the clapboard. Looking skyward, I saw the moon glowing behind a thin veil of clouds, portending rain by morning. But the scene was very pretty right then.

"Daphne?"

I realized I'd been daydreaming, and I turned to find Jonathan watching me. His eyes looked almost black, and he seemed serious again.

"Yes? What?" I asked a little nervously.

"Lean closer."

My stomach flipped in a funny way. "What?"

"Lean closer," he repeated, with a half smile. "Just do it."

I had no idea what was happening, but I did as he asked and leaned across the table, being careful not to burn my hair with the candle. I got so close to him that I could smell his cologne again and see the small scar that ran along his jaw.

What are we doing?

I wasn't sure if I said that out loud. And I didn't understand why Jonathan was reaching for my hair, too. He took some into his hands, held it for a moment, then tugged gently.

"Ouch!" I cried, sitting back. I wasn't sure what I'd expected would happen right then, but I hadn't anticipated getting my hair pulled.

What was he? A middle-school boy?

I rubbed my head, although it didn't exactly hurt. "Why did you do that?"

"Sorry," he said, grinning at me. He extended his hand across the table, then opened it to reveal a fairly big chunk of cheese that he'd removed from my curls. Apparently, he'd been serious when he'd commented on that earlier. "Much as you seem to like cheese, I didn't think you'd want to *wear* it all night."

Okay, that was strangely deflating and somewhat embarrassing. But a moment later, we both started laughing pretty hard.

And when we stopped, I felt traitorous for the second time that evening.

Should I be eating—and cracking up—with a man who might put my sister in jail?

Jonathan seemed to sense the mood change, too. The laughter in his eyes flickered out.

"Can you at least tell me how much trouble Piper is in?" I asked softly. "Give me a hint?"

He didn't answer directly, but he said enough. "She was smart to get a lawyer."

I took a moment to let that sink in. Then, although I knew I risked messing up a pretty nice evening, I said, "I know you can't tell me much about the investigation. . . ." He immediately put up his guard—it was like two gates closed behind his eyes—but I forged ahead. "But could I at least ask three questions?"

He was clearly reluctant, but he nodded. "If you understand that I will answer them only if the information is already public knowledge. Things I'm telling local reporters."

That wasn't a great deal—not even as good as an exchange of fries for cheese sticks—but I took it. "Fine. First question. Did you ever find out who's been staying at Steve Beamus's house?"

He shook his head. His nearly black hair gleamed by the candlelight. "No. I returned once, but there was no one there, and I can't stake out the place. There's not enough of a compelling reason to do it."

I had a feeling that his failure to dig deeper into that mystery indicated just how convinced he was of Piper's guilt, and I resolved to solve the puzzle myself, even if I had to break into . . . er, use a key to enter the house again.

"Question two," I said. "Has Axis been located?"

"No. But again, I'm not a dogcatcher."

Perhaps not. But I was pretty sure that he cared about dogs. A lot.

It wasn't the right time to bring up his past, though. I needed to focus on my sister's future. I moved to question three.

"Did you find the murder weapon?"

Jonathan took a sip of beer, but he didn't say a word. He could really do a poker face well. "Pass," he finally said in an even tone. "And that concludes this game. . . ."

"No!" I objected. "I get three questions that you actually answer!"

He hesitated, then sighed with resignation. "Fine. You get one more. But this is it."

"What was in the thermos? What kind of poison?"

I could tell he didn't want to answer, and at first I thought he was putting up that professional wall again. But when he did respond, I realized he'd been reluctant to upset me, although at first he seemed to be speaking gibberish.

"The thermos contained dimethyl ammonium chloride mixed with some other ingredients."

My brow furrowed. "I don't know what that means. . . ."

"It's a commercial-grade sanitizer," he clarified softly. "Sold under the brand name Clean Kennel."

My heart was already sinking, but I asked, "And this is used by?"

"Kennel owners," he said. "And veterinarians."

My heart hit rock bottom, and I didn't even know

what to say. Jonathan seemed unsure, too. We got very quiet, but this time the silence was less comfortable.

After a minute, Jonathan looked past me, as if something over my shoulder had caught his attention. "I think your boyfriend is about to play," he said. "He's arrived, and he's got his guitar."

I'd almost forgotten that I'd initially gone to the Lakeside to support Dylan, and I turned around to see him making his way through the tables toward what served as a stage at the end of the pier. He had his guitar slung over his broad shoulder, and he was smiling in his easy, infectious way.

"We really don't use labels like 'boyfriend' and 'girlfriend,'" I muttered, continuing to watch Dylan, who pulled the microphone closer to himself. "The terms wouldn't be accurate, anyhow. . . ."

I turned back to Jonathan, who had raised a skeptical eyebrow, like he didn't quite believe me.

However, before I could explain Dylan's and my thoughts on the perils of commitment, Dylan began his set without so much as an introduction—heck, everybody knew him—by announcing, "I'm going to play a song I just wrote today about someone who's here tonight and who means a lot to me. I call it 'Daphne.'"

Chapter 27

"I can't believe Dylan wrote a song about you!" Moxie said as we both walked down Sylvan Creek's main street the morning after my serenade. We were accompanied on that warm, humid day by Socrates and a floppy, lazy bloodhound named Charlie, whom I was watching for the next few days. Artie was with us, too, riding in Moxie's arms. He'd pooped out after we'd gone about a block. At least, he'd acted tired, lying down on the sidewalk with his tongue hanging out even farther than usual. Moxie waggled Artie's paws, as if they were *both* excited. "That must've been so romantic!"

"Actually, it was awkward," I said, popping a treat into Charlie's waiting, open mouth. Martha Whitaker, town librarian and Charlie's person, had advised me that he would lie down, too, if not occasionally provided with an incentive. Then I cringed, recalling how I'd sat stiffly as Dylan had sung my praises, and added, "More than awkward, really."

Socrates, who hadn't even been there, snuffled, like he found the whole scenario funny. I glanced down to see him trying *not* to wag his tail, which moved only on the rare occasions when something amused him.

"Not funny, Socrates," I complained. I tugged lightly on Charlie's leash, and although he was one of the most charmingly baleful dogs I'd ever had the pleasure of meeting, I also warned him, "Don't you get any ideas about laughing, either."

"What was so terrible?" Moxie asked. A light went on in her eyes, as if she had an idea. "Was it bad because nothing rhymes with 'Daphne'? Was the song awful?"

"Not *awful*," I said. "Although there were some unfortunate lyrics, including a not very successful attempt to rhyme 'Daphne' with 'decaffeiny-ated'—"

Moxie drew back, her brow furrowed. "Why 'decaffeinated'?"

"I don't know." I waved off the question. "It had something to do with the herbal tea I drink. It's not really the point."

Moxie shifted Artie to her other arm. "So . . . what *was* the point? If the song wasn't really bad, by folk standards, why didn't you like it?"

The funny thing was, I couldn't explain exactly why I wasn't happy with Dylan's decision to pay tribute to me in song. In a way, the gesture had been sweet, if too public for my taste.

And it wasn't like Jonathan and I had been on a *date*. . . .

As if reading my mind—which I sometimes swore she could do—Moxie turned to me, her eyes gleaming with smug satisfaction. "You didn't like Dylan acting like he's your boyfriend while you were having dinner with Detective Black, did you? He was still there, wasn't he?"

I felt my cheeks redden. "Yes, but . . ."

"You really do like him, don't you?" Moxie asked. "You didn't want to seem tied down—"

"I'm not tied down!" I interrupted her, growing defensive. "I'm not sure how I feel about either of them, and I don't want a *commitment* with anyone. Not with Dylan—and certainly not with Jonathan, whom I barely know."

Just to hear myself even mention the words "commitment" and "Jonathan" in the same breath suddenly made the beyond remote possibility seem especially laughable. He spent most of his time mocking me; he had been part of an organization that stood for everything I stood against; there was that gorgeous blonde from his past; and, last but not least, he was trying to pin a *murder* on my sister.

Dylan, meanwhile, was a perfect match for me. We didn't stress over professional achievement, to say the least. We both liked to wander. And we believed in all the same things. Peace. Harmony. The right of every human and animal to follow his or her bliss. Yet I couldn't imagine being bound to Dylan, either. There was no way we'd both thrive in some sort of formalized, let alone legalized, arrangement.

Was it odd that one of the things that brought us together was knowing we could be apart?

I was pondering that conundrum when a warm, damp nose nudged my hand, and I realized I hadn't offered Charlie a treat in quite some time. I reached into my pocket and came up empty.

Glancing across the street, I saw that the red-and-white sign in the window of Fetch! was turned to CLOSED. I knew, however, that Tessie was often in the shop during off hours and was happy to open up if someone knocked.

"I'm out of treats for Charlie," I told Moxie. "Let's run over and see if Tessie's in Fetch!"

"Sorry," Moxie said, shifting Artie again so she could check her vintage Mickey Mouse watch, which went very well with her Lucille Ball–style polka-dot, flared summer dress. She held out her arms, offering me Artie. "I've gotta go open the salon. I've got two early appointments."

"Why don't you keep Artie?" I suggested, stepping back. "You two could have a slumber party tonight. Watch old movies and eat snacks. I made Sweet Potato Puppy Crunchers last night, and I could drop some off. He loves them. They're made with yummy sweet potatoes, cornmeal, and cranberries." She didn't seem convinced, so I added, "I could make that special popcorn you like, too. The one with the toasted pecans and drizzles of dark and white chocolate."

Moxie bit her lip, indicating that she was tempted. "You know I love your Tuxedo Popcorn." We'd named it that because it was about as fancy as popcorn could get, and had the mix of dark and light chocolate. "But I also know what you're doing, and I cannot have a pet."

Of course, Moxie knew that I was hoping she'd get attached to Artie and keep him. She held out the dog again, so his tongue *and* his paws dangled in the air.

"As much as a movie night with Artie sounds fun—and the Puppy Crunch sounds delish, from a dog standpoint," she continued, "for the millionth time, the Flinchbaughs won't let me have a dog in the apartment."

I accepted Artie, but I told Moxie, "I don't believe that. They own a *pet store!*"

"Daphne!" Moxie said loudly, like she needed to get my attention. "I work crazy hours—and I live on the third floor, without a yard. It wouldn't be fair, even for a small dog like Artie, to try to cram him into my life or my house."

She was right. Of course, she was right.

"I know," I agreed glumly, nuzzling the Chihuahua under my chin. "I just want him to get a good home, with a good person."

Perhaps a tiny part of me also wanted Artie to remain in my life even after he'd been adopted.

Moxie smiled like she knew something I didn't. "He's going to find the right home, Daph. I promise. And he won't go far. You'll see him around."

Along with being a sometime mind reader, Moxie had a strong psychic sense.

"You really feel that?" I asked.

She grinned more broadly. "Yeah, I do."

The rain that the clouds and breeze had portended the night before finally began to fall, if only in the form of a light drizzle, and Moxie—no doubt wanting to keep her circle skirt stiffly starched—hurried off with a wave.

I waved back, then crossed the street with Socrates, Artie, and Charlie. Fetch! looked dark inside, but I set down Artie, bent close to the glass door, cupped my hands around my eyes, and peered inside.

At first, I couldn't see anything.

Then, as my eyes adjusted to the dim store interior, I saw Tessie *crying*.

Chapter 28

"Tessie?" I rapped on the glass, then cupped my hands around my eyes again, being careful not to tug Charlie's leash, because the lazy bloodhound had flopped down and stretched out on the sidewalk, leaving little slack. Socrates sat patiently at my feet, while Artie scratched wildly against the door, as if he also wanted to comfort Tessie. She was leaning against her sales counter, her face buried in her hands and her shoulders shaking. I could hear her sobs.

"Tessie?" I called again. "Please . . . let me in!"

She finally lowered her hands and raised her face. "Daphne?" she asked, peering through teary eyes. "Is that you?"

"Yes," I said. "Are you okay? Please, unlock the door."

"It's already open," Tessie said, sniffling. "Just come in."

Socrates sneezed. It sounded a lot like a barely stifled chuckle.

"Seriously," I grumbled at him. "Please stop laughing at me today!"

Socrates lifted his noble head, clearly offended by

the idea that he'd find anything amusing, but I knew he'd found my failure to try the door funny.

I looked between him and Artie, who considered the whole world entertaining.

Was Artie's exuberance rubbing off on Socrates?

"Come on, guys," I said, bending to rouse Charlie, who was snoring. He would open only one eye, until I noted, "There are treats inside."

That got him on his feet, and the four of us entered Fetch, our arrival announced by a strap of sleigh bells hanging on the doorknob. The cheerful sound was at odds with Tessie's tearstained face and red-rimmed eyes. After unhooking Charlie's leash, I took the liberty of turning on some lights, and I saw that Tessie's normally neat, conservatively styled graying hair was unkempt. Her seasonally themed shirt of the day, which featured a cute kitten sniffing a summer daisy, was rumpled, too.

"What's wrong, Tessie?" I asked, keeping a watchful eye on Charlie, who was sniffing around a basket of complimentary jerky treats on the counter. Fortunately, Artie barked, alerting the bloodhound to a bin of toys. A moment later, the two dogs were tugging on a stuffed elephant I'd have to buy, Artie putting up a valiant fight, although he was outweighed by about sixty pounds. Socrates watched their play with disapproval. Satisfied that they were all occupied, I returned my attention to Tessie. "What happened? Why are you crying?"

"I can't tell you," she said, wiping her arm across her eyes. She was drying her face—and hiding it. "I can't. . . ."

I drew closer to her and tentatively reached out, resting a hand on her shoulder. "Sure you can. I want to help."

Tessie lowered her arm. Her face was puffy, and the lines around her eyes seemed deeper than usual. She shook her head and spoke softly, her lower lip still trembling. "No, Daphne . . . I can't tell you. And no one can help. . . ."

I didn't know Tessie that well, but she was obviously carrying some sort of secret burden. One that was crushing her. "It's okay," I said quietly. "I am a *professional pet sitter*. I know how to keep secrets, if you have one you need to get off your chest. I promise, whatever you say won't go beyond these walls."

Even I wasn't sure what pet sitting had to do with keeping secrets—although I had seen some pretty weird stuff in people's houses during overnight stays, and I'd never said a word. Regardless, something about my promise to be discreet or my soothing tone must've struck a chord with Tessie.

Either that, or she just *really* needed to unburden herself, because all at once she blurted, her voice thick with misery, "You can't tell *anyone*, but I think Tom might've killed Steve Beamus!"

Chapter 29

The whole store went silent when Tessie came close to accusing her husband of murder. I sucked in a sharp breath and held it, while Artie and Charlie abruptly stopped tugging on the elephant, which dropped to the floor.

Plop.

Socrates, of course, hadn't been making any noise. His rolling eyes indicated that he found the drama a little over the top.

I, however, couldn't help getting sucked in, although I tried to remain cool and composed. "Why in the world would you think that, Tessie?"

The store was brightly lit, but I suddenly felt like we were all gathered around a campfire on a gloomy night, about to hear a ghost story. Tessie leaned toward me and confided softly, "Twelve years ago, almost to the date of Steve's death, there was a car crash. . . ."

All at once, before she even said more, I knew the rest of the story. I'd been away at college, but my mother had mentioned the accident during one of her frequent phone calls to remind me that I was wasting her money by studying philosophy. I let Tessie continue, though.

"Tom's sister, Angie . . ." Tessie's focus had shifted inward, but she met my eyes for a moment. "You remember her, right?"

I nodded. Angela Flinchbaugh had been a waitress at a diner called the Silver Moon, just outside town. My father used to take me and Piper there after he'd left Mom, but before he'd wandered out of our lives, too, and Angie used to give us all extra scoops of ice cream on our apple pie.

"She was driving home late one night, after work, and Steve was headed in the opposite direction, going too fast, when they both rounded a curve. . . ."

I cringed, because accidents like that weren't uncommon around Sylvan Creek. The roads—like the one to Steve Beamus's house—were twisting and narrow, lined with trees that were beautiful but unyielding if a driver missed a turn or had to steer to avoid an oncoming car. Say, one driven recklessly by a brash young man . . .

"You don't have to finish the story," I told Tessie, who was getting teary-eyed again. "I remember what happened."

She nodded gratefully but added, "I try to forgive, because Steve was young and stupid . . . practically a kid. . . ."

I did the math to the best of my ability and wanted to disagree. Steve hadn't exactly been a "kid." But I didn't contradict Tessie. She was being generous, trying to forgive an act many would find unforgivable, and I admired that.

As the Buddha said, "Holding on to anger is like drinking poison and expecting the other person to die."

I got a sick feeling in the pit of my stomach.

Had Tom Flinchbaugh consumed enough metaphorical "poison" to compel him to administer some literal toxins to the man who'd killed his sister? And then, when that hadn't worked, *crushed his skull?*

Tessie seemed to think it was possible. "Tom can't let go of his anger," she said, wiping again at red-rimmed eyes. "He *hated* Steve."

It was hard for me to imagine mild-mannered Tom Flinchbaugh despising anyone, but who could really know what sort of pain and anger simmered deep in people's hearts?

Still, I said, "Tessie . . . I can't really picture Tom hurting anyone." I recalled a particular area at the Philosopher's Tome. "He's dedicated a whole bookcase to philosophies emphasizing nonviolence," I reminded her. "The last time I visited the store, he was reading a collection of essays about Gandhi."

"Yes, he's always seeking answers in those books," she said, digging into the pocket of her slacks for a tissue. It was crumpled and looked damp, like she'd been crying off and on for a while. She swiped it under her nose. "But sometimes he gets very angry."

I wanted my sister's name to be cleared as soon as possible, but I hated watching Tessie suffer by thinking that her husband might have taken a life. I glanced at Socrates, who gave me an encouraging look, before I asked reluctantly, "Was he angry the night you and Tom were setting up the tent and Steve was there?"

Tessie nodded, her chin quivering. "He was frustrated with the tent—we'd never set one up before—and distracted by Steve's presence, too. He kept looking over at Steve and grumbling about how he should be in jail or . . . or someplace *worse*."

I was pretty sure she was talking about a grave.

Or someplace beyond a grave—like Hades.

"But you were with him the whole time at Winding Hill," I noted, grasping for anything that might reassure her. "Right?"

"Not the whole time," she said quietly. She buried her face in her hands, so her voice was muffled. "And after we went home, late, Tom didn't go straight to bed. . . ."

Oh, gosh. I did not want to believe that the gentle man who let me borrow books I should've paid for could be a killer, but Tessie was raising a lot of questions in my mind. And the fact that she—his *wife*—feared he could commit murder wasn't helping to quell my own growing doubts.

I rested my hand on her shoulder again, compelling her to look at me. "Just don't panic yet," I urged. "Please. Sometimes things aren't what they seem. You're probably worrying for no reason. Tom is a good man."

I believed everything I'd just said, including the part about Tom being a decent person. If he had killed Steve, he'd been pushed to an emotional brink over the course of more than a decade. It must've been hard watching Steve walk around town, not only still alive after the accident he'd caused, but also with his chest puffed out and his arrogant attitude, acting like he'd never done anything wrong in his entire life.

I felt myself getting agitated, and I took a deep breath, then told Tessie, "I'm kind of investigating the murder. Let me see what more I can learn before you get too upset, okay?"

Tessie gave me a funny look. "*You're* investigating?"

"Unofficially," I said. Recalling Jonathan's snarky comments, I added sarcastically, "It's not like I've been to the *police academy*, but I'm looking into the crime."

Tessie didn't seem to mind my lack of credentials or badge. "Thank you," she said, clasping both of my hands in hers. I kind of wished she'd put away the damp tissue first. "Thank you, Daphne. I feel better having talked to you."

I'd pretty much forgotten the dogs while I'd been talking with Tessie, and I looked across the store to see that Charlie and Artie were lying side by side, gnawing on the stuffed elephant. Or, more accurately, Artie was stabbing at the poor thing with his protruding front teeth, while Charlie's head was bobbing as he began to doze off.

Awww, cute.

Awww, crud!

I really do have to buy that thing!

I dug into a pocket of my jeans, while Socrates, still seated at my feet—the better to hear the human conversation—sighed at the folly of his fellow canines.

"We'll take the elephant," I said, unfolding a few wadded-up dollar bills.

Tessie pushed my hands back toward my pockets. "No, no, I couldn't take your money. You're being very kind."

I would've protested, but I had only three dollars, just barely enough to buy a handful of treats that would lure Charlie through the rest of the walk, so I gratefully accepted. "Thanks, Tessie."

She smiled, if weakly, and went over to retrieve the toy from the dogs. Artie bounced around on happy feet, like he knew it was going home with us, while Charlie's head thumped to the floor.

As Tessie placed the soggy object in a bag, I got a closer look at it. "That's really different," I said, noting the heavy canvas fabric. "It looks sturdier than most plush toys for dogs."

"Yes, that's the idea," Tessie agreed. She gestured to the bin Charlie and Artie had raided, and I saw that it was filled with stylized versions of other African creatures, like lions and zebras. "A seamstress from Milroy, a few miles down the road, makes them. It's a very small operation—a hobby, really—and they're sold exclusively at Fetch!"

I'd been headed toward a wall of bulk-purchase treats to get three dollars' worth of Salmon Snackers, but I stopped in my tracks, struck by a memory. An image of a giraffe, which I'd seen under Steve Beamus's couch when I was crouched by the end table, failing to hide from Jonathan.

But surely even insensitive Steve wouldn't have been so thoughtless as to darken the doorstep at Fetch!

Surely, he would've left the Flinchbaughs alone.

Plus, I couldn't imagine him spending money on expensive, whimsical toys. Rubber balls and rope pulls maybe, but a *giraffe?*

"Take as many treats as you want," Tessie urged, snapping me out of my reverie. "Please, fill up a bag."

"Okay. Thanks," I said, accepting that offer, too, and dumping a decent-sized scoop of Salmon Snackers into a plastic sack. "I appreciate that."

A few moments later, the dogs and I were at the door, ready to complete our walk. As I reached to grab the knob, Tessie stopped me, though.

"Daphne?"

I turned back to see that she looked very worried again.

"Yes?"

"Everything I said. . . You'll keep it a secret, right? As you promised?"

"I *am* a professional pet sitter," I reminded her, trying to smile. "Please, don't worry."

She forced a smile, too, and the dogs and I stepped awkwardly through the door, tripping over each other. A light drizzle continued to fall, and my mood was suddenly as dreary as the weather.

I hadn't expected to learn so much when I'd urged Tessie to confide in me, and as Socrates, Artie, Charlie, and I made our way through town, I kept wondering if I'd done the right thing by pledging secrecy.

What if my silence allowed Tom Flinchbaugh to get away with murder—and sent Piper to jail?

Could I really *not* tell Jonathan what I'd learned?

As I was pondering those moral and ethical questions, my phone, which had been dead all morning, suddenly became reanimated, and, after juggling Charlie's leash and the bag of treats, I managed to pull it out of my back pocket.

"Hello?" I said, shaking it three times as I put it to my ear. "Hello?"

Like sometimes happened, the display screen was dark, so I couldn't see who was calling, but I definitely recognized the male voice that greeted me.

"Hey, Daphne," the caller said. "Can we meet? Tonight in the park?"

Chapter 30

"What do you call this again?" Dylan asked, digging his hand into the tin of popcorn I'd brought to Petti-grew Park, an oasis of green grass and flowers in the heart of Sylvan Creek. We were sitting on a plaid blanket under the stars, waiting for the evening's free outdoor movie to start. "It's really good," Dylan added, talking with his mouth full. "Are you sure it's vegan?"

"Moxie and I call it Tuxedo Popcorn," I told him. "And believe me, I had to spend extra to get vegan chocolate, so you are safe to eat it."

Dylan grinned and nudged me with a shoulder that was strong from toting surfboards and hauling the occasional mastiff onto a table at Piper's practice. "Thanks, Daph. You're the best."

"Yeah, so you said in your song."

I hadn't meant to bring that up—had planned to studiously avoid the subject—yet suddenly, thanks to me, the topic was out there.

Why did I always blurt things?

Dylan had been resting back on his hands, his elbows braced, but he shifted, the better to talk face-to-face.

He was frowning, which rarely happened. "I'm glad you mentioned that."

"I'm not," I said. "So could we just—"

Dylan placed a hand on my wrist, shutting me up. The evening was getting cool, but his skin was warm, like he'd soaked up enough sun during his surfer days to last him a lifetime. "Daph," he said, "that's why I wanted to meet you here tonight." Releasing me, he glanced at the makeshift screen, which was a heavy sheet of white fabric strung between two trees. "Well, I really wanted to see *Casablanca* again, too. It's pretty amazing." He returned his attention to me. "But mainly, I wanted to talk to you. You've been weird ever since I sang to you. What's wrong?"

I shrugged, feeling uncomfortable. "You just said a lot of nice things about me."

Dylan grinned again. "And that's bad?" He seemed to understand what I was thinking, and said, "I didn't get down on bended knee and ask you to marry me. I said you had a good heart and a nice laugh and . . ." He twisted one of my curls around his finger, teasing me. "Really, really great hair."

I still felt strange about the serenade, and I picked at a loose thread on the blanket. "It was just very . . . *public.*"

"Hey." Dylan leaned even closer and rested his index finger under my chin, so I had to look at him. He searched my eyes, making me squirm even more. "Tell me the truth, Daphne. Did you care what most people there thought, or were you just worried about the detective you were with? What *he* might think?"

I pulled back, my eyes widening. "No! I didn't care what he thought!"

I spoke too loudly, and even though the movie

hadn't started yet, a few other couples on blankets around us gave me "shushing" looks.

"Moxie invited him to sit there," I told Dylan in a softer voice. "And I was asking him about Steve's murder—in hopes of helping Piper. It wasn't a date."

"I didn't say it was."

No, he hadn't.

My cheeks got warm, and I turned my face away and searched the crowd. The weekly movies in the park were a popular summer activity, and it didn't take me long to locate lots of familiar faces—including everyone who'd been at Winding Hill right before Steve's death.

Giulia and Christian were snuggling on a blanket not far from Dylan and me. Giulia wore a white sundress that showed off her tan, and Christian's thick, movie-star blond hair shined in the moonlight. They had brought along a bottle of wine and a wooden platter filled with bread, grapes, and some cheeses, which I wouldn't have minded sampling, if offered the chance.

The perfect couple.

As I watched them, Christian reached past Giulia and got himself some grapes. He popped them in his mouth without offering her any.

Or were they perfect?

Tom and Tessie Flinchbaugh were there, too, seated stiffly in the kind of folding nylon chairs parents took to their kids' soccer games. The movie screen was blank, but they both stared at it. Tom's bandaged hand rested in his lap.

Twisting, I craned my neck to see Virginia and Senator Mitch. They were also on lawn chairs but were part of a large group, and everyone was laughing, including Virginia. Right before I turned away, Mitch finished a joke or anecdote and placed his hand over Virginia's, squeezing her fingers.

She never stopped laughing, but she pulled back from his touch.

If I hadn't been watching them closely and felt the chill between them a few days before, I wouldn't have even noticed the gesture.

Turning to face Dylan again, I asked quietly, "Not to keep bringing up murder, but who do *you* think killed Steve? Do you have any guesses?"

I had recently glimpsed a new side of Dylan—a jealous side—and I was relieved to see his shoulders relax as he settled back again, pondering my question while digging into the popcorn.

"I think karma killed Steve," he finally said. "The individual—the murderer—was just the instrument, and karma will get that person, too. I got along with Steve well enough, but he crashed through most people like a human Banzai Pipeline and left them shredded on a reef."

I wasn't a surfer, but I knew Dylan was referring to the legendarily dangerous waves that broke on Oahu.

I also understood what he was saying about karma—and I believed in it. Karma had just "got" me in the woods near Steve Beamus's. Still, I noted, "I'm not sure we should just wait around for the universe to mete out justice."

Dylan gave me a curious look. "Who better?"

It was a good question. One I didn't have to answer, because without further ado, the movie started. The antique reeled projector clacked to life behind us, and the familiar story began to play out in fuzzy black and white on the sometimes fluttering screen. The old technology didn't diminish the story at all. Somehow, the tale seemed more powerful and poignant.

Yet I found my mind wandering now and then to that question Dylan had just asked.

Who better than the universe to mete out justice?

Perhaps someone who'd come to the movie late and who was watching the film alone on a wooden bench at the far end of the park, with his arms and legs stretched out in the territory-claiming way I was coming to associate with him?

Was the answer, perhaps, Jonathan Black?

He must've sensed me studying him, because he raised one hand, offering me the smallest wave.

I started to return his greeting, but my hand stopped short as a vehicle drove down the street at the edge of the park, passing right behind Jonathan.

It was a Jeep, moving slowly, as if the driver was trying to catch a few scenes of the movie.

I checked the screen and saw that Bogie was just about to say good-bye to Ingrid Bergman forever, and although I wanted to see that iconic farewell, I tapped Dylan's shoulder and whispered, "Sorry! I've gotta run!"

Chapter 31

I wasn't sure if I really expected to catch up with a Jeep, even a slow-moving one, on foot. Especially since I was wearing ill-fitting cowgirl boots I'd bought at a flea market in Tulsa and a flowing skirt that kept twisting between my legs as I flailed my way through the park, dodging lawn chairs and blankets.

"Hey!" a couple jointly complained when I stumbled through their picnic. "Watch out!"

"Sorry," I called over my shoulder. "I didn't see you!"

It was true. My eyes were trained on the Jeep, which had reached the end of the block.

What did I hope to gain by following it?

Did I plan to take down the license number—or maybe leap onto the hood, like Tom Cruise in a *Mission: Impossible* movie, to see who was driving?

As usual, I had no real plan, which didn't stop me from rushing headlong toward the street, getting free of the sea of people right as Rick told Ilsa that their problems didn't "amount to a hill of beans." I loved that part of the movie, and I couldn't help turning to glance at the screen just for a split second.

That was all it took for me to lose my footing, lose one of my boots, and lose my dignity, all in one fell swoop. The next thing I knew, I was facedown in the grass.

I lay there for a second, catching my breath and trying to decide if anything was broken.

When I finally raised my head, the Jeep was gone, but someone was standing in front of me, one hand extended to help me get up and the other holding a battered cowgirl boot.

"Are you all right?" Jonathan asked, bending down so I could reach his hand.

He was trying to show concern, but he was on the brink of laughter. I saw the corners of his mouth twitching.

"I'm fine," I grumbled, sitting up, brushing some grass clippings off my stained white blouse, and accepting his offered hand. "Embarrassed, but fine."

Jonathan clasped his fingers around mine. His hand was cool to the touch, and his grip was strong. He pulled me to my feet in one smooth motion, then quickly released me.

"Here's your slipper, Cinderella," he said, offering me the boot. I reached to accept it from him, but he pulled it back, warning me, "It's got a . . . *substance* on the toe. You might not want to touch whatever that is."

"Okay," I said, taking the boot from him.

I saw what he was talking about, and, since I was pretty sure I knew what the "substance" was, I gave it a sniff.

Jonathan drew back, visibly repulsed. "What are you doing?"

"It's just guacamole," I informed him, bending to

pull on the boot. I nearly lost my balance and hopped on one foot. "I stepped on somebody's picnic."

Jonathan reached out to clasp my shoulder, steadying me as I stood upright. Once again, he let go quickly, like he didn't want to touch someone who'd just sniffed her own boot.

"I'm almost afraid to ask, but what were you doing?" he asked.

Behind us, people started rustling around, and I glanced over my shoulder to discover that the credits were rolling and everyone was packing up their chairs and blankets. I couldn't find Dylan, and I turned back to Jonathan.

"I saw a Jeep just like the one at Winding Hill the night Steve got killed, and I was following it," I informed him. "I wanted to see who was driving."

He'd been close to laughing, but he grew serious and donned his professional persona. "Daphne, I'm going to ask you again to please refrain from investigating Steve Beamus's murder. Not only might your interference hinder my efforts to solve the case, but you could find yourself in a dangerous situation."

I crossed my arms over my chest and cocked my head. "Do you plan to follow up on the Jeep sighting?"

"Yes," he promised. "In fact, Detective Doebler has been working to identify the vehicle that was at Winding Hill that night—"

"Oh, Detective Doebler is the B team," I complained, nearly stamping my foot. I didn't mean to insult an officer who was probably decently competent, but it was true. Jonathan was the lead investigator. "I really think the Jeep is important enough for *you* to look into it."

In a way, I'd complimented Jonathan. But I'd also

come close to bossing him around, and I could tell that he was getting annoyed. "My partner is experienced and thorough," he said evenly. "He will get the job done."

Actually, *I* would get the job done. That very night.

I wasn't about to tell Jonathan that, though.

We stood across from each other in a tense standoff, until I felt an arm drape around my shoulders. Startled, I nearly shrugged free, until I realized who had joined us.

Dylan, of course.

Chapter 32

"Is it just me, or is Dylan getting a little clingy?" I asked Socrates, who was strapped into the front seat of the van, next to Artie. For once, Socrates was doing a decent job of sharing. Artie was only lightly pressed against the door, although his bulging eyes made it look like he was being squeezed half to death. "What was up with the arm around my shoulders?"

Socrates lowered his muzzle and shook his head sadly, so his long ears flopped back and forth. Clearly, he agreed that Dylan's behavior had been too possessive.

"Let's go, Daphne," Dylan had said after barely acknowledging Jonathan. Then he'd steered me away before we'd all even said our good-byes. Not that I'd been in the mood for exchanging pleasantries with Jonathan Black. I'd twisted around once to see him watching Dylan and me walk off. His arms had been crossed, and he'd had a disapproving look on his face, like he knew I wasn't going to stop investigating.

"I thought Dylan was going to follow me all night," I added, stepping on the gas, which I had plenty of, since I'd stopped to fill up the tank. The last thing I

wanted was to run out again on the way to or from
Steve Beamus's house. I glanced over at the dogs.
"Should I be flattered . . . or worried?"

Artie barked happily, which I took to mean "flattered."

"Oh, Artie," I grumbled. "You would say that. You're
kind of clingy, too. No offense."

The road got twistier, and for a few minutes I had to
focus solely on driving. I didn't want to meet the same
fate as Angela Flinchbaugh.

My fingers tightened on the wheel as I considered
how Angela must have felt in the final moments of her
life. Had there been time to be afraid when Steve
forced her off the road with his reckless driving? Or
had it all happened so quickly . . . ?

I shook the terrible questions out of my head, but I
couldn't help thinking that Tom Flinchbaugh wouldn't
be able to do that as easily as me. He was probably
haunted by similar thoughts every day.

But could he really have committed murder?

And should I ever tell Jonathan about my conversation with Tessie?

"He'd probably just laugh at me," I muttered. "Or
assign *Detective Doebler* to follow up on my *good* leads."

"Woof!"

Socrates's low, deep bark—so seldom heard—jolted
me out of my reverie, and I realized I'd almost missed
the turn onto Steve Beamus's property. "Thanks, Socrates," I said, hauling hard on the steering wheel and
guiding my van onto the narrow lane.

This time, the VW didn't conk out, and we bumped
along right up to the house, where I hit the brakes—
and swallowed hard.

I'd left the safety of town, hoping to learn who was
staying at Steve's and filling the fridge with tofu, but

now that I was out in the middle of nowhere, looking at glowing windows, which indicated someone was inside the log structure, I was suddenly a little anxious.

And although I'd run after a Jeep back in Sylvan Creek, I also had to admit that my nervousness was heightened when I spied a vintage army-style vehicle parked under the shadows cast by the trees.

I sat there for a while with the dogs, trying to decide if I should drive away.

Then I recalled how Jonathan had practically ordered me to mind my own business, and I hopped out, liberated Socrates and Artie from their harnesses, marched up onto the porch, and knocked on the door.

Only when I heard footsteps approaching inside did I remember that Jonathan had also suggested I might be putting myself in danger by poking around a murder.

It was too late to leave, though.

Someone was opening the door.

Chapter 33

When alive, Steve Beamus had bagged not only grizzly bears and squirrels but, by all accounts, a fair number of women, too. Therefore, I fully expected to be greeted by Steve's latest—and last—conquest. I pictured her as a health-conscious, outdoorsy woman who would drive a Jeep, eat natural foods, and not mind spending nights alone in a remote house populated by dead animals. She would be pretty but tough. The type of girl who might shun meat in favor of granola, but who would kill her boyfriend if she learned that he was cheating, say, with my sister, then squat in his house until she figured out her next move.

Yes, I had formed a pretty clear picture of who was about to greet me.

Needless to say, I was very surprised when the door was opened by someone entirely different from my imagined wronged girlfriend.

First of all, she was a *he*. And he was far from out-doorsy. On the contrary, the twentysomething guy who barely poked his head out the door was skinny, pale, and wearing nerdy, hipster eyeglasses that came off more nerdy than hipster.

"Who *are* you?" I asked, only to realize that I'd actually voiced that question out loud. I'd meant just to think it.

By rights, the person huddling in the dimly lit foyer should've been asking me the same thing.

But he didn't. Instead, he informed me in a soft, uncertain voice, almost like he wasn't sure of his own identity, "I'm . . . I'm Steve's *son.*"

Chapter 34

"Wow, I still can't believe Steve has a child," I said for at least the tenth time since Bryce Beamus had been nice enough to invite me and the dogs into the house. I knew I should stop myself, but I couldn't seem to shut up. "I never knew he was a father!"

"Not much of one," Bryce muttered, pouring us each a glass of soy milk. He set the carton down on the granite countertop and pushed his eyeglasses higher onto his nose with a slender index finger. "I had to track him down, and I was lucky if I got a birthday card. Which, I have to admit, is more than I get from my birth mother. It took me years to find her, and she won't even acknowledge me publicly."

I had known Bryce for only about five minutes, but he seemed as woebegone as Artie. They were both small, shaky, damaged and, apparently, homeless, since Bryce was crashing at his deceased, estranged father's house after leaving Seattle two weeks before, for reasons he hadn't explained. Given how he was over-sharing, I assumed he'd soon tell me that story, too.

Talk about a lost puppy!

I searched for Artie and found him in the living

room, spinning around in circles, chasing what little he had of a tail.

Actually, Artie—in spite of his overbite and missing ear—seemed in better shape than Bryce. At least Artie had spunk and joie de vivre.

Looking back at Bryce, I saw that he was glumly drinking his milk-like product, his shoulders slumped under a short-sleeved plaid shirt that could've been trendy on some guys but that skewed more toward geek than chic on him.

Was there such a thing as *mal de vivre*?

Still, Bryce had his good points. He'd invited me in and offered me a drink. . . .

I suddenly remembered that Steve had been *poisoned*, and I double-checked to make sure that Bryce was consuming his soy-based beverage, too. I'd already taken a few sips of the milk, so I was relieved to see that his glass was half empty.

At least, I assumed that was how he'd look at it.

I also liked how Bryce had made a big fuss over Artie and Socrates. Although the fuss had been a little *too* big for Socrates, who'd recoiled from an attempt to scratch that spot just above his tail, where most dogs loved to be scratched. Eyes wide with horror, Socrates had retreated to sit in front of one of the cabin's big windows and was staring fixedly at the blackness, like he wanted to leap into an abyss.

"Not to be rude, but who, exactly, are you, and what are you doing here?" Bryce finally asked a few questions that were long overdue. His cheeks flushed. "Were you one of my father's . . . ?"

At first, I didn't know what he was trying to say. Then I realized he was asking if I'd been one of Steve's romantic interests.

"No! No!" I cried, setting down my glass and raising my hands. "We were never involved like that!"

Piper had been "involved," though.

Did she know about Bryce?

He peered more closely at me with brown eyes that were reminiscent of Steve's. Bryce shared his father's thick sandy hair, too. That was pretty much where any resemblance ended. Yet I swore I saw something familiar in his other features. But I couldn't quite figure out who he reminded me of.

"So," he asked again, "what brings you here so late?"

For a moment, I was stumped by that simple question, although I should've anticipated it before knocking on the door.

Actually, I should've been preparing for it the whole time I was driving to Steve's. I'd come to the house on the hunch that I'd find the owner of the Jeep there.

"I'm looking for Axis," I finally semi-fibbed. I seriously doubted that the slight young man who was slouching on a stool was capable of homicide, but he'd clearly had issues with Steve. It didn't seem wise to admit that I was investigating the murder when I might be in the presence of the killer. Then, in case Bryce and Steve had been *really* estranged, I asked, "You know Axis, right? Your dad's dog?"

"Yes, of course." His eyes finally lit up with interest. "So Axis really is missing? You're looking for him, too?"

"Yes," I said. "I'm worried about him. He was always with Steve."

A shadow crossed Bryce's face. "I'm worried, too. Given how my father treated dogs, I never understood Axis's loyalty. But the few times I saw my dad, Ax was always with him. I was hoping one of my father's friends had taken him after the . . . the . . ."

He couldn't seem to bring himself to say "murder,"

which indicated to me that he probably couldn't have committed the act, either. Still, I remained guarded.

"Well, let's not think the worst yet," I said, although I was starting to fear that the worst was inevitable. Axis had been missing for quite a while. I also noted that the bottle of Lysodren was still on the counter. If the dog was alive, he wasn't getting his medication, which wasn't good, either. "Why did you say that about your dad's treatment of dogs?" I added, glancing over at the poor bear. I met Bryce's gaze again. "I didn't always understand your dad's relationship to animals, but he was a respected trainer."

In the blink of an eye, Bryce's whole aspect changed, and not for the better. His mouth drew down into a scowl, and anger flickered deep in his eyes.

"My father liked to *control* animals," he said, voicing something I'd also suspected. "He didn't care about them—except to the extent that their willingness to do his bidding reflected well on him. He thought he was a big man because dogs jumped, literally, when he told them to do so."

I sat quietly, letting him vent. The way he'd changed so quickly was unnerving, and the glimmer in his eyes was downright scary.

I looked at the bear again, trying to figure out how much it might weigh.

If Socrates, Artie, and I had to make a run for the door, and Bryce followed, could I push the grizzly over and knock Bryce down, gaining us time to run to the van?

And if I did that, would I be using the majestic creature wrongly, like Steve had done when he'd tossed a coat over its paw?

Or would I be giving it one last chance to attack, in keeping with its ferocious nature?

As I wrestled with that moral dilemma, Bryce set me more on edge by hopping off the stool and beginning to pace, staring at the floor. "My *father* kept most of his dogs, even Axis, kenneled much of the time," he continued, with a quick glance at me. "Did you know that?"

"No, no, I didn't," I admitted. "I never came here before his death. I didn't even know how many dogs he had. I only knew Axis."

"He always kept several dogs in pens, for breeding purposes," Bryce said. "He was always looking for 'breed perfection.'" He stopped pacing and turned to face me. I thought he was close to tears of rage—and disappointment. "Do you know how offensive that is to me, as a founding member of PUFAT?"

I noted that Artie and Socrates had drawn closer, both having sensed the shift in Bryce's tone and the altered mood in the house. Artie was confused, while Socrates appeared concerned. I was getting worried myself.

"*You* helped found People United for Fair Animal Treatment?" I asked, unhappily surprised to learn that Bryce was linked with a group that had a very unfortunate acronym and a short, but sometimes violent, history of using guerrilla tactics to protect animals the members believed to be in danger or abused.

I'd read that they'd once *blown up* a lab that tested cosmetics on rabbits.

Clearly, I had been very wrong about Bryce's potential for violence.

I pushed aside my soy milk and climbed down off the stool I'd been sitting on. "The dogs and I should really be going now."

But Bryce wasn't finished releasing his pent-up

frustration and rage against Steve. He resumed pacing, pounding one fist against his other open hand. "All his dogs might've been champions and well trained," he muttered, more to himself than me. "But they got no affection! No love!"

I had a feeling some father-son issues were bleeding into the soliloquy about dogs. I also thought he was going a little overboard about Steve.

Sure, Steve had enjoyed wielding power over dogs to feed his considerable ego, but I'd seen him with Axis. He'd respected the Lab, and I'd witnessed him doling out affection, if not in a gushy way.

I didn't think it was wise to counsel or contradict Bryce right then, though.

"I tried to tell him that nothing thrives in a sterile environment!" he concluded, eyes blazing. "That no creature should have to live in a box that's doused with toxic antiseptics every day, so even the smell of nature is denied to the inhabitant!"

I stiffened and hoped my wide eyes weren't betraying my thoughts.

Had he just referenced, in a very angry diatribe, Clean Kennel?

The toxin found in Steve's thermos?

There would be a certain twisted poetic justice in poisoning one's despised father with a chemical that had likely sparked many a heated argument.

I wanted to cue Socrates and Artie and get the heck out of there, both because Bryce Beamus was scaring me and because I could hardly wait to tell Jonathan that I had been right. Figuring out who drove the Jeep and ate tofu might have just broken the murder case wide open.

Seriously, if I made it out of Steve's house alive, I

was going to make Detective Jonathan Black eat the vegetarian version of crow—crowfu?—for his snide comment about my failure to attend the police academy. It seemed to me that I was doing *his* job pretty well.

Suddenly, however, I didn't have to wait to rub his nose in my successful investigation, because the front door opened.

For a second, I thought the grizzly had grown tired of playing doorman and was making an exit. The bear was so realistically posed that it was sometimes still hard for me to believe it wasn't alive.

Then I saw Jonathan Black stroll right into the house like he owned the place.

Chapter 35

"What are *you* doing here?" I asked Jonathan, who joined Bryce and me in the kitchen. "Did you *follow* me?"

Bryce, meanwhile, was still seething with residual rage and indignation. "Who are you?" he demanded sharply. "Huh?"

I could've told him that his attitude wouldn't go over well with his latest guest.

"I'm Detective Jonathan Black," Jonathan said, introducing himself and disregarding my questions. He also ignored Artie, who'd bounced over like a one-canine welcome wagon. The little dog had a Chihuahua-sized bladder, and he was so excited that I started to worry he might pee on Jonathan's shoes. But Jonathan didn't even look down. He was studying Bryce. "And you are?"

Bryce didn't supply his name. "What do you want? And what makes you think you can barge in here?"

Bryce was definitely pushing his luck, playing twenty questions with a man who was usually on the other side of interrogations, and I felt I had to intervene.

"Jonathan, this is Bryce Beamus," I said. "He's

Steve's son." I decided to seize the opportunity to cram a lot of information into my introduction, to bring Jonathan up to speed. "Bryce is also a founding member of PUFAT, disagreed with his father's use of chemical kennel cleansers, and arrived from Seattle about a week ago—in a *Jeep*."

Bryce shot me a confused, wary look. "Why did you say all that? And what does my Jeep have to do with anything?"

Jonathan, meanwhile, processed everything rapidly. "Is that your vehicle out front?" he inquired—without so much as offering me a look of gratitude for all the helpful knowledge I'd acquired in a short time. "And were you at Winding Hill Farm with your father the night of August eleventh?"

Bryce's face had flushed bright red during his tirade, but when Jonathan asked those two questions, all that color drained away, along with Bryce's macho, confrontational attitude. Suddenly, we were confronted with the lost puppy again. A lost, *petulant* puppy.

"I'm not answering anything without a lawyer," Bryce grumbled, hanging his head and wrapping his arms around his thin frame, like he was locking himself away. He pursed his lips, and he sounded like a pouting child when he declared, "I'm not speaking anymore!"

"That's fine—for now," Jonathan said. He managed to be intimidating, despite the fact that a Chihuahua continued to dance around his feet. "But don't go anywhere, because I have a feeling we'll be talking again. Soon."

Given that Bryce was staring straight ahead, pretending like he didn't hear Jonathan, it seemed like the evening was about to wrap up, so I went over to where Socrates was still staring out the window. He had a far-off look in his eyes, which indicated he was meditating, and I spoke softly, not wanting to jolt him. "Come on, Socrates. It's time to go."

He looked up at me and blinked a few times, gradually bringing himself back to the material world, while I straightened and realized I was right next to Steve Beamus's trophy-slash-bookcase. The one that had interested Jonathan the first time we'd been at Steve's. There was a lot of gold glittering in there on the trophies topped with dogs, but I was immediately drawn to the leather-bound book I'd noticed among the paperbacks.

Opening the case's glass door, I took it out and read the title.

What the . . . ?

"Daphne, are you coming?"

Jonathan's voice broke into my thoughts, and I looked up to see that he was standing in the foyer, next to the grizzly bear, both of them glowering. Artie continued to wriggle at Jonathan's feet.

Bryce was perched on his stool again, silent and slumped over, like a lifelike robot whose battery pack had died.

"Daphne?" Jonathan prompted. "Are you done here, too?"

"I'm coming. I'm coming," I said. I summoned Socrates, who had benefited from his time of quiet contemplation. He seemed like his old self again after the trauma of nearly being scratched at the base of his tail. "Are you ready to go?"

He was not only ready but eager, too, and trotted swiftly to the door.

I started to return the book to the shelf, then, on impulse, tucked it under my arm.

Jonathan held open the door for me and the dogs,

and we all passed through without a word—or a woof—to each other. Nobody even said good night to Bryce.

I had a few questions for Jonathan, regarding his un-expected appearance at Steve's, and I was pretty sure he was saving up some choice words for me, too, but we didn't talk the whole time he walked me, Socrates, and Artie to the van.

While I got in on the driver's side, Jonathan opened the passenger-side door for Socrates, who climbed onto the seat with effort. Artie could've easily jumped up, too, but he stood silently begging for help from Jonathan, who tried to wait him out but eventually muttered, "Fine," before lifting the Chihuahua. A few seconds later, he had both dogs buckled into their safety harnesses.

It seemed like I was going to get away without a lec-ture on meddling in murder investigations—assuming my VW would start.

Holding my breath and crossing my fingers on my free hand, I stuck the key in the ignition and gave it a turn.

Chapter 36

"Are you sure you put gas in your van?" Jonathan asked as I pulled my seat belt over my shoulder and across my lap. Actually, the seat belt belonged to Jonathan, since Socrates, Artie, and I were riding in his truck again. The front seat smelled faintly of lemony iced tea. "Maybe I should check . . ."

"No, I'm pretty sure I really broke down this time," I said, clicking the belt into place. "I put five dollars in the tank on the way here."

"Were you starting with an empty tank?" Jonathan asked. "Because you only put a few dollars' worth in using the gas can the other night. And Beamus's house is nearly ten miles from town. What kind of gas mileage does your van get?"

"I don't know," I said, wondering if maybe I should've put a *little* more gas in the tank for the round trip. "I'm not a mechanic or . . . or any other kind of car expert."

"You're not a detective, either," Jonathan noted as the truck bumped off the gravel lane and onto the road back to Sylvan Creek. "Yet you keep playing one."

The inevitable lecture was about to start. "Someone needed to solve the riddle of the mysterious Jeep," I informed him. "And so I did."

"'The riddle of the mysterious Jeep'?" Jonathan echoed. "Who are you? Nancy Drew?"

Okay, "riddle of the mysterious Jeep" did sound like the title of an old Carolyn Keene novel. But he was missing the point.

"I am a practically certified pet-care expert who got a lot of information out of Bryce Beamus just by sharing a glass of soy milk," I told him. "Meanwhile, the techniques *you* learned at the police academy earned you nothing but silence."

"Yes, I suppose that blank stare that managed to come off like a temper tantrum is some strategy he learned as an animal-rights protestor," Jonathan said. "And, I have to admit, it's pretty effective. Usually, when a subject goes silent during an interrogation, he does it defiantly or fearfully. But with Beamus . . . There was nothing in his eyes. It was like he was dead."

I wanted to ask Jonathan just how many "subjects" he'd interrogated, especially in his past life, but I couldn't do that without letting him know I'd researched him.

"If you thought Bryce's passive-aggressive resistance was annoying, you should've seen him when he was angry," I said. "It was scary."

"Which is why you shouldn't have been there alone."

I shifted in my seat, the better to watch him when I asked, "Why were *you* there?"

A muscle in his jaw worked, like I'd struck a nerve with the question. "I knew you were going to break into Beamus's again," he said. "I knew you believed that whoever drove the Jeep would be there. I told myself that, first of all, you were probably wrong. So you saw a Jeep coming in the opposite direction on this road the other day? That didn't necessarily mean anything. And even if you were right . . ."

"Like I was."

He pretended not to hear that. "And you barged in to find that someone was in Beamus's house—or you ran out of gas again late at night in the woods, with a hyperactive Chihuahua and a sluggish basset hound in tow. . . ."

Socrates once again broke his silence, woofing loudly in objection to that description.

"He's actually quite agile," I said in Socrates's defense. "He just doesn't *like* to move quickly."

Jonathan also ignored that comment. His fingers flexed, then tightened around the steering wheel. "I kept telling myself that nothing that might happen to any of you was my problem, even if you all got attacked by a bear. . . ."

He was starting to ramble, and I was grinning. "You were worried about me!" I said, laughing. "Admit it! You were worried that I might get myself into trouble!"

He looked over at me, his brows knit. "I don't see how a propensity for getting into trouble is amusing."

I didn't explain. Jonathan was again missing the point, which was that we were becoming friends. Friends who aggravated each other, but friends, nevertheless.

That was a good thing, right?

"Hey," I said more seriously. "Thanks for coming out to Steve's tonight. I honestly know how to take care of myself. I was nearly imprisoned in Africa once, and I survived that on my own. But . . . thanks."

He glanced at me again, frowning. "Africa? *Prison?*"

I dangled my beaded key chain from my index finger. "I told you, it's a long story," I reminded him, wishing I hadn't even brought it up.

"I'm sure you can fend for yourself," he agreed, with a quick look over his shoulder. "To be honest, I was mainly worried about the Chihuahua. That thing can't afford to lose any more body parts to bears."

Artie yipped gleefully, like he was grateful for Jonathan's concern, in spite of the accompanying insult. I was going to have to caution Artie about the dangers of one-sided bromances—after I convinced Jonathan that Bryce Beamus was very likely Steve's killer. A much stronger suspect than Piper.

"Can we please talk about Bryce now?" I requested. "I have a lot to tell you about his relationship with Steve, his involvement with PUFAT, and his hatred of products like Clean Kennel. He *really* resented Steve for using that."

"How did that even come up?" Jonathan asked. "You couldn't have arrived more than fifteen minutes ahead of me. How did you cover so much territory with him?"

"When not in the presence of a detective, Bryce is naturally prone to over sharing," I said. "Plus, people tend to open up to me."

As I made that boast, I realized that one person never shared anything with me. I was riding in a truck with him.

Maybe Jonathan and I weren't really friends, after all. I knew everything about Moxie, from her shoe size—six—to the fact that she suffered from chelona-phobia, or a fear of turtles. We'd discovered that together during a disastrous fifth-grade class trip to a small zoo called Reptiland.

But if Jonathan had any debilitating fears—and I doubted it—I wasn't going to learn about them that night.

All at once, he nodded to the book I'd forgotten was on my lap, and suggested, "How about you first recount highlights of your therapy session with Bryce and then explain why you *stole* that from a dead man's house?"

Chapter 37

I had learned more about Bryce than I'd even realized, and it took me almost all of the trip to bring Jonathan up to speed, since he asked questions every half mile or so.

Before I knew it, we had arrived at Winding Hill. As Jonathan pulled the truck into a small gravel parking area between the farmhouse and the barn, I noted that most of the windows in the house were dark. Piper had left the back porch light on for me, though, and a night-light glowed in the kitchen.

"Thanks for the ride," I told Jonathan. We'd ridden home with the windows open, enjoying the breeze, but now that we'd stopped, the heat seemed to close in around us. The air was heavy with the sweet smell of lavender and gardenias. Mr. Peachy, who did most of the gardening, had outdone himself that year. I moved to open the passenger-side door. "I guess I'll see you around. . . ."

But Jonathan wasn't calling it a night yet. He shut off the engine and got out before me, then pulled open the rear door on his side. "Seriously, Daphne," he said, picking up Artie, who squirmed and tried unsuccessfully to kiss Jonathan's cheek. In one smooth but effective move, Jonathan simultaneously pulled back and pushed Artie's muzzle away. "I don't know if Bryce Beamus committed murder," he continued, "but if he did, think of how dangerous your situation could've been."

"Yes, yes, I understand," I said, letting Socrates out, too. He shambled off toward the door, letting me know, in no uncertain terms, that he was ready for bed. "But nothing happened to me. I'm fine."

Jonathan had come around to my side of the truck, where he set down Artie, who collapsed at Jonathan's feet and promptly fell asleep. Apparently, spending so much time with the man he inexplicably worshipped had worn him out.

"You're fine—this time," Jonathan cautioned me. "But please stop investigating, all right?"

"I can't promise anything until I know Piper isn't your chief suspect," I said. "I'm sorry, but I can't."

I wanted Jonathan to say that Bryce Beamus was now the prime suspect in Steve's murder, but he didn't do that. All I heard were crickets and the creaking of the barn's old beams, although the night was very still and humid. In the distance, the sky was starless and ominously black. The wind would probably pick up soon, and the encroaching clouds would obliterate the full moon, which was bathing Piper's property in soft light, causing the white gardenias and moonflowers to glow like tiny lanterns.

"Do you need a ride to get your van tomorrow?" Jonathan finally asked. "Or can you find someone to take you?"

He'd done enough for me, and I said, "I suppose Piper can give me a ride. Or my mother."

The prospect of calling Maeve Templeton for help

was grim, but I'd probably have no choice. Piper had recently vowed never again to pick me up when the VW broke down.

Of course, that was assuming I'd actually suffered engine trouble.

"Hey," I said, acting far too nonchalant. "Although I'm *sure* I'll need a tow, you wouldn't have that gas can with you, would you?"

Jonathan went to the back of the truck, opened a cover, and pulled out a red plastic container. "I thought you'd never ask." He started to hand over the gas can, then pulled it back. "But before I give you this, as a gift, for you to keep . . ."

I opened my mouth to object; then I realized I might as well accept his offer. He would never run out of gas, and he probably had his oil changed more than once every few years, too.

"Before I give you this," he repeated, "you have to promise me that you won't confront Bryce again if he's there tomorrow, when you get your van."

I doubted Bryce would talk with me after how we'd left things, and I raised my hand and positioned a couple of fingers in what I hoped was a "Scout's honor" sign but which might've been Dylan's "hang loose" gesture. "I can promise that."

"Good," Jonathan said. "Although Scouts actually use the right hand." Then he gestured to the book I'd borrowed, not stolen. "Also, would you please tell me why you took that book, which also interested me when I first saw it at Beamus's?"

"You noticed this, too?" I asked, slipping the volume from under my right arm, where I'd had it tucked. That was why I'd used my left hand for the pledge. I held the book so we could both read the title—or titles—which were written in bold gold script on the dark cover.

Macbeth—Othello—Hamlet—King Lear.

"Why would a guy whose only other books were spy thrillers in paperback own a leather-bound collection of four plays by Shakespeare?" I mused aloud. "Doesn't it seem strange?"

"Yes," Jonathan agreed. He held out his hand. "May I see it?"

I didn't want to part with the anthology, since he obviously judged it as potentially important, and *I'd* been the one with the foresight to take it. But he kept standing there with his hand out, so I finally offered it over. "Here."

Jonathan opened the front cover, and I hoped he didn't intend to read four tragic dramas by Shakespeare while we stood there, with lightning starting to flicker on the horizon.

Jonathan didn't seem interested in the plays, though. He was looking at the very first page, which I would've expected to be blank. He bent closer, his eyes moving back and forth, scanning something illuminated by the moon.

"What is it?" I asked, because obviously he'd discovered something of interest. "What did you find?"

For a moment, he must've forgotten that I was a civilian. Or, more likely, given how late it was, he didn't want to deal with me badgering him for a half hour, until he inevitably told me what I wanted to know. He probably just wanted to go home to bed.

"There's an inscription," he informed me.

"Well, read it," I urged. "What's it say?"

After a moment's hesitation, Jonathan lifted the anthology again and read aloud. "Dear Steven, I fear that the fault was not in the stars, but in ourselves. Yet tragedy can also be beautiful, as these plays prove. I can only hope that someday our pain will yield fruit that is more sweet than bitter. Love always . . ." Jonathan's voice trailed off, as if he didn't want to tell me who had signed that curious, if somewhat melodramatic and cloying, note.

"Give the book back," I said, pulling it from his hands and reading quickly, in case he planned to snatch it away from me.

He didn't do that, though, and I skimmed the note, then checked the signature, although I doubted I'd know the author, if I could even read the handwriting. A lot of people just scrawled their names.

But that wasn't the case here.

In fact, although the signer had used only her first name, I recognized the distinctive script immediately—in part because I saw it all the time. On checks that I cashed for walking three rottweilers.

Virginia.

Chapter 38

"Can we please go get my van soon?" I asked my mother, who sat across from me at a table in an alcove at Giulia Alberti's café, Espresso Pronto. We were by a window, and outside the morning sun was shining on Sylvan Creek's pretty main street, which was starting to bustle with activity. I wanted to get moving, too, and I told Mom, "I have things to do today."

That was the wrong thing for me to say to Maeve Templeton, who maintained *two* computer-synchronized day planners, one for professional engagements and one for social ones. She'd been tearing open her third packet of Sweet'N Low for her coffee, a special blend Giulia had created just for her, appropriately called Seize the Day, but she stopped in mid-shred to raise her eyebrows slightly at me. "Do you, dear? Do you have plans?"

"Yes," I said, pulling apart my *cornetto alla crema*, a flaky, horn-shaped pastry filled with sweet, thick custard. I deserved one—or more—of Giulia's freshly baked sweets after the sleepless night I'd endured. That storm I'd seen rolling in while talking to Jonathan had been massive. I wasn't normally jumpy, but I'd huddled under my printed Indian coverlet, flinching at each too-close strike of lightning and feeling my chest rumble and the bones of the old house rattle when the thunder boomed. I also had a headache from Artie snoring in my ear all night. But how could I leave him shivering on the floor, given that Socrates had slumbered soundly, offering no comfort? "I promised Piper that I'd help Mr. Peachy today," I explained, because Mom was watching me skeptically. "Some branches came down during the storm, and she doesn't want him to clear them out alone."

My mother stirred the sweetener into her coffee, shaking her head and tsk-tsking the whole time. "I don't know why Piper continues to employ that old man if he can't do the job he's paid to do. And what do you even know about him? I don't know of any other Peachys in Sylvan Creek."

"First of all, Mr. Peachy does more before eight a.m. than I do all day," I said, immediately regretting the comment. I forged ahead before my mom could say anything. She was already opening her mouth. "And just because his family didn't come here on the Mayflower and stay forever, multiplying, doesn't mean there's something wrong with him," I added, eating a bite of my pastry and covering my mouth so I could keep talking. "He's a nice old guy."

Mom sipped her coffee, but she didn't respond—which indicated that she disagreed—so I reminded her, "You practically arranged a marriage for Piper and Jonathan Black the other night, and he's new in town. What do we know about him?"

Actually, I knew quite a bit about Jonathan. Things that I doubted my mother was aware of. But she knew the one thing that mattered to her.

"He is prepared to purchase a *four-bedroom home*, which indicates that he is more than ready to settle into our community and 'multiply,' as you so crassly put it," she countered. "And given that he is an *officer of the law*, I am confident that he will become a *pillar* of local society."

"You are *emphasizing* a lot of words but not convincing me," I said, lifting my mug to sip my chai tea. "Your logic would not stand up to dissection under the Socratic method."

The Socratic method wasn't really designed for debates like we were having—meaning pointless ones—but bringing up my philosophy degree had the desired effect of provoking my mother into action. She gulped down her coffee, set the mug on the table, and said, "Come along, Daphne. Let's go. . . ." She cocked her head. "Where did you say we're going?"

"The van's outside of town," I said vaguely. I hadn't yet formulated a story that would explain why my VW was at Steve Beamus's.

"Well, let's go purchase some gasoline and limp that old thing back to Sylvan Creek," Mom said. She shook her head again and sighed. "I can't believe you would just run out of fuel!"

As I'd cowered under my covers, I'd reluctantly come to the conclusion that five dollars' worth of gas probably hadn't been enough for the trip to Steve's.

Otherwise, my thoughts had been occupied by the inscription in the book, which Jonathan had ultimately taken with him.

Virginia? And *Steve*?

And what "tragedy" did they share that might someday yield fruit that was "more sweet than bitter"?

Finally, how many packets of artificial sweetener

had *Virginia* downed before inking that saccharine message?

"I have houses to show," Mom added, tossing the day's silk scarf—a red-and-navy geometric design—over her shoulder. She was wearing white slacks, so the effect was quite patriotic. As she walked toward the door, assuming I'd follow, she asked, without looking back, "Will you need to borrow money for the gas?"

Given that I'd searched all my pockets to come up with twenty dollars, I really resented that question. However, I didn't want to get into an argument with her.

In fact, I suddenly decided that I didn't want to accept a ride from my mother, either. Doing so would mean I owed her a big favor, which might result in me being forced to test for a license to sell real estate, the purchase of "sensible" clothes, and a lifetime of indentured servitude at Templeton Realty, Inc.

Things could easily spin out of control that way with Mom.

Meanwhile, I spied someone I wanted to talk with before I left. A person whose left ring finger was sparkling as she restocked pastries in a glass counter.

I might've had three *cornetti* that morning, depleting the supply.

"I'll catch up with you later," I told Mom, who was opening the door. "Don't worry about giving me a ride. I'll find another one."

My mother turned back, one hand on her hip. An oversize red Coach bag dangled from her wrist. "Honestly, Daphne, I will never understand your unusual whims."

Then she breezed out of the café without so much as a good-bye.

When my mom was gone, leaving the shop empty of other customers, I approached Giulia and asked what was probably a stupid question, given the impressive size of the diamond on her delicate hand.

"Are congratulations in order?"

Chapter 39

"Oh, goodness . . . You startled me," Giulia said, withdrawing from the case, straightening, then rubbing her head, which she'd bumped on the glass when I'd addressed her. Wiping her hands on a spotless white apron, she came out from behind the counter. "I didn't see you there!"

I wasn't sure how she'd failed to see me through a big pane of glass, but I apologized. "Sorry. I didn't mean to scare you."

She smiled, although she still seemed nervous. She ran one hand the length of her glossy black ponytail, unnecessarily smoothing it, since it was already perfectly sleek. "Of course you didn't," she assured me. "I don't know what's wrong with me lately."

Grinning, I gestured to the ring. "Maybe you've got pre-wedding jitters?"

I was joking, but Giulia didn't laugh. She fidgeted with the diamond. I didn't know anything about carat weights, but I knew that the rock on her finger was large by most standards. It was cut in a square shape and set in a wide silver—or perhaps platinum—band that complemented her olive skin.

"Yes, I suppose I have jitters," she finally agreed quietly. "Christian wants to get married very soon. I suppose I am nervous."

I almost asked, "What's the rush?" Then I realized that was none of my business. Instead, I said, "Well, congratulations again. The ring is beautiful."

"Yes, yes," she said, smiling wanly. "Christian has wonderful taste. He put much thought into this ring."

For a woman with a handsome, wealthy, and supposedly thoughtful fiancé, Giulia looked more like a prisoner on the way to the gallows than a bride on the way to the altar.

Well, maybe she didn't look that bad. But she didn't seem overjoyed, like most newly engaged people.

If she'd been happier, I probably wouldn't have burst her bubble by bringing up a sad subject. But since she already seemed glum, I said, "Hey, Giulia . . . I've been meaning to ask you. Did you see anything suspicious at Winding Hill the night of Steve's murder? It might really help Piper if you could think of anything unusual. . . ."

I let my voice trail off, because Giulia wasn't looking at me anymore. The café's door had opened behind me, letting in a rush of warm air and a customer whose presence was drawing Giulia's attention and causing her to take a step backward.

I turned around, not sure why Giulia looked unhappy to see the person approaching the counter, or why he, in turn, seemed displeased with *me.*

Chapter 40

Before the arrival of Jonathan Black, Christian Clarke had been the most handsome man in Sylvan Creek. That was an indisputable fact. With his blue eyes, dirty blond hair, and shiny white teeth, he was rural Pennsylvania's answer to Brad Pitt. And Christian had something else most local guys lacked: fashion sense. Most of the men in Sylvan Creek stuck to a wardrobe of T-shirts and jeans, but Christian—who did something in the banking industry—often wore tailored suits and sweaters that I thought looked like cashmere, although I couldn't be sure.

As Christian stood before me, glowering, I wondered if he was angry because a dark-haired newcomer was now in the running for his unofficial title.

Maybe Christian didn't think Sylvan Creek was big enough for two men with movie-star looks.

Then again, he might've been unhappy because I was asking nosy questions about Steve Beamus's murder.

"As Giulia and I told several police officers, we didn't see anything out of the ordinary the night Steve was killed," he informed me before I even had a chance to greet or congratulate him. He placed an arm around Giulia's shoulders and gave her a squeeze, along with a smile that I thought was forced. "Right, honey?"

Giulia tucked a few strands of hair that had slipped from her ponytail behind her ear. "Yes, we saw nothing," she agreed, with a similarly fake, shaky smile. "I was busy setting up my trailer."

She was telling the truth about being preoccupied. I recalled that she had been working hard—while Christian had been standing around, supervising. Or, more accurately, staring in the general direction of Steve Beamus's truck.

Christian drew Giulia even closer, his fingers flexing around her shoulder. "You must be very worried about Piper if you're going around asking questions, Daphne."

Christian had attended the same high school as me, but he'd been two years ahead of me and part of an entirely different social circle. He'd been the popular prom king, and I'd been . . .

What had I been?

Regardless, I'd never known Christian that well. And I wasn't exactly liking him right then. He was trying to sound sympathetic, but he didn't seem sincere.

He was also hiding something. But I wasn't going to learn anything more from him. He wasn't clamming up like Bryce Beamus, but he wasn't being forthcoming, either. He also wasn't going to let Giulia speak for herself. That arm around her shoulders might as well have been a gag on her mouth. I could see in her eyes that she felt trapped.

I wished I could withdraw the congratulations I'd offered Giulia. Unless I was completely wrong—and I didn't think I was—I didn't have high hopes for her being happy once they were married.

Why was a beautiful, successful, smart woman making such a bad match?

"I'm sure Piper's gonna be just fine," I finally told Christian. Then I addressed Giulia, changing the subject. "I don't suppose you'd share your recipe for *cornetti*, would you? I'd still buy them here all the time, but it would be nice to be able to make them at home, too. I might even adapt them for dogs. Fill them with peanut butter, you know? I think it might be cute! But if the recipe's a family secret, or you just don't want to give it out, don't worry. . . ."

I'd started babbling, because as soon as I'd asked for the recipe, I could tell Giulia was unwilling to share it.

All at once, though, she got a funny look on her face and said, "Yes, yes, Daphne. Of course, you may have the recipe. And I hope you make a special *cornetto* for the little dog with the funny face." She twisted slightly to free herself from Christian's grasp and lifted his arm from her shoulder. "Excuse me, dear."

He reluctantly let her go, and she headed behind the counter, toward the kitchen. Raising one finger, she promised, "I will be back in one minute."

"You don't have to get the recipe now," I told her, mainly because I was afraid she might have to copy it by hand, and I'd be stuck making uncomfortable small talk with Christian for way more than a minute.

It was too late, though. Giulia had already disappeared into Espresso Pronto's back room, leaving Christian and me alone.

He made no attempt at conversation. He just stared at me.

"So," I finally said. "You and Giulia are getting married, huh?"

"Yes," he informed me. "Yes, we are."

I refused to congratulate him. "So . . . umm . . . did you pick a place yet?"

"Yes," he said. "The chapel at Wynton."

He was referring to a charming, old stone building on the campus of Wynton University, which was a small but prestigious college just outside Sylvan Creek.

"Oh, that'll be really pretty," I said, forgetting for a moment that I thought Giulia was making a mistake. I could picture her walking down the aisle in a long white dress, under the chapel's ancient arched beams, while sunlight streamed through the stained-glass windows, painting the whitewashed walls with soft colors. "What a great place for a wedding."

I was so caught up in my fantasy that I also forgot I was in the midst of an awkward conversation with the groom-to-be, until Christian snapped me back to reality, noting, "Giulia's afraid our guests will keep thinking about Steve's funeral during our ceremony, but I told her that she shouldn't worry. Steve's service will be a distant memory in a few weeks."

That seemed like a cold thing to say.

And why was I just learning about Steve's funeral, which was apparently scheduled?

"Christian, no . . ."

Hearing a soft, dismayed voice behind me, I turned to see that Giulia had rejoined us. She was standing just outside the door to the kitchen and held a piece of paper in her hand. Her face was uncharacteristically pale.

Clearly, she also considered her fiancé's comment inappropriate. But she didn't say more, and Christian didn't respond to the mild rebuke. He acted like he hadn't even heard it.

"Here," Giulia said, approaching me and smiling again. But I saw concern in her dark eyes. "This is the recipe. I hope you make *cornetti* very soon and bring me one to try. Please?"

"Definitely," I agreed, accepting the folded paper. I stuck it in the back pocket of my jeans. "Thanks a lot."

"Good-bye," Christian said, dismissing me.

I gave them both a small wave and headed for the door. "I'll see you two later."

"Yes, I hope so," Giulia said, waving back at me. Her diamond glittered when her fingers waggled. "Ciao!"

Espresso Pronto was one of my favorite spots in town, but for the first time ever, I felt a sense of relief when I stepped outside into the sunlight.

What had just happened?

Why had Giulia acted like a hostage?

I pictured her expression as she'd handed me the recipe, telling me, "I hope you make *cornetti* very soon. . . ."

I was walking down the street, headed nowhere in particular, since I had no van, but I suddenly stopped in my tracks and pulled the recipe from my pocket.

Unfolding the paper, I saw not just a list of ingredients but also a note.

Please meet me Thursday at midnight on the bench near the creek in Pettigrew Park. I have something important to share, privately. Please come alone. G.

My heart started racing, but I also thought, *Really? A secret note? Why not just call or text me?* I was definitely on Giulia's list of contacts. She always let me know when she made my favorite honey-pistachio biscotti.

Then I read the postscript below Giulia's initial.

P.S. I tried to text you, but I think your phone is broken? I receive three error messages!

I jammed the paper back into my pocket, resolving to get a new phone.

I would also be at the park at the appointed time.

But would I really go alone, given how odd Giulia was acting?

I was trying to decide—and figure out how to get back to Steve Beamus's to reclaim my van—when to my surprise a very distinctive VW with a misshapen horse-dog on the side came rolling down the street.

Chapter 41

"I really don't understand why people have to wear uncomfortable clothes to funerals," I told Piper, who was driving us to the chapel at Wynton University. She'd given me the ride on the condition that I borrow one of her dark pencil skirts and a stiff, starchy blouse for Steve's memorial service. I couldn't even bear to look at my feet, which were crammed into one of her many pairs of sensible black pumps. I squirmed on the leather seat of her Acura sedan. "Something is itching me!"

"Tell me again why you're even going," Piper suggested. "We've established that you weren't Steve's biggest fan."

"I want to offer you moral support," I said, although Piper wasn't outwardly grieving anymore. She wasn't the type of person to weep for days on end. "And I found Steve's body," I added. "I feel like we share a connection now. I want to wish his soul good luck as it embarks on the next great adventure."

"Speaking of adventures," Piper said, downshifting to round a sharp curve, "what in the world were you doing at Steve's house?"

I had been avoiding that question for more than a day, and I tried to dodge it one more time. "Yes, thanks for taking Dylan to get my van," I said. "That was really nice of you both."

I'd been happily surprised when Dylan delivered the VW to me, with a full tank of gas, courtesy of Piper, who swore she'd bought the fuel only so she wouldn't have to bail me out again in a day or so.

Piper didn't acknowledge my gratitude. "I asked what you were doing at Steve's," she reminded me.

I smoothed my—Piper's—skirt over my knees and was suddenly struck by a question I should've asked when Dylan handed me the keys. "How did you guys know my van was at Steve's? Mom didn't even know exactly where it was."

"I didn't talk to Mom," Piper said. "I ran into Detective Black at Fuller's Market. He asked if you'd retrieved your 'rolling death trap' yet. When it was obvious that I didn't know what he was talking about, he told me where to find it, in case you didn't have a way to get it back."

"Oh."

"What's going on with you and Detective Black?" she asked. "And don't say, 'Nothing,' because I saw you two standing outside the house after midnight—reading together, for some reason."

I stopped fidgeting with the skirt and looked over at Piper. "You *spied* on me? Really?"

"Says the girl who not only watched me have an argument with Steve, but also ended up telling the police all about it."

"Sorry," I said. "You wanted me to be honest, though."

"Yes, that is true," Piper conceded as she drove through the university's tall, impressive iron gates. The students were still on summer break, so the pretty little campus was quiet. No one was on the footpaths that wound among the ivy-covered brick buildings, and the only cars were parked near the chapel, which was all but hidden in a shady grove of oak trees. "And I want you to come clean now about your trip to Steve's," my sister added, pulling into a parking spot near the tiny church. "What in the world were you doing at his house?"

We both exited the car and slammed our doors. "Investigating," I admitted.

We were running late, thanks to our protracted argument about what I should wear, so Piper was hurrying, but she glanced back at me. "You were doing *what*?"

I teetered on her low heels, trying to keep pace. "I'll tell you everything later," I promised right before she grabbed a wrought-iron handle on the chapel's wooden door and hauled it open. Now that I was admitting to sneaking around Steve's house, I got excited to share what I'd learned there, and I whispered, "I do think you'll be very interested to know that I met Steve's . . ."

I started to say, "son," but then decided not to finish that thought, since I was practically bumping into none other than Bryce Beamus, who stood at the very back of the chapel, as if he wasn't sure he belonged at his own father's funeral.

The service was already under way, so I nodded a silent greeting, which wasn't returned. Then I stepped up next to Piper, who had paused to search for a seat in the crowded church. My feet already hurt, so I definitely wanted to sit down, too, and I scanned the pews, seeking an empty spot big enough for both of us.

As I surveyed the crowd, I saw a lot of people I'd expected to attend Steve's memorial—as well as a few I'd never dreamed would show up.

I double-checked the congregation.

And at least one key individual was conspicuously *missing*.

Chapter 42

Piper and I never did find empty seats, so we made room for ourselves, squeezing into the next-to-last pew with some folks who looked pretty put out to be shoved out of their prime aisle spots.

As the minister, whose denomination I never did catch, wrapped up some opening remarks, I took the opportunity to observe the mourners.

Or could I really call all of them mourners?

I seriously doubted that Bryce Beamus, who'd moved to the front of the chapel, was grief stricken. I still thought there was a good chance he'd killed his father.

As for Tom Flinchbaugh, who sat two pews ahead of me, sweating in a polyester shirt, I couldn't understand why he was even there—and without Tessie. Steve Beamus had killed his sister, Angela.

Why attend Steve's funeral?

And why was Tom still wearing a bandage on his hand?

The dressing was smaller, but still noticeable when he wiped his brow with a handkerchief.

I looked to the other side of the chapel, where Giulia and Christian sat, cool and collected in spite of how warm the room was.

Well, Christian appeared cool. He wore a dark suit and a suitably solemn expression.

As I watched them both, Giulia bent her head and dabbed at her eyes. Christian immediately slid his arm around her shoulders.

Was he comforting his fiancée?

Or claiming and silencing her, as I'd felt he'd done back at Espresso Pronto?

I stole a peek at Piper, who was grim but was not shedding any tears, then looked at Giulia again. Her shoulders shook.

I was starting to believe that the rumors about Steve and Giulia must've been true. She certainly wouldn't weep over a casual acquaintance.

Christian pulled her closer, and I wondered how he must feel to be seated next to his bride-to-be, in the chapel where they'd get married, while she mourned another man.

Then I carefully searched the pews one more time, looking for Virginia Lockhart. It seemed to me that someone who'd given Steve a book of plays by Shakespeare, inscribed with a maudlin note, should be at his funeral.

Or hadn't the "always" part of "love always" been accurate?

All at once, I heard the door at the back of the chapel open on its squeaky hinges, and I turned, fully expecting to see Virginia slip into the church.

But I was wrong.

We had been joined by Detective Jonathan Black, who met my gaze for just a moment before taking his place with some other overflow attendees, who stood along the back wall.

I should've faced forward again, but for a few seconds, I couldn't stop looking at Jonathan. He had definitely usurped Christian Clarke's position as Sylvan Creek's most handsome man. His dark suit was impeccably tailored, and his hair looked a little shorter and neater, like he'd gotten it cut . . . out of respect for Steve?

I knew Jonathan was there as part of his investigation, but he seemed more like a genuine mourner than some of the people who'd really known Steve. I could've sworn I saw a shadow of pain in his eyes.

I know that he's buried someone important to him.

Maybe quite a few someones . . .

I was so preoccupied with Jonathan that I didn't even realize the minister had stopped talking until Piper nudged me, whispering, "Turn around! It's time for the eulogies!"

I did as she directed, only to discover that the first person to raise a tentative hand, asking for permission to speak, was the last person I would've expected to talk at all.

Bryce Beamus.

Chapter 43

I had to spin around and look at Jonathan again. I doubted that many other people—if anyone else—in the chapel knew who Bryce was or how much he'd resented his father.

Jonathan didn't look at me, though. His eyes were trained on Bryce, who trudged up to the lectern, his shoulders slumped even more than usual. If I'd worn the outfit I'd originally picked out—a black, drapey shirt over a long, olive-green, tiered skirt—I wouldn't have been half as underdressed as Bryce, who looked like he was leaving for a safari right after the service. His khaki shirt and pants combo had more pockets than a herd of kangaroos. I supposed the clothes were considered "professional wear" for members of a guerilla army.

When Bryce turned to face us all, I saw that his eyes were rimmed with red, like he'd been crying. But when he began to talk, I realized that he was probably suffering from a lack of sleep due to a guilty conscience, because the first words out of his mouth were a shaky confession.

My heart nearly pounded out of my chest, Piper grabbed my arm, and everyone in attendance gasped when Bryce buried his face in his hands and told us all, "Steve Beamus was my father, and I . . . I *poisoned* him."

Chapter 44

"Are you upset with me?" I asked Piper, who'd been silent during most of the ride home from Steve's memorial service, which had wrapped up quickly after Jonathan led away Bryce Beamus.

Their exit hadn't been overly disruptive. Jonathan had quietly approached the lectern and placed a hand on the younger man's shoulder, then had guided him out the door. If I hadn't known Jonathan was a detective, I would've thought he was a concerned uncle helping a grieving nephew through a breakdown. Still, Bryce's admission that he'd poisoned his dad had been a hard act to follow. Only three other people had stood up to eulogize Steve—including Piper, who'd given a brief, but classy, speech.

Now, however, my sister was deathly silent. She hadn't said a word since *I'd* confessed to knowing all about Bryce and snooping not once, but twice, at Steve's house.

"Piper?" I prompted as she turned the car onto Winding Hill Lane. "Are you mad? I was just trying to help you."

"I know," she finally said, exhaling with a sigh. "You were keeping a lot of secrets, though."

I slouched down in my seat, to the degree that the pencil skirt allowed me to move. It was like a strait-jacket made for legs. "Sorry," I grumbled. "I knew you'd disapprove of me breaking into the house and tracking down the Jeep."

"Yes," Piper agreed. "Because you might've been putting yourself in danger. Bryce seems unstable, to say the least, and you were alone in a house with him!"

"But it all worked out," I reminded her. "If I hadn't led Jonathan to Bryce, he might never have confessed to poisoning Steve. And now you're off the hook!"

Piper gave me a funny look. "How so?"

Had she missed the entire drama at the funeral?

"Bryce confessed," I said. "Case closed!"

We'd arrived at the farm, and Piper parked in the gravel spot near the barn. "Umm . . . Steve was *bludgeoned*," she pointed out. "Bryce didn't admit to that crime."

Oh, crud. She was right. How had I overlooked that?

Piper reached to open her door. "Just promise me that you'll stop meddling in this whole mess, okay?" she requested. "Let the professionals take it from here. Please."

I couldn't make any promises. I was meeting with Giulia that very night, in hopes of learning more about the murder.

Plus, I couldn't stop thinking about the book of plays with Virginia's inscription inside.

I *had* to find out what her message meant.

But first, I needed to get out of the sausage casing that was making my legs sweat, kick off the shoes that felt like vises on my toes, and take a nice, long nap.

Who would've thought *that* could go wrong?

Chapter 45

"Dylan, no!"

My own voice woke me from my nightmare, and I sat bolt upright in bed, my heart racing.

The sunlight filtering through my window had an eerie pinkish cast, and I checked the clock and was dismayed to realize that I'd slept for nearly five hours. It was after seven o'clock.

As I sat there catching my breath, I gradually recalled details from the dream I'd had, in which Artie and Socrates had gone missing, like Axis. They'd been taken away by *Dylan*, who'd chased me, brandishing a mallet and quoting Shakespeare. . . .

I shook off the memories, reminding myself that Dylan was a vegan peacenik who would never hurt an animal, let alone me. I didn't think he'd ever read Shakespeare, either. His tastes ran more toward Beat poetry than sonnets. The dream meant nothing.

Still, I moved to the edge of the mattress so I could see the floor next to my bed, where I expected to find Socrates and Artie sleeping. Lately, Socrates had been sharing a tiny corner of his pillow.

But neither dog was there, and although I knew

they had probably woken up before me, grown bored, and wandered off, I felt even more uneasy.

Slipping off the bed, I went to the window and drew back the curtain.

The sunset was beautiful, but bloodred and almost blinding.

Raising my hand to shield my eyes, I saw that someone was walking near the barn, in the direction of the network of trails that snaked through the woods.

I couldn't quite shake my sense of foreboding, but I really wanted to talk with the visitor to Piper's property, and I pulled on my cowgirl boots and ran off, headed for the forest as the sun set lower.

Chapter 46

"Virginia, wait!" I called, catching up to her under a thick canopy of trees that cast the path she'd followed in dark shadows. She and the rottweilers walked quickly and were already pretty deep into the woods, at a fork in the trails. "Wait up!" I repeated when she didn't turn around. Even the dogs were ignoring me—until I added more loudly, "Hold! Enough!"

Macduff, Hamlet, and Iago stopped in their tracks—and so did Virginia. As she turned slowly to face me, the rottweilers, off leash, came to her side.

I loved those dogs, and I knew they were friendly, but all at once I got the creeps. As they gathered around Virginia in the darkness, drawing close to one another, their black bodies seemed to blend together, so I was reminded of Cerberus, the three-headed dog said to guard the underworld.

Virginia was giving me the willies, too. "How did you know that command?" she asked in a low, even, unwelcoming tone. "I never told you to address the dogs that way."

Maybe if she had, I wouldn't have nearly lost control of them the night they'd been spooked by the storm.

I didn't mention that, though. She was obviously in a bad mood and probably wouldn't appreciate criticism from her hired dog walker.

Seriously, though . . . Why have a secret language for the dogs? Why not teach me the command, since I walked the rotties at least twice a week, when she was too busy with her law practice?

"I heard Steve address them that way once," I told her. "When Macduff, Hamlet, and Iago got loose in town."

Virginia didn't respond, although I thought she stiffened. "What do you want?" she asked, resting one hand on Macduff's head. In what little light was available, I could just barely see all three dogs' eyes glittering and their pink, panting tongues hanging out. "I'm working with my dogs," Virginia noted. "And it's getting late, so if you could please make it quick."

"You were here the night Steve was killed, weren't you?" I asked, moving closer to the pack and its leader. "I saw your SUV parked in its usual spot."

Virginia hesitated, then said warily, "Perhaps I was. Why do you ask?"

"You were also there when the police questioned Piper, so you know she's a suspect," I said. "I'm trying to help her. So if you saw anything that might be useful—"

"I've spoken with the two detectives," Virginia interrupted. "I told them everything I know. Which is nothing. I was out on these paths, walking the dogs."

"Really?" That was hard to believe. "But it was so late—"

Virginia spoke sharply, cutting me off again. "What are you trying to say?"

I raised my hands and took a step back. "Nothing!"

"I don't have time for this," Virginia grumbled. "I've got to go." She turned and summoned the rotties with a click of her tongue and the sharp command "Advance!"

Most people released their dogs with "Okay" or "Let's go."

"Virginia," I said, stopping her again. "Wait!"

"What?" She turned back, sounding exasperated. "I honestly can't tell you anything!"

I had a feeling that Virginia was being ruder than usual because she was grieving a man she shouldn't have been mourning. Maybe she and Steve had been having an affair when he died, or maybe the inscription in the book was old, and they hadn't been together for a long time—since before she'd married Senator Mitch. Either way, I suspected that she was hiding a big heartache, and at least one secret tragedy, that she couldn't share with anybody.

Sylvan Creek was a small town. If Virginia and Steve had told anyone about their "pain" and the "fruit" it might yield, word would've spread—with Moxie serving as a prime conduit. My best friend was on a first-name basis with all the skeletons that were hiding in closets around Sylvan Creek. But as far as I knew, everyone, Moxie included, believed Virginia's life was and always had been perfect.

"Are we done here?" Virginia asked.

"I guess so," I said. "But before you go . . . can I ask one more thing, just out of curiosity?"

"I suppose so," she agreed. I couldn't really see her face, but it sounded like she was gritting her teeth.

I forged ahead, anyhow. "Why are the dogs named for characters in Shakespeare's plays?" I asked. "And why do you train them with commands that sound

Shakespearean, too? Were you an English major before you went to law school or something?"

I didn't really expect Virginia to answer those questions, but she suddenly seemed to soften toward me. Her voice grew quieter and lost its edge. "Those plays once helped me through a very difficult time in my life," she said. "They mean quite a bit to me."

"Oh, gosh . . . What happened?" I was sympathetic, but I was also struggling to contain my excitement, because I was pretty sure she was referring to the tragedy that had inspired the inscription. "That is, if you don't mind me asking?"

"I do mind," she snapped, as if she realized she'd let her guard down too much. "And it was nothing, really!"

She was being rude again, but I felt sorry for her. Whatever happened hadn't been "nothing."

"Do you want me to walk the dogs tomorrow?" I asked, wishing I could give her a hug. Since I couldn't do that—it would baffle her, and I'd get pushed away—I offered her the only thing I could think of. A discount on my services. "I think I owe you a freebie," I added. "I'm starting a thing where every fifth walk is on the house."

She didn't answer me, and I worried that my nosiness had just cost me one of my best customers.

And would I have to follow through with that impulsive, impromptu change to my policies? Start giving all my clients punch cards for free walks?

Piper would not be pleased to learn that my profits were about to go *down*.

Sighing, I lingered for a moment, watching Virginia disappear down the gloomy path with her trio of Shakespearean pups.

When they were out of sight, and I realized I was alone, the back of my neck started to prickle, and I had the eerie sense that someone was behind me.

It was probably my imagination working overtime, fueled by the knowledge that someone had been murdered not far from where I stood. I was convinced that Steve had been killed by somebody who hated him, and I doubted anyone was really after me. Still, I started to beat a hasty retreat back to the house.

As I reached the open fields that surrounded the farmhouse and barn, I felt a sense of relief and wondered how Virginia could be so brave, heading farther into the woods at night, even if she was accompanied by three large dogs.

All at once, I stopped dead in my tracks.

Was there a chance Virginia wasn't worried about running into a killer because *she* had murdered Steve?

I resumed walking, more slowly, and slipped into the house. Checking the antique clock that hung on the wall, I realized I had a few hours to spare before my meeting with Giulia.

In fact, I had just enough time to visit someplace that had a tenuous, but perhaps important, connection to Steve's life—and possibly his death, too.

Plus, there would be pie there.

Chapter 47

"What, exactly, are we doing here?" Moxie asked. She dug her fork through a six-inch tower of flaky crust and sweet cinnamon-apple filling, then scooped up some rich, creamy vanilla ice cream, too. She shoveled all of that into her mouth, which didn't prevent her from continuing to talk. "I mean, besides eating the best pie in the world?"

We were seated in a red vinyl booth at the Silver Moon Diner, just outside of Sylvan Creek. I hadn't been to the diner in years, but nothing had changed, although some of the shine had worn off the iconic 1950s trailer. Inside, though, the black-and-white checkered floor still gleamed and customers swiveled on tall stools at the long Formica counter, their plates piled high with triple-decker cheeseburgers and heaps of french fries.

"I'm not sure why I wanted to come here," I admitted, maneuvering my own silverware through a tall slice of lemon meringue. "I just keep thinking about this place, and how my dad used to take me and Piper here. There was a waitress named Angela—"

"I remember her!" Moxie said. Dressed in one of

her many vintage outfits—a starched pink blouse with poofy short sleeves and a full black skirt—she looked like she could've been sitting in the booth, trapped in time, since the day the diner opened in 1952. Well, Moxie's spiked flame-red hair and the small tattoo on her wrist—a big-eyed kitten—would've been out of place back then. Otherwise, she could've tumbled sixty years back through history, landed on one of the swiveling stools, and ordered a shake without anyone looking twice. "She used to give me extra ice cream with my pie," Moxie added. "She was really nice."

"Hey, I thought she only did that for me and Piper," I said, feeling deflated. "I thought we were special."

"I'm sure you were." Moxie reached over to pat my hand. "I'm sure you were."

I did not need to be patronized; however, I *did* need napkins, because I'd dropped a big blob of meringue onto my lap. Leaning over, I pulled a few from a silver dispenser, which was next to a tabletop jukebox that featured songs by Elvis Presley, Chuck Berry, and a band I'd never heard of called The Four Lads. If I'd had a quarter in my pocket, I would've played their song, because I doubted anyone had thought of them in decades. It would've been nice to release their music to the world one more time.

Unfortunately, I had no change. Just a few wadded-up dollar bills.

I wiped at the stain on my jeans. "Did you know that Angela the waitress was Tom Flinchbaugh's sister?" I asked Moxie. "And that she died in a car accident?"

Moxie dragged her fork across her plate, trying to scrape up the very last ice cream–soaked crumbs of crust. "I kind of remember the accident. But I didn't know she was related to Tom." She looked at me and frowned. "Poor Tom. That's really sad, to lose a sibling."

"Yeah, and Tessie told me that he's still really broken up about it."

I had been keeping everything Tessie Flinchbaugh had told me locked away for quite a while, and I really wanted to confide in someone. I knew that Moxie, who might've spread her clients' gossip all over town, would keep *my* secrets. She was the only person in the world who knew that in fourth grade I'd stolen a pack of Juicy Fruit gum from the Stop 'n Save mini market—an episode that still gave me pangs of guilt and compelled me to leave at least two pennies in the "give a penny, take a penny" bowl near the market's cash register every time I bought something there. I knew I'd paid for that gum ten times over, but I couldn't stop trying to erase my moral debt. Moxie always advised me to let it go—and she'd never told a soul what I'd done.

Still, I leaned forward and asked her, in a whisper, "If I tell you something, will you *promise* to never tell another human being? Ever?"

Eyes gleaming with interest, Moxie dropped her fork and crossed her heart with her index finger. "I promise. Now spill!"

I glanced from side to side to make sure nobody would overhear me, even though someone else had put a quarter in one of the jukeboxes, so the diner was filled with the sounds of Frankie Valli singing "Big Girls Don't Cry." Then I said, "You probably don't remember this, but Steve Beamus caused the accident that killed Angela. He was young and was driving too fast. . . ."

Moxie's eyes were huge, but she let me keep talking.

"Anyhow, Tessie said Tom never forgave Steve." I leaned even closer and spoke a bit louder, because Frankie was really belting it out in his signature falsetto.

"She also can't account for Tom's whereabouts the night Steve was killed," I confided. "Tessie honestly thinks Tom might've committed the murder!"

I uttered that last sentence just as the song ended, and although I hadn't been talking too loudly, it sounded like I was shouting in the sudden quiet. My words echoed in the diner—and my heart sank down to my boots.

Moxie clapped two hands over her mouth, like she could somehow swallow my words.

Then, just when things seemed bad enough—a few people had swung around on their seats at the counter to give me funny looks—someone walked up to our booth. The diner was very bright and cheerful, but the person cast a shadow over the table, so my bright yellow lemon meringue pie suddenly looked a little less sunny.

All the color drained from Moxie's face, too, and I reluctantly turned to see who had joined us, although I had a feeling I already knew.

A very, very bad feeling.

Chapter 48

"Umm . . . what brings you here, Detective Black?" Moxie asked nervously.

Jonathan's arms were folded over his chest, and his eyes were trained on me, even as he answered Moxie with a single word. "Hunger."

"Oh . . . that makes sense," Moxie said, offering him a shaky smile, although Jonathan still wasn't looking at her. She scooched over in the booth, like she was making room for someone. Then she patted the seat next to her and inexplicably inquired, "Would you like to join us?"

What was she thinking?

I needed time to figure out how to explain why I'd just blurted out that Tom Flinchbaugh's own wife thought he'd committed murder. I'd obviously made a huge mistake by betraying Tessie's confidence once, and I really didn't want to share her secrets again—especially with Jonathan.

"There's plenty of room," Moxie added, pulling her big skirt closer to herself and patting the seat again. "Come on."

I kicked my best friend under the table with the pointy toe of my boot, and she shot me an injured look. "Ouch!"

Ignoring her, I smiled at Jonathan, too. "Please don't feel like you have to sit with us. I'm sure you . . ."

Before I could say, "would prefer to eat in peace," he slid into the booth next to Moxie, saying, "As a matter of fact, I am *very* interested to join this conversation."

Chapter 49

"I'm sorry, but I can't explain what I just said," I told Jonathan for at least the tenth time. He'd had a chance to peruse the menu, place his order, and receive his food—a turkey club—and we were still going around and around in a conversational circle. "I wish I could tell you everything—I really do—but I can't. I made a promise."

"You obviously broke that promise with Moxie," Jonathan reminded me.

"She's my best friend," I explained. "I have to tell her all my secrets. It's part of the girl code. You wouldn't understand."

"There's another 'code,' too," Jonathan said. "One that I do understand. It's called the *legal* code, and I'm pretty sure it trumps the 'girl code.'"

"I don't know about that," Moxie observed. She'd ordered a chocolate milk shake and was stirring it with her straw. "Back when Daphne and I were kids, we went to this little market where they sold gum and stuff. . . ."

I kicked her again, and she rubbed her shin. But she was the one who apologized. "Oops. Sorry, Daph."

What had gotten into her lately?

Jonathan leaned back in the booth. "So you're really not going to tell me anything more?"

"I think you heard enough," I said. He wasn't eating his potato chips, so I took a few from his plate. The chips were made in-house, cut superthin and fried in peanut oil. How could he resist them? "I'm sure you'll follow up with Tessie and Tom," I added. He didn't owe me any favors—in fact, I still owed *him* money from our evening at the Lakeside—but I ventured to ask, "Could you please somehow avoid letting them know why you're questioning them again? Is there a way you could *please* leave me out of it?"

Jonathan considered my request while he chewed a bite of his sandwich. I hadn't eaten meat for years, but I sometimes still missed bacon, a thick, crispy piece of which had fallen out from between the layers of turkey, lettuce, and bright red tomato. I had to admit, the sandwich looked pretty good.

"I'll do my best," Jonathan finally agreed. I reached for his plate again to get more chips, and he pulled his dinner closer to himself. "Did you ever consider asking if I'd like to share?"

"I guess it crossed my mind," I said, reaching farther and grabbing another handful. "But you don't seem to be eating these."

He looked to Moxie, as if for support, but she sipped her milk shake, then shrugged. "You snooze, you lose."

"Hey, whatever happened with Bryce Beamus?" I asked, changing the subject. "Why are you even worried about Tom Flinchbaugh, now that Bryce has confessed—at least to the poisoning? Doesn't it make sense that he probably bludgeoned his father, too?"

Jonathan set down his sandwich and rested back in the booth, brushing crumbs off his hands and shaking his head. "No, Bryce didn't kill his father. He's a very troubled kid, with a lot of anger and guilt, but he's not a killer. He only put a small amount of Clean Kennel in the thermos, hoping to prove to his dad that it wasn't safe for animals. He was trying to convince Beamus that dogs lick their paws and could get sick. It was a stupid stunt, but far from homicide."

I couldn't believe Jonathan was so readily dismissing Bryce as a suspect. "But . . . but . . . Bryce was angry . . . and I saw his Jeep at Winding Hill. . . ."

"Bryce left the farm long before his father was killed," Jonathan said. He stretched out his long legs, and they bumped into mine under the table. We both pulled away. "He has an alibi for the time of death."

"What kind of alibi?" I demanded. Jonathan had never told me exactly when Steve had been killed, but since I'd seen Steve working late at the farm, then found his body in the morning, I felt confident in saying, "The murder must have happened in the middle of the night."

"Yeah," Moxie agreed. "And not to get too personal about it, but even if Bryce was sleeping with somebody, how can you trust her—or him—to tell the truth?"

"Actually, it was pretty easy to find verifiable evidence of Bryce's activity for most of the night," Jonathan informed us. "And he was a busy guy."

Furrowing my brow, I chomped down on a chip. "What do you mean?"

"At one a.m., Bryce was in town, at a mini market." He was probably referring to the only market open all night in Sylvan Creek, Stop 'n Save, and I shot Moxie a warning look, in case she had a sudden urge to talk about stolen gum.

She pursed her lips and made a motion like she was locking them, then throwing away an imaginary key.

Satisfied that she'd stay silent about my past misdeeds, I resumed listening to Jonathan.

"The clerk on duty that night remembers, because Bryce went a little crazy, berating him for selling meat products. When the clerk asked him to leave, Bryce knocked over a display of beef jerky. It's all captured on time-stamped security footage, too."

Moxie raised one hand to her mouth to stifle a snicker that wouldn't quite be contained. "That should be on YouTube," she said. "I would watch that."

I would, too, but I wasn't about to admit that to Jonathan. He was giving Moxie a pretty funny look.

"Maybe Bryce was agitated because he'd just killed his father," I suggested. "Did you ever think of that?"

"That's not possible," Jonathan said. "Beamus was still alive at that time."

"Well, the whole beef-jerky incident couldn't have taken more than a few minutes," I pointed out. "How do you know Bryce didn't return to Winding Hill and kill his dad later?"

Jonathan finally ate some of his chips, and he raised a finger, indicating that he needed to chew and swallow—whereas Moxie and I usually just kept talking. When he was ready, he said, "Bryce went to Beamus's house, where he made a phone call to a friend on the West Coast, using his father's landline. We verified the time. Then he spent the rest of the night on a dating Web site. His profile—under the screen name animalluvr582—was active from about one thirty to three thirty a.m."

Moxie cringed and made a face. "Animal lover five-eighty-two? That is a very unfortunate choice for a dating site. That could be incorrectly interpreted in several ways. I can't believe five-hundred eighty-one other people chose it, too!"

Jonathan didn't seem to know what to say, while I was considering the timeline he'd just laid out for us.

"How do you know Steve was still alive at one a.m. and dead before, say, four?" I asked.

I still wasn't prepared to let Bryce off the hook. He could've driven back to Winding Hill after three thirty. He might've been even more agitated, too, if he'd been repeatedly shot down online for several hours. From what I'd seen of Bryce, I doubted he'd inherited his father's talent for winning over the ladies.

"The coroner was able to pinpoint the time of death pretty accurately," Jonathan said. "And we know for sure that Steve was alive at one, because he sent a text message at one twelve."

"To who?" I asked. I couldn't believe how nocturnal people were. Bryce had been hitting on women in the middle of the night, and Steve had been texting. Tessie didn't know where Tom had been the night of Steve's murder. Didn't anybody in Sylvan Creek sleep? "Who'd Steve text so late?"

All at once, Jonathan's expression became guarded. I was reminded of how Virginia had acted when she thought she'd shared too much with me. Only Jonathan didn't snap at me. He just grew quiet.

I stared into his blue eyes, trying hard to read them, and thinking about how Steve had been at Winding

Hill when he'd sent that late-night message after having an argument with Piper.

Folding my arms on the table, I let my forehead sink down to rest on them, so my voice was muffled when I asked, with a groan, "He was texting Piper, wasn't he? He was trying to meet for a post-argument"—I shuddered and barely got the words out—"booty call, right?"

Jonathan's silence spoke volumes.

I wasn't sure if I was mainly upset by the fact that the text represented more evidence against Piper—if she'd agreed to meet Steve, she was probably the last person to see him alive—or if I was just sickened to think about Steve trying to lure her. . . .

Ugh.

"I should go now," Jonathan said, pushing the plate with the last few chips toward me and checking his wristwatch. "It's getting late."

I suddenly remembered something and grabbed his wrist and twisted his arm so I could see the time, too. It was after eleven o'clock.

"Oh, no," I said, releasing him. "I've also gotta run. I'm going to be late for a meeting." I turned to Moxie. "Let's go, okay?"

Jonathan stood up to let Moxie out of the booth. "Why am I concerned about you having a meeting so late at night?" he asked, sounding unhappy. "Why do I feel that I will eventually be involved?"

"It's nothing that should—or will—concern you," I told him, taking Moxie's arm and leading her toward the door. "Don't think twice about it."

He had a skeptical look on his face as Moxie and I left the diner.

Only when we were about a mile away, headed back

to Sylvan Creek, did I realize that we'd stuck Jonathan with the entire bill. Again.

All at once, I slammed on the brakes—not because I intended to turn back and give Jonathan some money. I'd repay him someday, soon enough. I stopped the van because I'd seen something by the side of the road.

"Moxie!" I cried. "Did you see that, too?"

Chapter 50

"My shoes are not made for hiking," Moxie complained, picking her way through some gravel and weeds at the side of the road. She was much more adept at wearing heels than me, but the footing was terrible and she teetered on her red stilettos. "Why are we doing this?"

"I just want to see the memorial up close," I said over my shoulder. I was striding along in my very sensible, if oversize, cowgirl boots. "It might be important."

I'd parked the van as soon as I could find a safe spot next to the road, but we still had to walk about a hundred feet back in the dark. Fortunately, there wasn't much traffic that night.

"There it is!" I cried, locating the small wooden cross I'd seen while driving. It was set back a few feet from the road, under some trees, and I probably wouldn't have even noticed it if it weren't so vividly white.

"I'm not going into the woods," Moxie said. "These shoes are vintage Roger Vivier. I had to do at least twenty Brazilian blowouts just to pay for them!"

It took me a second to realize she was talking about an expensive process to straighten hair.

"Just stay there," I told her, trudging up a small rise toward the cross. "I'll be right back."

After taking a few more steps, I bent down to read the neatly painted inscription:

ANGELA FLINCHBAUGH
D. AUG. 10, 2007
~ NEVER FORGOTTEN ~

I was struck first by the date. As Tessie had mentioned, Steve Beamus had been killed very close to the anniversary of Angela's death, a time when Tom's grief and anger probably spiked.

And the cross looked brand new, like it had just been installed. The plastic flowers that were wired to the wood were bright and clean, too.

I was fairly sure there had been a roadside memorial at that spot for years, but it had been shabby and worn. I'd never really paid much attention to it until that night, when the fresh white paint caught my eye.

Had someone updated the marker to commemorate the anniversary of Angela's accident?

Or to get closure symbolically after avenging her death?

I could see how restoring the small personal monument might provide an individual with a sense of resolution. . . .

"Are we done here?" Moxie asked, interrupting my thoughts. "You have some 'appointment' to keep, right?" She slapped at her ankle. "And I am getting eaten alive by mosquitoes."

"I'm coming," I promised, heading for the road. "Have you ever considered wearing boots instead of heels—"

I was starting to lecture Moxie on the advantages of practical footwear when I suddenly sounded—and looked—foolish, because I stumbled. Catching myself, I looked down and saw that I'd tripped on something that was half hidden under the many years' worth of dead leaves that blanketed the ground. Bending, I picked up the object.

"What is that?" Moxie asked. "What did you find?"

"A hammer," I said, peering at it more closely and frowning. "One stamped with the initials WHF."

Moxie had no idea why that was significant, and I was a little confused, too.

Why in the world was a tool bearing the Winding Hill Farm imprint—which my prudent sister placed on every object that might be loaned or "accidentally" removed from the farm—at a memorial for *Angela Flinchbaugh?*

Chapter 51

"The big question is, 'Do I tell Jonathan?'" I mused aloud to Moxie, who was riding in the passenger seat, scratching all her bug bites. "Does he need to know about the hammer?"

"While I would gladly share secrets with Detective Black—"

"Yes, I know," I interrupted. "You almost shared mine."

"I said I was sorry," Moxie reminded me. "There's just something about him that makes me want to talk. And talk. And stare into his eyes. And talk some more. And then . . ."

"Moxie!" I spoke sharply before she could get carried away.

"Anyhow," she continued, getting hold of herself, "I really don't think the hammer is important. I'd just put it back in the barn, or wherever you keep hammers at Winding Hill, and go on with my life."

I wasn't sure I agreed with that advice.

Tom Flinchbaugh had been setting up a tent at the farm the night of the murder. He might've borrowed the hammer to help with that task. Then he could've intentionally or, more likely, accidentally kept it and used it to repair the wooden cross.

But why abandon a tool in the woods, under the leaves?

I'd set the hammer between Moxie and me—the VW had its original bench seats—and I gave the tool a wary glance, then reached over and nudged my best friend's shoulder.

"Umm, Moxie?"

She'd been preoccupied with scratching her ankles, but she looked over at me. "What? What's wrong?"

"What if I just found the *murder weapon?*"

Chapter 52

"Promise me you won't do anything hasty," Moxie urged. "Just hold on to the hammer for now, okay?"

We were standing outside the Philosopher's Tome, where I'd parked so she could go upstairs to her apartment, while I would have to walk only a block to the park to meet Giulia.

The bookstore was dark, but Tom had forgotten to change the OPEN sign to CLOSED. Not that customers would be breaking down the doors at dawn to get their hands on a 1930 first-edition copy of Bertrand Russell's *The Conquest of Happiness*—which Tom was kindly allowing me to read for free.

I got a little sick to my stomach.

Tom was my friend, and a good person, but I was starting to think Tessie was right to be worried about him.

"What if it's really the murder weapon?" I asked. "Don't I have to turn it over to Jonathan?"

"Daphne, it's *Piper's* hammer," Moxie reminded me. "What if her prints are on it?"

Piper was a practical, can-do kind of woman. I had

no doubt that she'd used a hammer many times. That could be problematic.

I suddenly realized that my prints were all over the handle, too. That was also bad.

"Besides," Moxie added, "not to be gross, but there's no blood on it, right? You really have no reason to believe it's the murder weapon. So why make such a big deal out of it?"

"There's no blood that we can see," I said. "But someone could've wiped it clean. Plus, don't you think it's kind of strange to find an object that could deliver blunt force trauma—and that was at Winding Hill at some point—half hidden in the woods near a memorial to a woman killed by Steve Beamus?"

The wind blew, and the Philosopher's Tome's wooden sign, which hung from an iron bracket near the door, creaked. It was a reproachful sound, and I felt like the whole store was accusing me of betraying Tom. I'd been picturing him cleaning off the hammer and concealing it after restoring a cross for the sister he'd avenged.

"What would your philosophers do?" Moxie asked. "Don't they offer you any answers?"

"I think I need to figure this out on my own," I said glumly. "I think this moral dilemma is uniquely mine."

Moxie planted her hands on her hips. "Do you want a hairstylist's advice? And a lot of people do. Probably more people than consult Plato these days."

I'd once paid forty-three dollars for one of those Brazilian blowouts that supported Moxie's shoe habit, and the process—which she'd sworn would give me straight, sleek hair—had resulted in me looking like Andy Warhol. Otherwise, she seldom steered me wrong.

"Go ahead," I said. "I'm listening."

"I think you should sleep on it," Moxie suggested. "Not the hammer, literally. Don't put that under your pillow or anything, just in case you're right about where it's been. But sleep on the idea of telling Jonathan about it. Tomorrow morning you might not think it's so important."

I hadn't expected Moxie to quote Confucius, but I'd hoped for something a little more profound.

"That's it?" I asked. "Sleep on it?"

"Yeah. Pretty good, huh?"

Moxie was so proud of herself that I didn't contradict her. "I'll call you tomorrow and let you know what I decide," I promised. "And thanks for going with me to the diner."

"My pleasure." Moxie was opening a small door on the side of the old Victorian building. A staircase inside would give her access to her upstairs apartment, but she paused on the sidewalk. "Are you sure you don't want me to come with you to this 'meeting'? And why won't you tell me who you're going to meet?"

I smiled. "Good night, Moxie."

She grinned at me. "Say hi to Dylan for me. You *are* meeting Dylan, right?"

If I didn't answer, I didn't have to lie, so I let her believe what she wanted to believe. "Talk to you tomorrow."

As I headed down the street, she called after me, "I want details about your date, too!"

Then I heard her door close, leaving me alone in the dark, sleepy town. The night was growing cool and breezy, and the leaves on the trees that lined Market Street were rustling overhead. The sound was eerie, and I picked up my pace, my boots clicking on the pavement.

I really wished I'd brought Socrates and Artie, but there was no time to go back to Winding Hill for them. I was already late for my meeting with Giulia.

Maybe too late, because the bench where she was supposed to be waiting, on the bank of the creek that gave the town its name, was empty.

Then I saw that someone was sitting in the gazebo at the edge of the park, in a grove of trees. I could see the person only in silhouette, but I could tell that her back was to me, and I assumed Giulia had forgotten where, exactly, we were supposed to meet.

"I'm sorry I'm late," I said as I approached the gazebo. "I was eating these potato chips, and then I had to stop along a road, and I lost track of time. . . ."

Giulia didn't turn to greet me, and I reached out to tap her shoulder.

"Giulia?"

She still didn't turn around, so, assuming that she was taking a nap, I shook her—only to realize that the person I was trying to rouse wasn't Giulia.

And something was terribly wrong.

As I watched in horror, Virginia Lockhart tumbled stiffly off the bench and hit the floor of the gazebo with a lifeless thud.

I stood there in shock, unable to move, until I heard deep, low growls, right behind me.

Turning slowly, I discovered that I'd been joined by three rottweilers, whose leads were dangling from their collars.

And the normally sweet dogs did *not* look happy.

Chapter 53

I stood a few yards away from the gazebo, alternately wrapping my arms around myself and petting Macduff, Iago, and Hamlet to comfort them.

The dogs seemed very sorry for growling at me, and they were spooked by the flashing red lights and the activity, too. The park was swarming with EMS workers and police officers, including Detective Doebler. Coroner Vonda Shakes was also there. It was like the scene at Winding Hill all over again, only in the dark.

"It's okay, guys," I promised the rottweilers in a soothing voice. Holding their leads in one hand, I used the other to stroke their broad heads and scratch behind their ears. "I know when you growled at me, you were scared and were trying to protect Virginia. And I'll take you home soon."

Someone had other plans for me, though. A person who had been conspicuously missing from the scene but who had arrived at some point and was approaching me with a purposeful stride and a frown on his face.

Detective Jonathan Black, who informed me, in a

no-nonsense tone that told me he had adopted his official persona, "You're not going anywhere until we talk about why your 'meetings' inevitably involve me— and we discuss your curious propensity for discovering *victims of homicide.*"

Chapter 54

It was nearly 2:00 a.m. when Virginia's body was finally taken away and Jonathan could walk me and the rottweilers to my van. By that time, he was apparently so tired that he couldn't entirely maintain that wall he liked to keep up between his personal and professional lives.

"Honestly, Daphne," he said, rubbing the back of his neck, "I don't really consider you a suspect. Who would be stupid enough to report *two* murders she committed?"

I hoped he wouldn't answer that, and I shuddered, too, to recall how I'd had to dig for Virginia's cell phone in the pocket of her Windbreaker to call 911. I *really* needed a new phone.

"But you have to admit," Jonathan continued, "stumbling across two bodies is rather strange."

"Nobody thinks it's stranger than I do," I agreed, stumbling again when Iago pulled on his lead. All three rotties were still out of sorts, and my boots were too big for dog walking.

Jonathan reached over and wordlessly took Iago's

lead from my hand. The dog fell in step next to him, like they'd been partners for years. I wasn't surprised.

"What were you doing in the park?" he asked. "And don't give me some vague answer about a 'meeting.'"

I had planned to do exactly that. Then I realized that while Giulia had asked me to come to the park alone, she'd never told me to keep our appointment a secret. Plus, she'd stood me up.

"I was supposed to meet Giulia Alberti," I said. "She asked me to be at the park at midnight tonight. But she didn't show up."

Jonathan bent slightly to study my face. "Why meet her so late, in a park?"

"I have no idea," I said, with a shrug. We'd reached the van and stopped walking. The dogs should've sat down, but they remained restless. "I told you, she didn't show up."

"You must've known *why* she wanted to talk." Jonathan sounded exasperated. I was having that effect on people lately.

"No, I didn't know," I said, handing him the two leads I had and digging into my back pocket. I was wearing the same jeans I'd worn the day Giulia'd handed me the note, and sure enough, I found the paper with the recipe for *cornetti* and the mysterious request. It had gone through the wash and was worse for wear, but the ink was still legible. Taking back two of the leads, I handed Jonathan the message. "Here. Read."

With a single gesture, he placed Iago in a sit and dropped the lead, clearly confident the dog would obey him. Then he carefully unfolded the fragile, damaged paper and read aloud. "Two cups flour . . ." He looked up at me, eyebrows arched. "What is this?"

"The other side!" I said, grabbing his hand and turning it. "Read the other side!"

Jonathan shook free of me and flipped over the paper. He read silently, then looked at me again, frowning. "And you have no idea why she wanted this private conference?"

I shrugged. "None."

Jonathan bent to pick up the lead; then he released Iago from his sit and absently stroked the dog's head. "What are you going to do with the dogs?" he asked.

"I'm taking them to Virginia's house."

"I don't think anyone will be there. No one's been able to reach Mitch Lockhart. According to the assistant who staffs his district office, he's at the state capital for a few days, working there. She also claims he normally turns off his cell phone at night."

I could tell Jonathan wasn't sure about any of that. Or, at the very least, he wasn't convinced that Senator Mitch hadn't made the two-hour trip from Harrisburg to Sylvan Creek, killed his wife, then taken off again.

"I guess I'll just keep the rotties until I hear from him," I said. "Unless you'd like one or two?"

"No, thanks," Jonathan said. He removed his hand from Iago's head, and I wished I hadn't pushed him to take the dog, even temporarily. "But if you recall anything more that you noticed this evening, please call me first, before you do anything else on your own."

"I do have something to tell you," I said. "About Virginia."

I saw a flicker of interest in Jonathan's eyes. "What about her?"

"I talked with her this evening at Winding Hill. She was walking the dogs, and I followed her down the path to ask her about the night Steve got killed."

Jonathan tilted his head back and sighed deeply. It was kind of a groan, too. I thought he was going to interrupt me for one of his public-service-announcement lectures about the dangers of meddling in murder, but he didn't, so I kept talking.

"She was in a really bad mood and wouldn't tell me anything," I said. "Until I asked her why she'd named her dogs after characters from Shakespeare's plays."

"You were trying to learn more about the inscription."

Jonathan didn't sound pleased about that or impressed by my subtle attempt to broach a sensitive topic.

"Yes, that's what I was doing," I told him.

"And what did you learn?"

"Nothing," I said. "Except that the plays helped her get through a difficult time in her life. That's what she said. But I guess we sort of knew that already."

"Yes, that seems apparent from the inscription." Jonathan moved past me to open the rear door of my van. With a click of his tongue, he sent Iago into the VW. "Please don't follow any more people into the woods, all right?"

"Okay," I agreed as Macduff and Hamlet leaped to join their brother. "It *was* eerie."

Jonathan leaned in to pet the dogs one last time; then he pulled back and closed the door, slamming it firmly. When he turned to me, he looked grim. "You know, I'll have to talk to Piper again. I shouldn't tell you that, but I imagine you've already assumed that she'll be questioned, since Virginia was on her property right before her death."

I had *not* assumed that. "But . . . but . . . I found Virginia in the gazebo. . . ."

Jonathan crossed his arms over his chest.

When had he changed into a suit? Because he'd been wearing jeans and a light blue Henley at the diner. The color had gone well with his dark blue eyes.

"We don't know that Virginia was killed in the park," he said. "In fact, that seems unlikely."

I took a moment to digest what he was saying—which was that Piper's situation might've just gotten worse, thanks to me telling Jonathan about Virginia's visit to Winding Hill.

I knew, though, that he would've traced Virginia's movements that day on his own, and that hiding information probably wouldn't really help things in the end.

Which was why I ignored Moxie's sage advice and abruptly made a decision about the hammer.

Opening the front door of my van, I said, "Before you go . . . I should probably also tell you that I think I might've found the weapon used in the *first* murder."

Chapter 55

I'd intended to get up early and tell Piper all about finding Virginia's body and the hammer, and about the fact that Jonathan would be in touch with her, but I didn't get home until nearly 3:00 a.m.—after being subjected to Jonathan's longest lecture yet, about mishandling evidence, with more warnings about wandering in the woods, too. Not surprisingly, I slept right through my alarm, which had no snooze button, because it was a live rooster that wandered with some really free-ranging chickens on Piper's property. The moment Cluck Taylor had stopped celebrating the sunrise, I'd rolled over and promptly fallen back asleep, with Artie pressed against my face, three rottweilers on the floor, and Socrates snoring in his bed, which he'd dragged to a far corner of the room to get some privacy.

By the time we all woke up, it was nearly 11:00 a.m., and Piper was already at work, so I made the dogs and myself omelets for brunch. Luckily, Cluck's harem had been busy the past few days, so I had nearly two dozen eggs, which would still barely be enough to put a dent in the rotties' huge appetites.

While the dogs all went outside for some fresh air—with Artie joyfully leading the way for his guests—I cracked all the eggs into a huge bowl and mixed in a little water so the omelets would be fluffy.

After pouring some of the mixture into a pan, I waited until the beautiful deep yellow, almost orange, eggs began to cook through, then added some cooked rice, peas, and chopped ham.

When those less conventional, but perfect for pups, omelets were all prepared and cooling, I made my veggie version with a mixture of ricotta and mozzarella cheeses and some chopped basil from a pot on the windowsill.

Plating everything—in dog bowls for the rottweilers and Artie, and on human plates for me and finicky Socrates—I then went to the door to call everyone inside. I almost hated to interrupt the moment, though.

For the first time I could recall, Socrates was deigning to *play*. He was actually running across the grass with Iago, Hamlet, Macduff, and Artie. His big paws were flying, and his ears were streaming behind his head.

Not surprisingly, the Chihuahua was in the lead, his eyes bulging and his tongue flapping like an out-of-control kite as he tore in my direction.

A few moments later, having smelled their breakfasts, all five dogs tumbled through the door and were soon up to their eyeballs in eggs, snuffling and snorting as they ate.

Well, Socrates didn't snuffle. He seemed slightly embarrassed to have been caught scampering around the yard. He ate slowly and didn't meet my eyes.

"It's okay to have fun," I told him, shoveling down my omelet with about as much decorum as the rottweilers and Artie. I was starving, since my entire dinner the night before had consisted of pie and a few potato chips. "You should play."

Socrates pretended not to hear me, but I had a feeling he would sneak in some future romps. In the meantime, I thought it might be nice to spend some quality time with him while Artie was preoccupied with the visitors. They had all finished their meals, and Artie was proudly leading Hamlet, Iago, and Macduff into the living room, presumably to show them his favorite sunny napping spot near the fireplace.

"How about you and I go into town?" I asked Socrates, who was already at the door.

He could read my mind almost as well as Moxie. Maybe better.

I went to say good-bye to the other dogs, but they were already asleep. Artie was draped across Iago's head, and Macduff and Hamlet were curled up together.

How could Piper, a vet, not want *at least* five dogs?

Returning to the kitchen, I waved to Socrates. "Let's go."

He trotted next to me, we both got into the van, and soon we were driving down Sylvan Creek's main street. The town was peaceful, and it was hard to believe I'd found Virginia's body the night before.

Nothing, it seemed, had changed.

I stopped at an intersection and looked to my right, over Socrates's head.

Correction.

One thing had changed in Sylvan Creek.

Espresso Pronto, Giulia Alberti's café, had a big hand-lettered sign on the door.

One that said CLOSED INDEFINITELY.

Chapter 56

"Where do you think Giulia is?" I asked Piper and Dylan, who were bustling around one of Piper's exam rooms, getting ready to perform a minor procedure on an iguana. Socrates was sitting as close to the door as possible. He was not a fan of modern medicine. "Why is the café closed?"

"I don't know," Piper said, sounding grumpy. "But I really could've used coffee today." She was arranging some scary-looking instruments on a silver tray, and she raised a scalpel at me in a threatening way. I didn't think that was wise for a murder suspect. "Why didn't you wake me up and tell me about the hammer?" she demanded. "And about Virginia!"

"Easy there, Dr. Piper," Dylan urged, nudging my sister out of the way. He gently removed the sharp object from her hand and took over organization of the instrument tray. "I'm sure Daph didn't want to upset you in the middle of the night."

"What were you doing at the park so late?" Piper asked me. "What were you up to?"

"I was supposed to meet Giulia. She was upset the

last time I saw her, and wanted to talk. But she didn't show up for our meeting. And now the café is closed!"

No one else seemed to think that was as strange as I did. Then again, Piper and Dylan hadn't seen the odd way that Giulia and Christian had been acting the other day.

"She's probably just on vacation, Daph," Dylan said, still trying to mellow out the mood. "Relax, okay?" He turned to Socrates. "You should chill, too. You're not getting any shots today."

Socrates wasn't normally a crybaby, but he whined softly at the word *shot.*

Dylan grinned. "Sorry, pal."

He was wearing board shorts under his lab coat, and while I thought his tanned legs looked pretty nice, I was sure his attire was contributing to Piper's bad mood. At least his shoes were closed-toe, knockoff rubber Crocs, as opposed to flip-flops.

"I'm going to get Sparky," Piper said through gritted teeth. "When I come back, you need to leave, Daphne. Unless you and Socrates want to assist in draining an abscess on an iguana's jowl."

"No, I suppose we'd rather not. . . ."

I didn't finish that thought. Piper had left the room and closed the door behind her, a little too hard for a place of business.

"She'll be okay, Daph," Dylan promised. He pushed aside the tray and came over to where I was standing, next to the exam table. He leaned against it and crossed his arms, searching my face and frowning. "But I'm worried about you. You must be pretty shaken up to find Virginia like that, after seeing Steve's body, too."

"I'm trying not to get too upset." I shrugged. "'For anything that men can tell, death may be the greatest good that can happen to them: but they fear it as if they knew quite well that it was the greatest of evils.'"

"Socrates?" Dylan guessed.

"Yeah," I said, gesturing to a still worried basset hound. "The philosopher, not him."

I probably hadn't needed to clarify that.

Dylan smiled in the way that made his eyes crinkle. "Well, even if you are okay, you could probably use a night out. Why don't you let me take you to the Lakeside tonight?" He must've seen that I was suddenly concerned, because he added, "I promise I won't sing to you. I won't even bring my guitar. We'll just get some of your favorite cheese and hang out by the water."

That did sound pretty good. "Okay. How about I meet you there at nine?"

There was no reason to put a strain on Dylan's car by forcing him to drive it up Winding Hill when my van could coast right down.

"I'll see you then," Dylan said.

He moved to close the blinds, so people walking by on the sidewalk wouldn't have to witness an iguana's draining abscess, and when I looked out the window, I saw Tom Flinchbaugh crossing the street, presumably headed for the Philosopher's Tome to reopen the shop after stepping out to get some lunch. He carried a paper sack in his hand, which still sported a small white bandage.

"I've gotta run," I told Dylan—and Piper, who was opening the door awkwardly. She had a large, drowsy lizard cradled in her arms. "I'll see you two later." I paused to stroke the iguana's head. "And good luck, Sparky. I hope you have a speedy recovery."

Socrates couldn't get away from that room fast

enough, and we both hurried out of Templeton Animal Hospital, then followed Tom to his shop, where he stood at the front door, fumbling for his keys with his free hand.

"Tom!" I called. "Wait!"

Hearing my voice, he turned, and Socrates and I both stopped short.

What was that expression on his normally placid face?

Was that *fear*?

Chapter 57

"I'm sorry that I'm so jumpy these days," Tom said, standing back so Socrates and I could enter the Philosopher's Tome first. As soon as we crossed the threshold, we both paused to take a deep breath, inhaling the delightfully musty smell of *profound thoughts*, captured on old, yellowed paper and passed down for generation after generation to contemplate. Tom followed us inside and closed the door behind himself, so the always soothingly dim space got even darker. "Between Steve Beamus getting killed and now Virginia Lockhart . . ." Tom shook his head. "Sylvan Creek doesn't feel safe anymore."

Since I was starting to fear that Tom was the killer, I was surprised that he brought up the murders. Then again, how could the topic be avoided?

I watched Tom as he shambled behind the small sales counter and opened the bag that held his lunch, then pulled out a plastic-wrapped tuna fish sandwich and a container of macaroni salad, which I knew came from the Delightful Deli.

I *loved* that salad. And could I really believe that the

man who was wordlessly offering it to me, along with a plastic fork, was capable of murder?

No. It was impossible. No matter what the evidence suggested, Tom Flinchbaugh couldn't be a killer.

Right?

"Is everything all right, Daphne?" Tom asked.

I realized he was still holding the macaroni salad, waiting for me to take it, and I gratefully accepted the container. "Yeah, I'm fine," I said. "Thanks for sharing your lunch."

We'd performed this ritual many times, and I didn't even bother to refuse politely anymore.

Popping off the lid, I dug the fork into perfectly al dente macaroni, just the right amount of mayonnaise, crisp celery bits, and the secret ingredient—a hint of pickle relish.

Tom opened a glass jar filled with bone-shaped biscuits that he kept on the counter for Socrates and bent to place three on a plate that waited on the floor. Socrates, as always, tried to act like he wasn't overly eager to accept the treat. He turned his face away, ostensibly reading the titles on the lowest shelves of the section devoted to German idealism—a school of thought that I knew didn't even interest him. He was definitely an existentialist.

Then Tom unwrapped his sandwich, but he didn't immediately take a bite. "You . . . you found Virginia," he ventured. "At least, that's the talk around town."

Moxie!

"The talk is correct," I said, taking a seat on a worn, crimson-velvet upholstered chair. "I found her body in the park." I paused, then asked quietly, "Did you see anything odd the night of *Steve's* death? Because everything the police turn up seems to point to Piper—and we both know she's no killer."

Some of the color drained from Tom's cheeks, and he picked at his sandwich, averting his eyes. "No, I'm sorry, Daphne. I didn't see anything. I was busy with that vexing tent." He raised his face and smiled wanly. "You can imagine I'm not good with things like that."

Forgetting that I shouldn't know how he injured himself, I poked my fork in his direction. "Yes, I see that you really hurt yourself, trying to erect that thing."

For a moment, Tom appeared confused. Then he looked down at his bandaged hand. "Oh . . . Oh, yes! That! It's healing now. Getting better every day."

He was hiding something.

"Tom?" My heart started beating a bit faster, and I confessed, "I was standing at my window, looking out, when you got hurt putting up the tent. But it didn't look like you cut yourself. How did *that* happen?"

During a scuffle with Steve Beamus perhaps?

Tom's face got ashen, and he didn't answer me. The store grew deathly quiet, except for the sound of Socrates finally chomping down on a biscuit.

I wanted to fill that uncomfortable silence, but I forced myself to wait it out, and my rare show of patience was rewarded when Tom leaned closer. His eyes were darting everywhere, although we were definitely alone. "Daphne," he whispered, "can you keep a secret?"

Chapter 58

"I know that Tessie thinks I killed Steve," Tom confided. His hands rested on the counter, and he balled up his fists. "You can imagine how that hurts, to have my own wife believe I'm capable of murder!"

My cheeks flushed, because I sometimes feared that Tom was guilty of homicide, too.

"I doubt she really believes that," I fibbed to make him feel better. "Everyone is just on edge lately."

Tom's shoulders rounded, and he spoke more softly, his head hanging low. "I suppose I really can't blame Tessie. I *hated* Steve Beamus." He looked up at me again, misery in his blue-gray eyes. "And Steve and I . . . we argued the night he was killed."

I felt my eyes grow wide, and I set the container of macaroni salad next to me on the chair, so I could give Tom my full attention. "Did you tell the police?"

"No!" Tom said that too loudly. He lowered his voice again. "And you can't, either. I didn't kill him. I swear it! The police don't need to know that I confronted him. I just wanted him to know that I would never forgive him for what he did to my sister."

"Yes, I know about the accident," I said. "I'm so sorry."

Tom swiped a finger under his eyes, which were teary. "Yes. I'm sorry, too. All these years later, the pain never goes away. Aside from Tessie, Angela was my only family."

Socrates and I exchanged sorrowful looks, and I gave Tom a moment to compose himself. Then I asked, "Did you do more than argue with Steve that night?" I gestured to his hand. "Is that how you hurt yourself? In a *physical* fight?"

Tom laughed, but ruefully. "No. Can you imagine me throwing a punch, let alone at Steve Beamus? I would've received more than a cut on my hand if I'd hit him—as I probably should've done!"

The tension had eased enough for me to resume eating. I picked up the container and dug in, asking, "So, how'd you get the cut?"

I was mainly being nosy at that point. I was fairly sure that I believed Tom's story—although I did wonder where he'd gone during the time Tessie couldn't account for his whereabouts.

Fortunately, he was about to tell me.

"I couldn't sleep that night, after Tessie and I left Winding Hill," he said. "As I tossed and turned in bed, I kept picturing Steve's smug face. And I could hear him telling me over and over again that there was nothing he could do about the past. He didn't even sound sorry. So I got up and went to Angela's grave. I took small hedge clippers to clean it up, like I do every year, near the anniversary of the accident." He raised his hand and smiled wanly again. "I was agitated, and I shouldn't have been using a sharp blade in the dark."

Ouch.

"Did you tell Tessie where you went?" I asked. I

couldn't help congratulating myself for getting so much information out of Tom, compared to a certain police academy attendee who didn't even know that Tom had argued with Steve. "Maybe she'd be less suspicious. . . ."

Tom shook his balding head. "I can't tell her. Tessie thinks I'm obsessed with Angela's death. She thinks I need to let the past go."

Tessie was probably right. Tom did seem a bit fixated on the tragedy.

"When you said you were at Angela's grave, you really meant the roadside memorial you made for her, right?" I asked. "Because I passed that the other night, and it looked nice, with the fresh coat of paint."

I wanted to let him know that his effort to keep his sister's memory alive—while perhaps borderline unhealthy—was noticed. I also wanted to ask him about the hammer, if I got the chance. A *tiny* part of me still had doubts about Tom's innocence.

But Tom got a funny look on his face. "No, I meant her actual grave. I have no idea who created or maintains that little cross in the woods!"

Chapter 59

Spilling so many secrets exhausted poor Tom Flinchbaugh, and at my urging, he packed up his sandwich and went home to take a quick nap while I minded the store.

That was another one of our standard arrangements, like the sharing of Tom's lunch.

It was actually very easy work. Since I was usually the only customer, and I rarely bought anything, I never even had to use the antique cash register.

After opening the shop's door to let in some fresh air—the musty smell of deep thoughts could get overwhelming after a while—I moved behind the counter, suddenly curious.

If I ever opened the register, would there even be any money inside to make change?

"What do you think, Socrates?" I asked. "Is there any cash in this thing?"

Socrates was reclining on the velvet-covered chair I'd vacated and didn't even open an eye as I began pressing a few of the sticky old keys.

Nothing happened, so I abandoned that endeavor and leaned on the counter, surveying the store, in search of a book or a topic that might pique my interest. I couldn't focus on philosophy, though. Nor did I feel like cleaning, although there was a feather duster under the counter, and the beams of hazy sunlight that filtered through the tall, narrow windows were filled with dust motes that swirled in the air.

I was too busy thinking about murders and hammers and roadside memorials to do anything but stand around and think—which was an appropriate activity for a shop that promoted philosophical inquiry and reflection.

Then I glanced at the one modern convenience in the Philosopher's Tome.

Tom's computer, which really wasn't that up to date, either.

With its clunky beige monitor and battered tan keyboard, it probably qualified as vintage technology.

But it was connected to the Internet.

I knew because Tom was always online, searching for more stock for his already overstocked enterprise.

I'd never used the computer, but I doubted that Tom would mind if I logged on to surf around just for a few minutes.

Still, I checked to make sure that Socrates, who would disapprove, was sleeping before I sat down on Tom's office chair, which probably dated back to Charles Dickens's days. Seeing that Socrates was sleeping soundly, I shook the mouse on a pad that looked like an antique Turkish carpet, and brought the monitor to life.

Then, although I knew I should stop snooping into his life, I called up a search engine and typed in "Jonathan Black." Knowing from previous inquiries that I'd be inundated with links to the wrong man, I narrowed down the results by adding, "Navy SEAL."

Chapter 60

I'd already seen most of the information that I found on Tom's computer the first time I'd researched Jonathan online, but I couldn't stop scrolling through everything again. In particular, I focused on the pictures I found, some of them posted by Jonathan's friends in the military, some on Navy newsletters, and some in the archives of mainstream media sites.

Was I impressed or repulsed by images of Jonathan in full combat gear in Afghanistan?

As a dedicated peacenik who also appreciated my freedom to believe as I wished—a freedom protected by men like Jonathan—I honestly wasn't sure.

But I was definitely fascinated by the photos of Jonathan with Herod, the Belgian Malinois who had been his partner in combat. There was even a picture of them skydiving together, the dog wearing nearly as much gear as his human.

I took a moment to consider the image. Then I clicked on another link, which led to a picture of Jonathan and Herod in a desert setting. Jonathan was sitting on the ground, smiling, and Herod was at his side. They both wore camouflage.

Was it right to send a dog to war?

My first instinct was to say, "No."

And yet Herod appeared proud. That was the only way I could describe his stance. Alert and proud.

I recalled Jonathan's mild rebuke when I'd called Axis Cookie Puss.

Please call the dog Axis. Retrievers are working dogs, and some of them are warriors. They deserve respect.

I kept studying the photograph. Clearly, Jonathan had respected—no doubt loved—Herod.

Surfing away from that image, I followed one more link, to a 2010 article in an online newspaper called *Navy Times.*

Injured in the firefight was . . . Jonathan Black . . . killed in action that day . . . Herod . . .

I treated Socrates, especially, like a person, and the Navy seemed to treat Herod that way, too. His death was recorded just like those of the men who'd perished in what must've been an intense, if small, skirmish.

I still believed that death was merely a portal to somewhere else, but my heart got very heavy, weighed down by losses both recent and a few years in the past. I felt sorry for Steve and Virginia, and I was sad for Herod—and Jonathan, too.

I would be devastated if Socrates met such a tragic, if valiant, end. Maybe I wouldn't ever be able to open my heart to another animal.

Was that why Jonathan seemed to keep his distance from dogs now?

And what type of injury had *he* sustained?

Had he earned his scar that day?

I left the site and found myself looking at a picture

on a tab I hadn't closed. That image of Jonathan in the desert. The sunlight was bright and conspicuously glinting off a gold ring on his left hand. A wedding band.

Last but not least, what had happened to *Mrs.* Jonathan Black?

That wasn't my business, and I suddenly felt guilty. I'd pried too much into the life of someone I barely knew.

Jonathan clearly agreed.

When I turned around, he was standing just inside the open door, staring at me with his arms crossed and a cold, closed-off look in his eyes that was somehow worse than anger.

Chapter 61

"What . . . what are you doing here?" I asked Jonathan.

I was clicking the mouse frantically, for some reason unable to find the x that would let me close down the picture of him. I was also fervently and futilely wishing that Tom hadn't decided to position his monitor so anyone walking in the door could see the screen.

Who *did* that?

Of course, I knew the answer.

People who didn't spy on other people!

Jonathan stepped farther into the shop, and Socrates opened his eyes and raised his head, awakened by the friction in the room.

"Are you *snooping* into my past?" Jonathan asked just as I managed to close the image.

"Not so much snooping as trying to learn more about you . . ."

I was splitting hairs, and Jonathan knew it, too.

"I think that's the definition of *snooping*," he said. His tone was even, and he'd reinforced those walls he sometimes put up in his eyes.

"I'm sorry," I said, with a glance at Socrates, who was rubbing his paws over his muzzle and shaking his head, as if to say, "You've done it now, Daphne!" I turned to Jonathan again. "I was just curious. You don't say much about yourself. . . ."

"Did you ever think there might be a reason for that?" An edge crept into his voice. "That I might like my privacy?"

I considered telling him that privacy was a luxury relegated to the past, before cell phone photos and Facebook posts. I also wanted to point out that friends didn't keep *everything* about themselves secret. Especially not the big things, like the fact that they'd been married, and part of an elite fighting force, and suffered heartbreaking losses.

Friends shared things like that.

But I wasn't sure we'd ever really been friends.

I was the type of person who accepted everyone into her life, and I might've imagined that Jonathan and I had come to share some sort of rapport.

"I'm really sorry," I repeated, hanging my head. "It won't happen again."

Jonathan didn't feel the need to respond to my promise. "What are you doing here?" he asked. "I thought you were a pet sitter, not a bookstore clerk."

I stood up and nervously wiped my hands on my jeans. "I was talking with Tom," I admitted. "About the murders."

Jonathan was trying to keep his temper in check, but I saw a glimmer of anger in his eyes. "So you continue to meddle in the investigation, too, although I've warned you not to do that."

All at once, *I* got mad at *him*. "You can ask me to stay out of your personal business, but you can't tell me what to do with every aspect of my life. Two people I know were killed, my sister is a suspect, and I have every right to ask questions. I'm not doing anything wrong."

Jonathan didn't argue with me. He just stared at me.

"Why are you here?" I asked him, mainly to break a charged, tense silence.

"I was walking by the store, and I saw you," he said quietly. "I thought I'd stop in and let you know that the hammer was the murder weapon. Lab tests turned up trace amounts of Beamus's blood. I wanted to tell you, as a favor, since this further implicates Piper."

My throat got tight. "Were there prints?"

"Only yours. The handle had been wiped clean before you touched it."

My heart thumped in my chest. "Am *I* . . . ?"

"No," Jonathan said. "I still don't really consider you a suspect. Although you are on Detective Doebler's radar."

I lowered my head, ashamed to have pried into Jonathan's life and sorry that I'd snapped at him— although I still believed everything I'd said was true. I had every right to conduct my private investigation. "Thank you for letting me know all that."

"The information about the hammer will be public knowledge soon," he said gruffly. "I was just giving you a heads-up."

Because we *were* becoming friends.

However, thanks to me, that was in the past, just like all the other things Jonathan had buried.

He turned and left the store without another word, closing the door behind himself.

I stood there, stuck in place for a long time, trying

to figure out how so much had gone so wrong so quickly. I couldn't even look at Socrates, for fear of seeing the blame and disappointment in his brown eyes.

Around me, the store grew incredibly silent. I usually liked the Philosopher's Tome's peaceful atmosphere, but I began to feel suffocated, closed in by the many rows of tall bookcases.

Suddenly, though, the silence was broken by the trill of a cell phone.

A soft sound, coming from *my jeans.*

That made no sense, because my phone's ringer had been dead for several days, and I knitted my brows as I pulled the device from my back pocket, only to realize that I was holding someone else's cell.

The phone rang again, and I hesitated, then answered.

"Hello?"

There was a millisecond gap before the caller spoke to me, but in that moment, I figured out whose phone I'd accidentally taken—from a murder site.

Virginia Lockhart's.

I must've slipped it into my pocket after calling 911, and since I'd fallen asleep in my clothes and not bothered to change after waking up so late, I still had it.

"Hello?" I ventured again.

The person who'd called also sounded uncertain. "Er . . . Mother? Is that you?"

I froze in place, my brain struggling to identify the somewhat familiar voice.

Who among my acquaintances spoke in a tentative, put-upon, yet self-righteous whine?

Who could convey years' worth of pent-up pain and frustration with the single word *Mother?*

Only one person I knew.

As my heart nearly pounded out of my chest and my palms started to sweat again, I asked, with barely controlled excitement, "Bryce? Bryce Beamus? Is that *you*?"

Chapter 62

"I can't believe Virginia and Steve had a child together—and that child is *Bryce*," Piper said. I was glad that she didn't seem overly upset by the news. I got the sense she was starting to see her ex-boyfriend more clearly in hindsight. "You are talking about the kid who confessed to poisoning Steve, right?"

"Yes," I said, taking a sip of lemonade. "My best guess is that Virginia was away at college or in law school, so she was able to hide the pregnancy from everybody in Sylvan Creek. Then she and Steve gave Bryce up for adoption—which was devastating for her." I thought about how Bryce had accused Virginia of dodging him for years and added, "At least, it was devastating at first."

"How do you know all that?" my mother inquired, pushing her Fendi sunglasses up into her dark, bobbed hair, the better to peer at me. We were all sitting around the table on the patio at the farmhouse, enjoying a late-afternoon snack of iced tea and lemonade with fresh sprigs of mint from the garden, accompanied by some old-fashioned thumbprint cookies with apricot jam filling. Socrates, Artie, and the rottweilers were licking bowls full of mashed strawberries in yogurt, which I'd frozen to make dog-friendly ice cream. "How do you know Virginia was devastated?" Mom added. "Surely, you two weren't so close that she would confide in you, her dog walker!"

I ignored what felt like a jab at my admittedly humble, but beloved, career. "I read an inscription she wrote in a book she gave Steve. It was all about a tragic event that might hopefully someday 'yield fruit that is more sweet than bitter. I'm pretty sure the tragedy was an unplanned pregnancy, and the 'fruit,' pretty literally, was . . . is . . . Bryce."

Piper grimaced, and not because her lemonade was too sour. "Oh, ugh. That is so sappy."

"How did you see this book?" Mom asked. "It sounds rather private."

I slouched down in my wicker chair. "That's a long story. One that I don't feel like telling right now."

All day long, I'd kept reliving my confrontation with Jonathan, and I wasn't in the mood to recount one of our happier exploits. At least I'd found aspects of our mutual sleuthing enjoyable. In retrospect, I was pretty sure he'd been genuinely frustrated with me the whole time.

My mother, who probably hadn't really wanted to hear the tale, anyhow, sighed wistfully. "You girls are so lucky to have a mother who is completely devoted to you."

I nearly snorted out my lemonade, while Piper rolled her eyes.

Our mother had spent the better part of our childhoods building her mini real estate empire. That was partly out of necessity after our father left, but it was primarily due to Maeve Templeton's relentless ambition to be Sylvan Creek's foremost Realtor, with a capital *R.*

Fortunately, our "completely devoted" mother didn't notice how Piper and I had reacted to her comment. She was pointing the toe of a navy-blue pump at the rottweilers, as if she didn't want to get her fingers too close to the "terrifying creatures," as she'd called them when she first saw them at the house.

"How long will these *extra* animals reside with you?" she inquired. "When is Mitchell coming to claim them?"

"I have no idea," I said. "I tried calling him once—with Virginia's phone, which I accidentally have—but it went to voice mail. I suppose he's overwhelmed right now."

Neither my mother nor Piper bothered to ask why I was in possession of Virginia Lockhart's phone.

"Poor Mitchell," Mom muttered, getting a distant look in her eyes.

I had a feeling she was both sympathizing with Senator Mitch and wondering if he'd soon be putting a mansion on the market. The house was too big for one person.

As if to prove my hunch right, Mom opened up the laptop that was never far from her fingertips. "I must make a note to contact him after a suitable period of time has passed." Then she leaned closer to the screen and tapped a few keys. "And what have we here . . . ?"

Piper and I exchanged looks and mutual shrugs. We were used to our mother checking her messages and making deals during social visits.

We each ate a cookie while Mom typed in her quick, efficient way—just like Piper typed.

I glanced at my sister, who hadn't fallen far from the tree, while I'd rolled down a hill, across a road, and into a proverbial river to the sea.

Or did I take after my father, who became more indistinct in memory with each passing day?

Abruptly pushing away the laptop, Mom sat back and sighed again with exasperation. "I don't know what else to show him." She tossed up her hands. "He's turned down another house. I honestly don't know what he wants!"

Piper leaned over and used a napkin to wipe up a sweat ring my drink had left on the table. She slid a coaster under my glass. "Who is 'he'?"

"Jonathan Black," Mom informed us. "I've shown him a dozen suitable houses, but he is remarkably particular, bordering on vexing."

I'd been avoiding the topic of Jonathan, but I had to know more about my mother's dealings with a client who refused to be steamrollered. "What, exactly, are you showing him?"

Mom began to list properties on her fingers. "The pink Victorian on Poplar Street. The white cottage on Abbott Lane. Three lovely new houses in the Avalon Acres development. And several large condos at the development by the Rolling Green Golf Club. He could walk right onto the course."

"The pink Victorian is way too girly," I said. "And the cottage is a mess. I walk dogs past it all the time. The roof is falling down!"

My mother raised her nose and sniffed. "For your information, I primarily showed him those properties so he'd realize that a new build or a condo is best for a single man."

"Avalon Acres is bland," I countered. "Every house looks exactly the same. And Jonathan's way too private for a condo. I don't think he'd like having neighbors right on top of him." I pictured Jonathan jumping out of a plane with a combat-ready dog and rolling into battle, then tried to imagine him wearing plaid pants on a putting green, chasing a small white ball. "I doubt he's into golf, either."

"How do you know so much about *Jonathan*?" Piper asked. "Seriously, what is going on with you two?"

"And what do you know about real estate?" my mother added.

"Nothing, and nothing," I mumbled, sinking lower and pulling Mom's laptop closer to myself. I opened her browser and found a bookmark to an MLS, or "multiple listing service," Web site.

"It's my job to find a *suitable* home for him," Mom reminded me. "One that will meet his needs—whether he's aware of them or not."

I tuned her out. I was busy checking a brand-new listing. A very intriguing one.

"Who is that coming up the hill?" Piper asked, rising slightly out of her chair and craning her neck. "Are either of you expecting someone?"

"No," I said, shutting the laptop and moving so I could see the road, too. "I don't think I recognize the car."

"Oh, I do," Mom said, smiling as a black, sporty convertible crested the rise. "I believe Senator Mitchell Lockhart is here to claim his dogs."

I really hoped she didn't intend to offer a grieving widower a business card.

And as I stood to greet our visitor, I also hoped Senator Mitch had a plan for cramming three rottweilers into a car with only *two* seats.

Chapter 63

I didn't know how to address Mitch Lockhart—
"Senator Lockhart" seemed too formal, while "Mitch"
was awfully familiar for a man I barely knew—so I
avoided the issue by going straight to condolences.

"I'm so sorry about Virginia," I said, approaching
his car, which he'd parked in the gravel spot. I'd hurried off the patio to intercept him, in hopes of pre-
venting my mother from foisting a card on him. "How
are you doing?"

Mitch stepped away from the BMW, and I noted
that he'd gained a nice tan since I'd last seen him. I
could imagine *him* chasing a little white ball around
on the grass. In fact, he was wearing khakis and a golf
shirt, like he'd just come from the course—although I
knew that couldn't be the case.

Could it?

"I'm coping," he said, reaching out to shake my
hand. He smiled, hopefully out of habit, then seemed
to think the better of that and quickly grew serious.
"I'm sorry for you, too. It must've been very traumatic
for you that evening."

"I'm okay," I assured him, ending the handshake and reaching into my back pocket to retrieve Virginia's phone. I didn't want to forget to hand it over to him. "I accidentally took this when I was trying to call for help. I'm sure you'll want it back, to give it to the police."

"That's Virginia's?" he asked, sounding oddly eager. Before I could answer, he took the phone from me and stared at the dark screen. "Yes," he said softly. "Yes, I'll definitely want this. I'd been wondering what happened to it."

There was something weird about his tone of voice. Then again, I didn't know what was normal for him.

"I suppose you want the dogs," I said, turning to summon them.

I also thought it was strange that Macduff, Iago, and Hamlet hadn't run to greet the man with whom they lived. They remained on the patio, eating their ice cream.

Piper and my mother were still seated at the table, too, although Mom was half out of her chair. I could tell she was watching to see if I'd invite Mitch to join us or if she'd need to swoop down to offer her overwrought brand of sympathy, accompanied by that business card.

I didn't want that to happen and called, "Macduff, Iago, Hamlet! Come!"

Luckily, they obeyed that non-Shakespearean command and started loping in my direction.

When I turned back to Mitch, he was opening his wallet. "I'd actually like you to keep the dogs for a while—at least until after the funeral," he said. He continued to dig for cash but looked up at me. "That is your business, right? You don't just walk dogs. You sit for them, too, correct?"

My van was parked next to his car, so there was no denying I was a pet sitter, even if I'd wanted to—which I didn't.

"The whole pack is welcome to stay here for a while," I said. "But I couldn't take any money for watching them. Not under the circumstances."

"No. I want to pay you," he insisted. "You'll be helping me during a busy, difficult time."

I was about to protest again when he grabbed my hand and pressed a wad of cash into my palm. He folded my fingers around the bills and squeezed them. "Here's five hundred dollars. That should pay their keep for a while. But I can pay you more, if need be."

"That's a lot of money," I said, trying to give back the advance. The rottweilers had joined us, and I felt sorry for them, in case they understood that they were being abandoned, even temporarily. "Please . . . I can't take this. Let me watch them as a favor."

"Of course you should be paid," Mitch said. I couldn't believe he hadn't even looked at the poor rotties. He really hadn't been joking when he'd suggested I keep them the day I met him on the porch. He released my hand and took a step backward. "Thanks for returning the phone," he said. "And I'll be in touch about picking up the dogs. Soon."

I didn't say anything more. I watched, cash in hand, as he hopped into his sporty car, put it in gear, and drove off.

"Well, he left in a hurry," my mother said, wobbling in her rush to cross the uneven ground, although she was obviously too late. The BMW was leaving a trail of dust as Mitch beat his hasty retreat. "I didn't even get a chance to express my condolences."

"I don't know if condolences are in order," I said, continuing to follow the BMW with my gaze as it sped down the hill. "I don't think he's too broken up about Virginia's death."

I also didn't think Senator Mitch was ever going to claim his dogs. In fact, I wouldn't let him. He'd sell them or put them in a shelter.

I rested my hand on Macduff's head and forced myself to smile at the leader of the small pack. He was looking up at me with confusion in his eyes. "It's okay," I assured him. "I'll take care of you all."

"You can't do that," my mother protested. "You can't take on three huge beasts! Piper will not allow it."

"Trust me, I'm being well compensated," I said, opening my palm to show her the money. "Five hundred dollars—for starters."

For once, Mom was impressed with me. "Well, that's decent remuneration," she said. "And with the chance of more to come."

The whole situation didn't feel right to me, though.

I didn't trust a man who didn't greet his own dogs, no matter how much he smiled or how many people voted for him. And he'd seemed so eager to get his hands on that phone.

Had I just taken money from a guy who'd killed his wife—and given him a device that might have damning evidence on it? Like an angry text or a call placed at the wrong time?

Then I remembered how Bryce had complained about his mother's failure to acknowledge him publicly. If Mitch had just learned about Bryce's existence, he'd probably hated Steve, too.

It would certainly be rough to learn that your spouse had kept a massive secret from you for years. A secret she'd shared with her past lover.

Bryce's arrival in town might've turned Mitch's world upside down—and given him motive for two murders.

I rested my hand against my stomach, which was churning.

"Mom?" I asked. "Can you *please* give me Detective Black's contact information? And loan me your phone? I think I've done something really stupid."

Chapter 64

"Would you believe my mother is *still* invoking 'Realtor-client privilege'?" I asked Moxie, who was on speaker. My mother had refused to let me touch her phone to contact Jonathan, but Piper had been nice enough to lend me hers so I could call my friend while I got ready to meet Dylan at the Lakeside. In spite of complaining about the addition of three dogs to the house, Piper was pleased that I was finally earning some real money. She'd taken the wad of cash from my hand and counted out three hundred dollars for herself as partial payment on rent and food. "Mom said *she'd* contact Jonathan about Virginia's phone."

"Do you hear yourself?" Moxie asked. Her voice sounded crystal clear, like she was in my bedroom with me. I was starting to see the advantages of keeping up with the latest technology, as Piper always did. "You are way too deeply involved in this investigation. Just let the police figure it out."

"Yeah, I can't do that," I said, searching through my closet for a new outfit. Piper'd made me bathe all the dogs, who were drying off outside, and I'd gotten soaked when they'd shaken off the hose water. Since the evening was hot, and Dylan and I would be sitting outside, I selected a spaghetti-strap maxi dress with a sweet washed-out pink floral print. The look was bohemian meets shabby chic. "Even if I didn't feel like I need to protect Piper, I'm too intrigued at this point to let it go."

"Are you intrigued by the murders or the detective who's *getting paid* to solve them?" Moxie asked.

"The murders," I said too quickly. I immediately felt guilty. Didn't girl code dictate that I be honest with my best friend? "Okay, I might be somewhat intrigued by Jonathan. Enough that I researched him online, got caught doing it, and ruined a potential friendship."

The phone was so good that I could hear Moxie suck in a breath. "Ooh . . . What did you learn? Because I will readily admit to being fascinated with Detective Black!"

I hesitated, then said, "I know we share all our secrets, but I'd rather not share his. Is that okay? And could you please not hunt them down, either? He's pretty upset with me. I'd like his past to lie dormant for a while."

"Okay," Moxie agreed. "I'll just wait for the regular gossip mill to start churning. Somebody else will delve into his history at some point and talk."

"Thanks. I appreciate that."

After slipping on the dress, I moved to my mirror, which was an intricately carved piece I'd bartered for at a Thai market, gaining it in exchange for most of the items in my backpack.

"Can you tell me one thing?" Moxie asked. "Although I think I know the answer."

I pulled my hair into a loose updo. I'd been promised cheese, and I didn't want to get a glob in my curls again. Then, on a whim, I put on some silver hoop earrings that I rarely wore, and slipped a bunch of delicate silver bangles on my left wrist. "What's the question?"

"His past—it's pretty interesting, isn't it?"

I wasn't sure I approved of Jonathan's decision to become an elite soldier—not that he'd ever sought my approval. And I felt sorry about the losses he'd suffered. But I couldn't deny that his former life was interesting. "Yes," I said. "It's all pretty fascinating stuff." Then I checked the clock on my nightstand. It was past eight o'clock. "Oh, gosh! I really have to go!"

"Dylan will be at least an hour late," Moxie reminded me. "I think he still lives on West Coast time."

That was true, but on the off chance he'd arrive on time, I signed off with Moxie, grabbed a pair of sandals, and hurried out of the house, stopping only to say good night to Piper and the dogs, who were still on the patio, enjoying a cool breeze.

"Do you think you should go inside?" I asked my sister. "It's getting dark, and there is a killer running around. . . ."

"I don't think whoever killed Steve and/or Virginia is after me," Piper said. She nodded toward the barn, and I saw light coming from the windows. "And Mr. Peachy is working late, replacing some rotting wood in one of the stalls. If anything happened, I'd just call for him."

That reassured me, and I headed for my van. About twenty minutes later, I pulled into the Lakeside's parking lot. The place was packed, and I ended up parking in a grassy area near some trees, outside the official patch of gravel.

As I got out of the VW, someone approached me, stepping out from behind another car.

At first, I thought it was Dylan. The man was built about the same.

But when he greeted me, I got a cold feeling in the pit of my stomach.

"Hello, Daphne," he said, with a smile that was far from warm and welcoming. "How fortunate for me that you showed up here, where we can talk—in private."

Chapter 65

"I don't have anything to say," I told Christian Clarke, who blocked my way to the gravel lot.

Sidestepping him, I headed for that more open area, out from under the trees, but he grabbed my arm. His grip was firm.

"What do you want?" I asked, trying to shake free. He held me tightly, though, and I snapped, "Let me go!"

Christian ignored my demand. "I think you know where Giulia is," he said in a low growl. "I know she was going to meet you the night before she disappeared."

"How do you know that?" I asked more softly. I wanted to keep him calm. His eyes were glittering with anger.

His grip on my arm tightened. "I knew she was up to something when she said she wanted to get some air so late at night. So I followed her to the park, but she saw me and ran away to her shop. She locked me out. . . ." He must've realized that he was casting himself in a terrible light. Painting himself as a stalker. He tried to smile and changed his tune just slightly. "I was worried about her wandering around alone at midnight, when there's a killer out there. I was trying to look out for her."

Yeah, right. That was why she'd run away and locked herself in a building.

I resisted the urge to try to yank my arm away again. I needed to wait for the right moment, when he let his guard down. He was still holding me tightly. But I took a tentative step forward, trying to move us both to where we might be seen by people on the pier. "What does this have to do with me?" I asked.

"As I was walking home, I saw you heading into the park. Why else, if not to meet Giulia, who'd handed you a note, acting suspiciously the whole time?"

"That was a recipe. And I don't know what you're talking—"

"You do know!" He squeezed even harder. He was going to leave marks. Yet he'd been so blinded by his rage that I'd managed to maneuver us into a less secluded spot. People eating outside might be able to see us. "Has she contacted you?" he demanded. "Where is she? What did she tell you about me?"

I was scared. And I had no answers for him. I had no idea where Giulia was. But I was glad she'd had the courage to escape Christian's grasp. Now I needed to do the same.

"If you don't let me go in two seconds," I warned him, starting to pull against his grip, "I will scream so loudly that every person in the Lakeside will come running. Then, although I am a pacifist at heart, I will punch your face so hard that your pretty nose will never look the same. Do you understand?"

I didn't have to make good on my threats. Two people had seen us and were coming to my aid.

One of them strode across the parking lot and

said in a calm but commanding tone, "Let her go, Clarke. Now. "

The other followed at a more relaxed pace and urged, "Let's everybody take a few deep breaths and chill. No need for anybody to get hurt."

What else would I expect from a warrior and a surfer?

Chapter 66

"Detective Black looked like he was ready to throw a punch, huh?" Dylan mused over a plate of iceberg lettuce and sliced tomatoes, which were normally used to top burgers at the Lakeside. The menu didn't include a salad, with the exception of coleslaw, which contained non-vegan-friendly mayonnaise. He shook his head and prodded the lettuce gently with a fork. "If you ask me, 'peace is the only battle worth waging,' as Camus would say. Use words first, right?"

Actually, Jonathan *had* used words. Sometimes very strong, even threatening words. He'd told Christian, in no uncertain terms, never to touch or even approach me again, lest Christian find more than his nose ruined. Then he'd dismissed Christian, nodded curtly to me, and walked back to the restaurant before I could even thank him for intervening.

I looked down the pier at Jonathan, who was sitting at one of the barrel tables with Detective Doebler and a woman I didn't recognize. She had curly brown hair and looked to be in her midforties. Perhaps Detective Doebler's wife? They were all sharing a bushel basket of crabs and a pitcher of beer. As I watched, Jonathan lifted a mallet and neatly cracked a crab in half.

"You definitely have two different styles," I said, returning my attention to Dylan. "I appreciated them both tonight."

Dylan poured some malt vinegar, meant for fish and chips, onto his makeshift meal. "What was going on there with Christian?"

I hesitated, not sure how much I should share. "I wouldn't want this to reach Moxie and the gossip mill. . . ."

Feigning an injured look, Dylan leaned back on his stool and pointed at his chest with both index fingers, as if to say, "Really? You think I'd blab?"

No, he wouldn't.

"I'm pretty sure Christian was abusing Giulia," I confided quietly. "Emotionally or physically . . ." I rubbed my arm, which was starting to bruise. "Probably both. She apparently got up the courage to leave him, and he thought I might know where she'd gone."

Dylan knitted his brows. "Why would he think that?"

"Remember, I was supposed to meet Giulia the other night? And she didn't show? I guess she did go to the park, but Christian followed her and scared her off. He saw me there, too, and assumed she meant to confide in me."

"Well, I hope she's someplace safe," Dylan said. "Nobody should have to live in fear or be controlled by another person."

I was afraid we were about to embark upon a discussion of the pitfalls of committed relationships before my double-cheese nachos even arrived, and I tried to steer the conversation in another direction.

"I also wondered if Giulia was going to tell me about something she saw the night of Steve's death. Maybe something involving her hotheaded boyfriend, who was with her at Winding Hill. I saw him that evening, staring daggers at Steve's truck."

Dylan appeared confused. "Why stare at a truck?"

"Because it was *Steve's*," I explained. "Surely, you heard the rumors about Steve and Giulia being an item?"

"No, never," Dylan said. "Not a peep."

Of course he hadn't heard anything. He probably hadn't visited Moxie's salon in months. His blond hair was, as usual, drawn back in a ponytail.

"Anyway, if there was even a grain of truth to the gossip, a possessive guy like Christian might've flown off the handle." My nachos arrived, and I took a moment to thank the waitress. Then I added, "Heck, maybe the rumors wouldn't even need to be true. He might've sought out Steve, started a fight, and killed him."

While Dylan was considering all that and I was opening a small plastic container of *pico de gallo*, I heard five muffled but distinctive notes from the Beach Boys song "Surfin' U.S.A."

"Uh, oh," Dylan said, reaching into his back pocket. He pulled out his phone and read the screen, muttering, "Aw, too bad."

"What's wrong?"

Shifting on the stool, he shoved the phone back into his pocket. "That was Piper. I've gotta go. Sparky's abscess is worse. We need to do emergency surgery."

I tried not to picture an oozing iguana jowl before I ate gobs of melted white cheddar, and said, "Oh, poor Sparky!"

I felt sorry for the iguana—and for myself. I was all dressed up, and I was going to be stuck eating alone. I'd learned from experience never to take nachos

home. The Lakeside concocted the best cheese sauce—
a warm, gooey mixture of butter, milk, and sharp
cheddar—and the freshest *pico de gallo,* made only in
season with local tomatoes, sweet onions, and cilantro.
But the meal didn't travel well. The chips would be
soggy by the time I got halfway to Winding Hill. And
the guacamole would be brown before I even left the
parking lot.

"I'll call you later," Dylan promised, sliding off the
stool. He grinned. "Stay out of trouble, okay, Miss
Marple?"

That was actually worse than being called Nancy
Drew.

"I'll do my best," I assured him. "Tell Sparky good
luck."

"Will do."

Dylan made his way through the crowd, leaving me
alone with my dinner—and the check. I realized that
too late.

Oh, well. I doubted the Lakeside even charged him
for the garnishes he ate. And the vinegar was free, too.
There was a bottle on every table.

Bending over my plate, I started eating, although
I felt self-conscious. I didn't know where to look
most of the time, so I stared at the candle flickering on
my table, which was why I didn't even know Jonathan
had approached me until he said, "I think I owe you
an apology."

Chapter 67

"No, you don't owe me anything," I assured Jonathan, blinking up at him. I couldn't see his face. I'd stared at the flame too long, so everything was momentarily black. I pointed in the general direction of the stool Dylan had vacated. "Would you like to sit down?"

"Are you okay?" Jonathan asked. "You're acting a little strange."

There was an unspoken "even by your standards" hanging out there.

"I just temporarily blinded myself," I admitted.

I heard the stool scrape across the wooden floor, indicating that he was accepting my invitation. "Why am I not surprised?"

Things were gradually coming into focus, and I saw him examining Dylan's plate, poking at the contents with one finger, like he didn't understand the garnishes-to-sandwiches ratio, which was about twenty to zero.

"I can see you now," I informed him, blinking a few more times. "I just stared at the candle for too long."

Jonathan didn't want to grin, but he did. "I'm glad

you're okay. And, as I said, I wanted to apologize for earlier today. . . ."

I held up a hand, stopping him. "There's really no need. I shouldn't have snooped."

"No, you shouldn't have."

So this was going to be one of those unconventional apologies, which would end up making me feel worse.

"Before you continue," I said, "why aren't you upset about the phone? I thought you'd be furious."

Jonathan grew wary. "What phone?"

"Didn't my mother contact you?"

"She contacts me all the time," he said, still watching me with suspicion. "So often that I don't always respond. So why don't you tell me what you're talking about."

Oh, I did not want to do that. But I had no choice.

"I saw Mitch Lockhart today, and I gave him Virginia's phone." I cringed in anticipation of Jonathan's inevitable reprimands. "I accidentally took it after I used it to call nine-one-one."

His eyes registered disbelief mingled with confusion. "You used *Virginia Lockhart*'s phone . . . ?"

"Mine's not working, so I found hers in her pocket, and I called for help. . . ."

I didn't bother finishing my explanation. He got the picture, which would show me moving Virginia's body around, touching things that shouldn't have been touched, taking away evidence. . . .

I let my shoulders slump. "I'm so sorry. I guess I'm not police academy material, after all."

Jonathan didn't disagree.

"I've had men combing the park for that phone," he said. "And now it's in the hands of a suspect, who might erase evidence or 'lose' the entire thing." He took out his own cell and began tapping the screen. "I'll try to get it back, but I'm sure it's too late. I guarantee you that anything important is already gone." In spite of feeling chastened, I was slightly gratified when he added under his breath, "I blame your mother, too. Her and her insistence on showing me twenty condominiums."

"Sorry," I repeated, then bit my lower lip. "I swear, this time I wasn't trying to meddle. Senator . . . er, Mitch . . . came to pick up the dogs, which I still have, and I didn't even think twice about giving him the phone. Not until he acted like a jerk toward the poor rotties, refusing to take them home. . . ."

I gave up trying to explain.

Jonathan had put away his phone and was bending his head and rubbing his eyes. Then he took a deep breath—a strategy Dylan would've endorsed. He didn't speak for a moment.

"At least this time you didn't purposely interfere," he finally admitted, if grudgingly. "I will give you that. However, you did make a very, very bad decision."

"I know that," I said. "You can stop pointing it out. I feel terrible."

Jonathan stared at me for a long time. Then he said, "I believe you. You're not even eating your cheese. I suppose that speaks volumes."

"It really does." I pulled the plate closer to myself, but it was too late. The nachos were past the point of no return. Covering them with a napkin, I looked across the table at Jonathan. "What if there was a way I could make amends for both things I did wrong today?"

He grew wary again. But he was curious, too. "How, exactly, would you do that?"

I grinned. "You'll have to take a short ride. And trust me."

"I don't think the 'trust' part is possible."

He was only half joking. At least, I hoped he was joking to some degree.

"Oh, come on," I said. "I'm trying to help you."

"I keep asking you to *stop* doing that—"

"This has nothing to do with police work or investigating. I promise."

I crossed my fingers under the table, because I did intend to discuss the murders if I convinced him to come with me. I also avoided telling him that we'd have to use my van for the ride.

Even without that knowledge, Jonathan deliberated for so long that I was sure he'd decline.

Then he stood up and said, "I can't believe I'm saying this, but let's go."

Chapter 68

"Why did I agree to ride in this thing?" Jonathan muttered. He rested one hand on my van's dashboard, as if he didn't trust the seat belt to save him if we had an accident. Probably because he'd given the belt a few sharp tugs before we'd set out, and it hadn't always worked. That was no doubt unacceptable to a man who almost certainly used to pack his own parachute. "Tell me again why we couldn't take my truck."

"Because I would've had to tell you where we're going," I said. "I have to drive."

"Actually, this route is familiar. Please tell me we're not going to—"

"Don't worry about the destination," I said, cutting him off before he could guess. "Just enjoy the ride."

"That's impossible." He tried to stretch out his legs, and some veggie burrito wrappers rustled on the floor. "Have you considered professional auto detailing? Or a *trade-in?*"

I gave him a quick, sharp glance. "Hey!"

He seemed to realize he'd taken the teasing too far. "Sorry."

We rode in silence for a few minutes. Then I asked,

"If I bring up the murder investigation, will you get angry?"

Jonathan stared straight ahead. "Probably."

"Well, I'm going to do it, anyway," I said. I pressed on the gas pedal, trying to get the VW up a small hill. Happily, my van was up to the challenge. I looked over at Jonathan again. "Not only did I accidentally take Virginia's phone, but I also answered it once, when it rang."

That small muscle I sometimes saw working in Jonathan's jaw twitched. "And . . . ?"

"I'm pretty sure I found out what—or who—the 'fruit' of the tragedy is."

"It's Bryce," Jonathan informed me. "He's Virginia and Steve's son. I already knew that."

Well, that was deflating. I'd hoped to drop a huge bombshell on him, but it had fizzled like a damp firecracker. "How did you find out?"

Jonathan reached for the dash again as I steered around a curve. "Bryce keeps in touch with me. He's back in Seattle—"

I nearly justified Jonathan's concerns about his safety by almost driving off the road. "How can that be? He *poisoned* Steve. Isn't he going to trial?"

"He was never charged, since there was no real intent to do harm," Jonathan explained. "His defense attorney and I argued that he's a confused kid who needs guidance, not jail time. In fact, I think jail would destroy a fragile person like Bryce."

I glanced over at him, not believing my ears. "What? *You* argued for leniency?"

"Yes," Jonathan said, meeting my gaze just for a moment. I was surprised to see sympathy in his eyes. "He's a very troubled young man. But he's not a criminal at heart."

"And you still speak with him . . . ?"

Facing the road again, Jonathan nodded. "Yes. He calls me every few days."

"What do you talk about?"

Jonathan shrugged. "Whatever he wants to discuss. Little things that happened to him that day—or big things, like the loss of his parents. It depends on his mood."

I was having trouble accepting the idea of Jonathan Black as a confidant. And yet I could see how a lost, fatherless soul like Bryce might look to Jonathan as a mentor. He was steady, grounded, and confident. Probably a dream big brother for a guy with Bryce's abandonment issues, insecurities, and anger.

"I think that's really nice of you," I said.

"It's nothing. All I do is answer the phone and listen."

I wanted to tell him that some people wouldn't even do that, but we'd arrived at our destination. I turned the van onto a lane that was growing familiar to me and probably to Jonathan, too. Only this time, the property was marked by *two* signs.

One for Blue Ribbon K9 Academy.

And one that said FOR SALE.

Chapter 69

"What are we doing here again?" Jonathan asked, following me up onto the porch at Steve Beamus's A-frame log cabin. "I've gone over this place thoroughly. There's nothing more to see."

There was a lockbox hanging on the knob, but I bent to find the spare key, which was still under the flowerpot. I inserted that into the lock and opened the door. "Just come inside and check out the house one more time—as a person looking for a new home, not a detective."

Jonathan appeared skeptical, but he followed me into the foyer. "How did you know it was on the market?"

"I was using my mother's laptop." I switched on some lights. "I saw it on an MLS site."

Jonathan peered around the cabin, as if seeing it for the first time. He looked up to the ceiling and checked out the exposed beams. "Why hasn't your mother mentioned it to me?"

"She probably thinks it's wrong for you," I said, guessing. "I bet she'd say, 'A busy single man doesn't need a home with so much upkeep—or the outbuilding that housed the K9 Academy.'"

"She'd probably be right," Jonathan noted. But he continued surveying the place and wandered into the living room.

I took that for potential buyer's interest and said, "I think this house could be great for you. It's very masculine and private. Just try to imagine the space without the ugly antler furniture, the tacky elk painting, and the poor bear, who should get a decent burial."

As I imagined the cabin with new furniture—maybe an antique Turkish rug on the floor and some over-stuffed, nap-worthy couches accented with soft, cozy throws—*I* was starting to want it.

"And just picture a roaring fire in the big stone fireplace on a snowy day," I added, completing the scene. "Wouldn't that be great?"

Jonathan ran his hand over the river rocks on the feature I'd just described. "You know you sound just like your mother, right?"

I froze in place. "Take it back."

"Sorry," he said. "I can't."

He moved into the kitchen, and I followed, then watched him open and close cupboards.

"It is a great house in many ways," he admitted. "But I honestly don't need a dog school on my property."

"If you trained Herod, you must have a gift for working with dogs," I said, forgetting that he might not appreciate me bringing up his past. "And I saw you with Iago. You didn't say a word, and he obeyed you perfectly—off leash. You could help people and their pets in your spare time. There are a lot of misbehaving dogs around here. I know, because I sit for them."

Jonathan got even quieter than usual, and I knew I'd said too much.

Who was I to suggest he become Sylvan Creek's resident dog whisperer?

And why had I brought up Herod?

"I'll think about the house," he finally said. "But I doubt I'd keep the outbuilding. I don't work with dogs anymore. I'm not with the local K9 unit."

I wished he would tell me more about Herod and what had happened in Afghanistan. Talking about the past could be therapeutic. I doubted he ever opened up to anyone, though.

At least he was still considering the property and was seeing past Steve's awful decor—not to mention the mess Bryce had left in the kitchen.

I wasn't the tidiest person in the world, but there was a lot of junk on the counter. Dirty dishes, plastic bags from local markets, and little grains of rice, an indication that Bryce had spilled one of the Thai Palace take-out containers that should've been put in the trash but which still littered the area near the stove.

Two important objects were missing, though.

A bottle of pills and instructions for their use, printed on Templeton Animal Hospital stationery.

Chapter 70

"You had another late night," Piper noted, looking at me over the rim of her coffee mug. She was sitting at the kitchen counter, reading the morning news on her tablet. "I hope that doesn't mean Dylan caught up with you after the procedure and will be moving even slower than usual today."

I took a container from the refrigerator and began to scoop a mixture I called PowerPup Breakfast into five bowls while Artie, Socrates, and the rottweilers waited patiently.

"Why did you hire Dylan and keep him on if you think he's such a bad worker?" I asked, setting the bowls down one by one. I was extra careful with Socrates's delicate china. "He seems to drive you crazy!"

Macduff, Hamlet, and Iago sat on their haunches, waiting for me to release them to eat, but Artie broke ranks and dug right into the blend of chopped chicken, ground beef, barley, veggies, and fruits.

"Okay," I said, with a wave of my hand, giving the rotties the go-ahead to chow down, too.

In less than ten seconds, most of their food was gone, and I gave them each an extra scoop.

My two-hundred-dollar share of Mitch's money might not stretch that far, after all.

Socrates lingered a few moments without eating, so I'd know he wasn't really following the command. Then he shuffled over to his special plate.

"Dylan's actually a good employee," Piper conceded. "His calm nature rubs off on the animals. I have fewer problems with biting and struggling when he's around. But I do wish he'd wear pants."

"Hey, speaking of your practice . . ." I went to the stove, turned a knob to get a gas flame going, and set the tea kettle on a burner. "Do you remember prescribing something called Lysodren for Axis?"

"Yes, of course," Piper said. "For his Cushing's disease. How do you know about that?"

"I saw the bottle at Steve's the first time I sneaked into his house. But it was missing last night, when I showed the property to Jonathan."

Piper had taken a sip of coffee, and she choked. She patted her chest with her hand until she could speak again. "You 'showed' him the property? As in 'tried to get him to buy it'?"

"Well, Mom wouldn't even tell him about it." I opened a tin and pulled out a hibiscus-and-watermelon tea bag, thinking the cheerful blend would be perfect on a gloomy morning. The day was misty, with the promise of downpours in the afternoon. "She keeps trying to sell him condos."

My sister rolled her eyes. "I am giving up trying to figure out what, exactly, you do for a living, and what sort of relationship you share with Detective Black."

"That's probably a good idea, because I can't figure out those things, either." I poured boiling water into my mug. The aroma of the tea filled the room. All the dogs, who were scattered around the floor, relaxing, lifted their noses to get a good sniff. Even Socrates took a whiff. "Anyway, getting back to the medicine . . ."

"Oh, yes," Piper said. "What about it?"

I leaned against the counter, sipping my tea. It was nice and warming on an unseasonably chilly day. "Why would someone take it? Would a human want it? Is it expensive?"

Piper shook her head. "No, it's not very expensive. I can't imagine anyone bothering to resell it on, say, the black market. It *is* used to treat adrenal cancer in humans, but I don't know why someone battling that would take a dog's pills. I'm sure the dosage is different for people."

"I think someone took it for Axis," I said. "I still think someone has him. That person saw Axis growing sick but couldn't risk taking him to a vet. So he or she went to Steve's and found the medicine."

"Oh, Daphne . . ." Piper looked sad. She pushed aside the tablet and stood up. "I'm pretty sure whatever happened the night Steve was killed scared Axis enough that he ran off. I put 'lost dog' flyers in my waiting room, but no one has seen him. He's probably long gone by now."

I didn't know if she meant far away or deceased. I had a feeling she was being purposely vague.

"I don't believe Axis would leave Steve willingly," I said. "He was a loyal dog. He would've stayed by Steve's side, even after death."

"Yes, he was loyal. They were a good pair."

Piper sounded wistful. I'd upset her by bringing up Axis and Steve.

"Hey, do you want to grab dinner tonight?" I asked, trying to cheer her up. "We could go to Franco's. I'll call Mom, too. I'm sure she'll want to celebrate my first successful real estate deal."

Piper was at the door, pulling on a light jacket. She frowned. "You didn't really sell . . . ?"

"I honestly think he might buy it," I said. "It's perfect for him. It's got an open floor plan, a big private lot, and a masculine vibe."

Piper zipped up her Windbreaker. "You know you sound like Mom, right? Except for the word *vibe*. Maeve Templeton would say 'milieu.'"

I didn't dignify that second comparison to my mother with a response. I was clearly the complete opposite of Mom. "So, Franco's?"

"Sure," Piper agreed. "You make the reservations— after you walk all those dogs at least two miles. Artie's getting fat."

I looked down to see the Chihuahua dozing on the hardwood floor, his intact ear bent at an awkward angle, his top teeth jutting, and his belly bulging.

"I guess I'm feeding him too well," I said. "We'll walk extra today."

"And please check your mail, too," Piper suggested, pointing to a basket near the coffeemaker. "You have quite a few letters, including one from Volkswagen. I think they finally recalled your van."

I couldn't tell if my sister was joking. She didn't do that very often, but when she did attempt humor, it was usually deadpan.

"I'll go through everything," I promised, reaching for the basket. "In fact, I'll get the mail out of the way first."

"Good."

Piper headed out the door, while I began sorting through the envelopes addressed to me.

Reminder about unpaid traffic ticket.

Pet Sitter's World magazine.

Notice regarding overdue student loan.

I set those things aside, planning to deal with one of them later, then dug into the basket for the next envelope.

It was business size, but the address was handwritten. And there was no return address.

That was weird.

Curious, I slipped my finger under the flap to unseal the letter.

Removing the folded piece of paper, I opened it—and gasped.

Chapter 71

I sank to the floor, sitting cross-legged, and the dogs gathered around me. Socrates took the prime spot at my right side, resting his head on my knee, and Artie jumped into my lap, while Macduff, Hamlet, and Iago pressed as close as they could, too.

I hardly noticed the canine cocoon they were forming around me.

I was absorbed in the letter I'd received from Giulia Alberti.

I should've recognized her distinctive, elegant script.

Dear Daphne,

I am sorry to have missed our meeting the other evening. Christian followed me, and I had to leave hastily.

You have probably determined by now that I am still running from him—perhaps will run for the rest of my life.

He is a violent and dangerous man who can exhibit great charm, so by the time one is aware of his devious, controlling nature, it is too late. At least, it was nearly too late for me. I nearly lacked the courage to break free of him. Only when

I sat in the chapel at Steven's memorial service, weeping for my future—and fearing that someday soon I would end up dead, too—did I decide that I would leave Sylvan Creek.

You are probably curious about what I planned to tell you in the park.

First, I wished to share that Christian hated Steven. He wrongly believed that Steve and I shared a secret relationship. But that was not the case. Even if I had wanted that, which I didn't, I was too afraid of Christian to ever stray.

I do not know if Christian killed Steven. I was honest when I said that I saw nothing the night of the murder. But I would not be surprised to learn that Christian committed the crime. We were not always together that evening. At one point, Christian left me to take a walk, while I worked hard to set up my coffee truck! What a jerk, as you Americans would say!

I was too fearful to share any of that information with police. At Christian's urging—or should I say command?—I lied to the handsome detective and his partner, telling them that Christian and Steven were on friendly terms, and that Christian was with me the entire night.

Perhaps you could share this letter with the police, so they know the truth? I am too afraid to contact them. They might insist that I return to Sylvan Creek so they can ask more questions—or punish me for my untruths. But I cannot turn back now.

I write to warn you, too. You are a beautiful woman.

Should Christian ever approach you, walk carefully away, as you would from a snake about to strike. Do not turn your back on him, ever. But always keep your distance.

I know you sensed that something was wrong the other day and agreed to meet me in an effort to help. I thank you for your kindness, and I wish you, your sister, and your furry friends—especially the little one who lacks an ear—best wishes for much happiness.

Ciao!

Giulia

P.S. I trust that you would never betray my location to anyone, but please know that the postmark on the letter is not my permanent place of residence. That is a secret for now.

P.P.S. Get your phone fixed! I wasted quite a bit of time putting these thoughts into a text that bounced back!

Chapter 72

I folded the letter, silently wishing Giulia the best as she started her new life, although I was pretty sure that with her business savvy and arsenal of biscotti recipes, she'd land on her feet.

Carefully freeing myself from all the dogs, I rose and returned the note to the basket so it wouldn't get lost before I could share it with Jonathan. Then I tore the envelope into little pieces and threw those in the trash, getting rid of the postmark on the off chance that the police would want to track Giulia down. I thought it would be better for Giulia if no one even knew in which direction she'd headed.

"Once again, girl code trumps legal code," I told the dogs, who were all standing at the door, clearly eager to walk. Artie was spinning in frantic circles, a string of drool hanging from his overbite, and even Socrates was restless. He shifted on his big paws, and his droopy eyes said, "I am prepared for an outing at your earliest convenience."

I was convinced that if Socrates could speak English, he would talk like one of my former philosophy professors, Dr. Orson Pennington, who wore a lot of tweed, smoked a pipe, and spoke with a vaguely British accent, although his online faculty profile said he'd been born in Cleveland.

"I'm coming, I'm coming," I told the dogs.

Reaching for a bunch of leashes that hung on a peg near the door, I chose three and began to clip them to the rottweilers' collars. "Sorry, guys," I said, securing Macduff. "But I don't quite trust you to obey my 'Hold, enough!' if you see a squirrel."

Macduff woofed, like he accepted the apology.

"Come on," I told them all, opening the door. "Let's go."

Artie darted out, and the rest of us followed, pausing for a moment on the patio to adjust to the gloomy day. The chilly gray mist swirled around me, and I debated going back inside to get a jacket. Then I decided we'd all warm up once we got moving.

But which way?

I looked around the property, trying to pick a direction.

We could follow the road down the hill. But that would mean following it back *up*, too.

That might be a bit too much exercise for Socrates's short legs. I would be fine.

Another option would be to cut across the fields, but Mr. Peachy had fallen behind on the mowing. The grass was far too high for Artie to navigate.

Then I turned toward the most logical alternative: the trails that led through the woods.

"What do you guys think?" I asked the dogs.

I wasn't too eager to follow those paths, especially on such a dismal day. Then again, it was mid-morning, and I'd be accompanied by three rottweilers . . . who had failed to protect Virginia.

"I am being a total scaredy-cat," I admitted to the dogs, who were watching me expectantly. "What did Seneca say? 'We suffer more from imagination than reality'?"

Artie obviously didn't care about a first-century Roman philosopher's opinions on fear. And he wasn't scared of the woods or anything that might lurk within them. He really needed to use the canine facilities, and he scurried off, headed for the nearest tree.

"I guess it's decided," I said, signaling for the rott-weilers to follow. "Trails, it is!"

I tried to sound cheerful. Yet I couldn't shake a nagging feeling of misgiving as we entered under the thick canopy of branches and leaves.

Chapter 73

"See? We're fine," I reassured the dogs, who didn't seem nervous at all. Well, Socrates looked uneasy to me. His tail was dragging lower than usual, and his head was sweeping back and forth as he scanned the surroundings. "There's nothing to be scared of here," I promised. "Nothing!"

I kept telling myself that, but as we reached the spot where I'd last seen Virginia alive, a shiver went down my spine. Even the rottweilers, who were walking so nicely, had seemed different that night. I remembered how their eyes had glittered.

I glanced down at Hamlet, who was right by my side, and he raised his face, so I could see that his eyes were quite normal. Still, I decided that we would turn back and walk down the hill. On second thought, a little extra exercise might benefit Socrates.

Before I could turn around, though, all the dogs stopped in their tracks, their ears pricked, as if they'd heard something.

I stopped, too, and tried to listen.

I couldn't hear or see anything, which didn't make me feel better.

Then the rottweilers strained against their leashes, and Macduff whined, a high, nervous sound.

"Let's go," I said, giving their leashes a tug. "Retreat! Advance!"

I was starting to get scared, and I couldn't think of the proper command.

It didn't matter. Macduff, Hamlet, and Iago pulled harder, trying to go farther into the woods, while Artie stood at attention, his whole body quaking even more than usual. He was facing down a path I rarely took.

"Socrates . . . ?" I looked to the most sensible member of our party, hoping he would offer me some sort of guidance. I really didn't understand what was happening. "How about we head home?"

I expected the prudent basset hound to support my decision to go back to the house.

But he didn't do that.

For the second time in just a few days, he *ran*—right down the path I didn't want to take.

I had no choice but to follow him, especially since the rottweilers started running, too, hauling me in their wake. I probably shouldn't have wrapped their leashes around my hands.

Artie also took off at a sprint and quickly caught up to Socrates.

I had stumbled along for about fifty yards, trying futilely to call them all back, when I heard the noise that their sensitive ears had picked up first.

The sound of barking.

A deep, repeated *woof*, which I *swore* I recognized.

Chapter 74

"Axis!" I cried, bursting into Mr. Peachy's cottage, along with Socrates and Artie. I'd taken just a moment to tie the rottweilers to the railings that enclosed the porch, so we wouldn't overwhelm the chocolate Lab. "It's really you!"

Axis was wriggling like crazy, and I knelt down next to him and held out my arms. He let me embrace him but kept struggling to lick my face, nearly bowling me over.

Swept up in the excitement, Artie was popping up and down and yipping wildly, while Socrates—exhausted from leading us to Axis—plopped down onto his stomach, sighed, and let his muzzle drop onto his paws.

"Oh, Axis," I said, hugging him and scratching behind his ears. "I was starting to think Piper was right, and you were gone." I pushed him away so I could look into his brown eyes. "But what are you doing here?"

Of course, he couldn't tell me that, and as he began to play with Artie, I stood up and looked around Mr.

Peachy's home. I'd never been inside the cottage before, and it was perhaps the cutest little place I'd ever seen.

A small fireplace with arched stonework graced the corner of the miniature living room, which was just big enough for an overstuffed love seat and a worn wooden rocking chair. A tightly spiraling staircase led up to a cozy loft under the eaves. I could imagine how soothing the rain would sound on the tin roof at night. And the kitchen, off the living room, had just enough space for a small spindle-legged table and two chairs, perfect for chatting with a friend over a cup of tea. Mr. Peachy had painted the cabinets a soft shade of blue green, and pots of herbs were growing on the windowsill. The kitchen door led to a tiny screened porch, where more plants grew next to a wicker chair and matching side table.

"What a sweet little space . . ."

"I'm glad you like it."

I spun around, my hand pressed against my chest. Then I smiled. "Hey, Mr. Peachy! I didn't even hear you come in. I guess Artie and Axis were making too much noise." I glanced at the dogs, who were alternately tussling and nuzzling each other. "They seem to really get along."

Mr. Peachy removed his cap with one hand and hung it on a hook near the door. I had a feeling that ritual was repeated quite often. "It's okay, Daphne." He smiled, too. "You're always welcome here."

"Where did you find Axis?" I asked. "He's been missing for so long. Did he just show up . . . ?"

I didn't quite finish that question, because Socrates was once again acting strangely. I'd thought he'd been sleeping, but he suddenly stood up and walked to the kitchen—giving Mr. Peachy as wide a berth as possible in the tight quarters.

He stopped in front of the cabinets, near the sink, and pointed his nose upward.

At first I assumed he wanted a drink after his run, and I followed him, asking over my shoulder, "Is it okay if I get Socrates some water?"

As I entered the kitchen, though, I saw something on the counter.

A bottle of pills.

Lysodren.

My heart stopped beating for a moment, and I turned slowly to face Mr. Peachy, who had taken a step closer to me, boxing me into the small space.

"You . . . you didn't just find Axis, did you?" I asked. My voice was shaky. "You've had him for a while, haven't you?"

"Yes," Mr. Peachy said. He had a funny look on his lined face. One that mingled amusement and regret. It was not attractive. "I've had him since I killed Steve. Axis wanted to stay by the body, but I couldn't allow that. He's such a clever dog. I feared that he would somehow lead the police to me."

My stomach iced over, and Artie and Axis stopped playing. Socrates stood stock-still, too.

"You did . . . what?"

"I killed Steve Beamus," Mr. Peachy admitted again. "I had to do it."

I took a step back and glanced over my shoulder. I couldn't see a door leading from the screened porch. It looked like a dead end. I turned back to Mr. Peachy. "Why? Why would you kill him?"

"He killed Angela," Mr. Peachy said. "The sweetest lady who ever lived." Growing thoughtful, he frowned and shook his head wistfully. "She always said I was like family. Took time to talk with me, really talk, even when the Silver Moon was full. And she never gave me pie without adding an extra scoop of ice cream."

Unlike Moxie'd done with me, I didn't shatter his illusions about the ice cream. Apparently, everybody had gotten that treatment, and Angela had made us all feel special.

She and Mr. Peachy really must've shared a bond, though.

"We used to talk most every night, until Steve ran her off the road!" he snarled.

His eyes glittered with anger, and his fist, at his side, curled into a tight ball.

I realized then that his other hand was behind his back and had been the whole time.

Oh, no . . .

"You created the memorial for Angela, didn't you?" I asked, trying to buy time. I also tried to defuse his rage with a compliment. "It's really lovely. I saw that you put new flowers up."

"I keep it nice for her," he said a little more calmly. "Somebody has to remember her."

"Tom does," I assured him. "He takes care of her grave."

I glanced warily at the spot where Mr. Peachy's hand should be if he weren't hiding something from me.

Will I be in a grave soon?

"That's nice," Mr. Peachy admitted. "But I want folks who drive past the spot where she died to remember her—and what Beamus did to her."

His eyes were gleaming again, and I rested one hand against my throat, which was getting tight.

"What happened the night you . . . you . . . ?"

I couldn't finish the question, but Mr. Peachy understood what I was asking.

"I reminded Steve that it was nearly the anniversary of Angie's death. Asked him what he planned to do to show his remorse."

"And he said . . . ?"

"Nothing. He said he planned to do nothing. Told me he'd made peace with the past, and that I should, too. Then he took out his phone and said, 'Get moving, old man. I've got business to take care of here with a lady.'"

My hand was still on my throat, and I glanced at the dogs. Artie and Axis remained quietly watchful, while Socrates seemed to be biding his time. I was reassured by his calm presence.

"And . . . what happened next?" I asked, although I didn't really want to hear the rest. I just needed to keep him talking. "What did you do?"

"I said, 'Who are you talking about?' Because I'd seen him fighting with Piper." His eyes narrowed. "I didn't like the way he treated her from the start. He *never* made her happy. And I knew what he meant by 'taking care of business.' I'm not *that* old!"

I realized that Mr. Peachy, who was always around the property, quietly working in the background, had probably observed quite a bit during Piper's time with Steve.

"Piper . . . She's nice to you, too, isn't she?" I ventured.

"Yes. Very nice." Mr. Peachy gestured around the cottage with the hand I could see. "She lets me live here for free. Pays me good and treats me good. I think of her like a daughter."

For a split second, I felt sorry for Mr. Peachy. He was

so lonely that he grasped for family among waitresses and employers.

I also hoped that his affection for Piper boded well for me, Piper's sister. If worse came to worst, maybe I could remind him that Piper would be heartbroken over my loss.

In the meantime, I pointed out, "Piper wouldn't want you to hurt anybody on her behalf."

He had softened for a moment but quickly grew bitter again. "Somebody had to stop Beamus. For good. He ended Angela's life—and he was trying to ruin Piper's, too."

As he said that, he finally slowly revealed what he'd been holding behind his back.

A hammer—bigger than the one that he'd used to kill Steve.

He tapped it lightly against his palm.

I felt my eyes grow huge, and I took another step backward, stumbling against the table. I reached back and steadied myself, while Mr. Peachy moved forward.

"Did you kill Virginia, too?" My voice sounded strangled, and I wished I'd brought the rottweilers inside with me. Maybe they could've helped this time. "Was that you?"

He didn't answer me directly.

"She was walking those dogs . . . always walking those dogs where she had no business going," he muttered. "She was on the paths the night I killed Beamus."

So, Virginia had been telling the truth about her late-night walk. Although I suspected she'd been at Winding Hill to see Steve, too.

"I was half afraid she'd seen something then," Mr. Peachy continued. "Then she *came back*—and heard Axis. I had to keep her quiet. Just like I have to shut you up now. Sorry as I am for that . . ."

He raised the hammer, and I saw my life flash before my eyes.

It looked a lot like a Chihuahua with a severe overbite.

"Artie!" I cried as the little dog launched himself, to the degree that he could launch, at Mr. Peachy, who laughed and kicked Artie away.

The sound died on his lips, though, when I cried, "Axis! Attack!"

I had no idea if Axis understood that command. But he clearly grasped that I was in danger. With a deep growl, he ran at Mr. Peachy, who was already crying out in pain, because a basset hound who was normally given to deep thoughts was deeply sinking his teeth into Mr. Peachy's calf.

To my relief, he dropped the hammer, which narrowly missed Socrates's head.

As Axis leaped on Mr. Peachy, setting him off balance, I bent to claim the weapon, and although I was usually a peaceful person, I raised it high, prepared to defend myself and the dogs.

Before I had to do that, though, someone burst into the house and said sharply, "Axis! Off! Daphne! Off!"

Chapter 75

"I can't believe you used the same command on Axis and me," I complained to Jonathan as uniformed officers who'd arrived on the scene took Mr. Peachy away in handcuffs. "Really? You couldn't just say, 'Hey, Daphne, put down the hammer'?"

"I reacted on instinct," Jonathan said, moving slightly to let Iago walk past him and join his brothers in the living room. It was very cramped in the cottage, now that we'd let the rottweilers inside. The house was built for two dogs, maximum. "You had a crazy gleam in your eyes."

His eyes were gleaming, with amusement.

"How did you know I was here?" I asked, opening a box of dog treats I'd found in Mr. Peachy's pantry. Winding Hill's caretaker might've been a killer, but he obviously had a soft spot for Axis. He'd even broken into Steve's house to get the Lab's medicine when the dog had shown symptoms of illness. I began to hand out the snacks, tossing biscuits first to the rottweilers in the living room, then bending to drop some for Socrates, Artie, and Axis, who were in the kitchen with Jonathan and me. I gave Artie an extra treat, since he'd been booted aside by Mr. Peachy. "How did you find me?"

"I wasn't looking for you," Jonathan informed me. "Although I wasn't overly surprised to discover you here, wielding a weapon and surrounded by a pack of furious canines. I half expected to stumble upon some kind of scene—"

"Well, if not me, what brought you here?" I asked, cutting him off.

I got the point. I had a tendency to get in trouble.

I'd also solved a murder. I noticed he hadn't mentioned that.

"I stopped in at Spa and Paw—I can't believe I just said that—for a shave." Jonathan rubbed his jaw. "Moxie does a really great job."

I made a rolling motion with my hand. "And . . . ?"

"I asked her if she'd noticed anything out of the ordinary the night of Virginia's murder, and she recalled seeing, in her own words, 'a really cool old truck, with crazy fenders and wooden slats in the back.'"

"Mr. Peachy's truck!"

"Yes, although she couldn't name the owner."

"Moxie doesn't go into barns," I explained. "She's probably never seen it parked at Winding Hill."

"Well, she said the truck went past her apartment building, headed out of town, just as you were walking to the park. She noticed it because it was—"

I supplied the word. "Vintage."

Jonathan nodded. "Yes. And it was the only vehicle on the street at that hour. Meanwhile, I recalled seeing a truck that matched Moxie's description when I searched your property after Beamus's murder. So I came to Winding Hill to ask Piper and Mr. Peachy a few questions. Piper wasn't around, but I saw three rottweilers running loose."

Mr. Peachy had untied the leashes and had let Macduff, Hamlet, and Iago run off so they wouldn't make noise when he entered the cottage.

"The dogs led me here," Jonathan added. "And the rest is history."

I almost mentioned that he'd teamed up with canines again, if only informally, then thought the better of it. I couldn't hold my tongue on another subject, though.

"When are you going to admit that *I* solved the murders?"

"Never," Jonathan said. "If anything, the dogs solved the case. You said they heard Axis and went running."

"I do have to share credit with them," I conceded. "Especially Socrates. He led the way to Axis."

Jonathan and I both got jostled as the rottweilers tried to crowd into the kitchen with us. Socrates ambled off, but Axis and Artie wagged their tails, happy for the company.

"I guess I'll be adding Axis to the pack for a while," I noted, reaching down to stroke the Lab's silky ears. "Poor, homeless orphan."

I thought Jonathan was going to ignore my hint and the way I'd stuck out my lower lip to emphasize Axis's plight. For a long moment, he didn't say anything.

Then he exhaled loudly. "All right. I will take Axis . . . for a while."

I could hardly believe my ears. "Really?"

"Yes. But only because you are obviously overwhelmed right now."

I wasn't, really, but I said, "Thanks so much. I am stretched to the limit with the rottweilers—and Artie. Who is also technically homeless."

Jonathan hesitated even longer than before. Then he bent down and picked up Artie, who'd seated himself on Jonathan's shoe. "Fine. I will take this thing, too—again, temporarily. And only because dogs need a pack, and he seems to get along with Axis."

I really, really wanted to hug Jonathan, but I restrained myself. I didn't want to risk messing up Axis's, and especially Artie's, adoption.

I didn't care what Jonathan said. Those dogs were going to live with him permanently. Someday he might even admit that he loved them.

"Come on, you two," Jonathan said, summoning Axis with just a look. The Lab followed him to the door.

As they left the cottage, Socrates deigned to woof a good-bye to the first canine friend he'd ever made.

Artie squirmed so he could look over Jonathan's shoulder. The Chihuahua's big eyes gleamed with happiness, and a string of drool dripped onto Jonathan's shirt.

I was sure Jonathan would learn to love that, too. Eventually.

Chapter 76

"Here's to Daphne solving two crimes," Moxie said, raising a glass of red wine. "Just like Julie Barnes on *The Mod Squad*!"

Moxie's affection for vintage things wasn't restricted to clothing. She rarely watched TV shows produced after 1975. I was pretty sure I could picture the character she'd just referenced, though. She'd been played by a young, hip, and very bohemian Peggy Lipton.

Finally, someone had aptly compared me to a fictional sleuth, unlike certain men who'd likened me to Nancy Drew and, heaven forbid, Miss Marple.

"Thank you, Moxie," I said, raising my glass, too. "And don't forget that Socrates, Artie, and the rottweilers helped, too."

Piper and my mother, who'd joined us at Franco's, also lifted their merlots. "To Daphne and the dogs," they agreed in unison, but without much enthusiasm.

"I'm just glad you didn't get killed," Mom said in a tone drier than the wine, which was pretty dry. She lowered her glass. "I still don't understand why you were wandering around the woods in the rain."

"It was barely drizzling. . . ." I stopped myself before I got stuck arguing a point that had nothing to do with the larger story. I slid lower in the booth. "Oh, never mind."

"I know that I keep saying this, but I can't believe Mr. Peachy could commit murder," Piper murmured, fidgeting with the stem of her wineglass. "He always seemed like such a nice man. Conscientious, reliable, polite . . ."

"And profoundly lonely, to the point of being desperate and disturbed," I reminded her, sitting up straighter again. "Mr. Peachy really considered Angela Flinchbaugh—and then you—family, Piper. He honestly believed he was avenging Angela's death by killing Steve. An eye for an eye. And he hated the way Steve treated you, too. When Mr. Peachy thought Steve was going to string you along again . . ." That was sort of insulting to Piper, and I gave her an apologetic glance before adding, "He snapped."

"Perhaps the first murder was a rash act committed by an unstable individual," Mom conceded, quickly clarifying, "Not that his actions can be justified or excused!"

For once, I agreed with my mother, who also pointed out, "But your Mr. Peachy calmly and deliberately *silenced* Virginia Lockhart, and he was fully prepared to do the same to you, Daphne."

"Yeah, he was rational enough to want to save his own skin," Moxie agreed, sprinkling Parmesan onto a big plate of lobster ravioli. "He wasn't acting on impulse when he cornered you in his cottage!"

No, Mr. Peachy hadn't been swept up in a moment of rage when he'd stood before me with that hammer in his hand and a strange gleam in his eyes. . . .

I shook off the memory and was grateful when the conversation shifted in a slightly different direction.

"Looking back, I also can't believe what a fool I was about Steve," Piper grumbled, picking at her pasta. We were both having the night's special, which was linguini in a basil-infused cream sauce, topped with roasted zucchini and toasted almonds. "That whole relationship—if I can even call it that—was a mistake from the start. And to make matters worse, other people got dragged into the mess."

"*I* initially considered Steve a good prospect," Mom said, sympathizing, as she neatly sliced her fork through the balsamic-glazed salmon she'd ordered from the few light selections on the pasta-heavy menu. "Like you, Steve was a successful professional with a well-respected business. You two seemed like a good match!"

Once again, my mother was talking as if romantic relationships should be built upon compatible accomplishments and property ownership, while I knew that Piper, for once, had followed the whims of her heart. Unfortunately, those whims had dragged her in the wrong direction.

Moxie also understood that my sister had simply lost her oh-so-rational head for a while. "Every girl falls for the wrong guy at some point in her life," she said, with a wave of her hand. "You shouldn't beat yourself up!"

Piper didn't appear comforted. "I also feel partially responsible for Virginia's death," she said glumly. "She was on my property."

"Virginia was just in the wrong place at the wrong time," I assured my sister. "That is not your fault."

Piper's shoulders remained slumped, and my mother, sitting next to her, reached over to squeeze her favorite daughter's wrist. "Please don't blame yourself for anything that horrible man did, dear." Mom withdrew her hand and turned to me, her mouth drawn oh so slightly down at the corners. "I recently tried to warn Daphne about the dangers of hiring drifters with no roots in Sylvan Creek. But she refused to listen."

First of all, Mr. Peachy wasn't exactly a "drifter." He'd been in Sylvan Creek since before Angela Flinchbaugh's death, which had occurred over a decade ago. And how had his actions become my fault? *I* hadn't hired him. Once again, though, there was no sense in arguing. Henceforth, I would be the irresponsible child who'd allowed a murderer to live in our midst.

Still, I couldn't help reminding Mom, "Remember how this conversation started? With you all toasting me for *solving two murders . . . ?*"

But my mother was holding up one finger, silencing me, because her cell phone was ringing softly in the Stella McCartney bag that rested on the booth, next to her hip.

As the rest of us ate in silence, she pulled her cell out of the depths of the bag and answered in her firm but pleasant professional voice. "Hello. Maeve Templeton speaking."

A moment later, my mother actually *smiled*, earning two puzzled frowns from Piper and me. "Excellent," Mom said. "I will tell Detective Black right away." Then she ended the call without a good-bye and slipped the phone back into her bag, still smiling like a cat who'd gorged on canary, although I hadn't seen her take more than two bites of her salmon.

"What was that about?" Piper inquired, right before I asked the same question.

Moxie, not surprisingly, had latched onto a name that had also caught my attention. She leaned forward, itching for news. "And what do you need to tell Detective Black?"

"I *finally* sold Jonathan Black a house," Mom informed us, getting her grin under control before any permanent damage could be done. She slid to the edge of the booth, like she was leaving. "His offer was accepted, and I *must* go give him the news in person. I am sure he will be happy to know that a search I sometimes found extremely vexing has come to an end."

I could've told Mom that Jonathan had also been "vexed," but I didn't want to burst her bubble. Instead, I pushed aside my empty plate, asking, "What house? Where is it?"

Mom lifted her chin so we would all understand that she didn't exactly approve of the purchase. "He is buying Steve Beamus's property—although I cautioned against it." Upon rising, she carefully folded her cloth napkin, set that on the table, then smoothed her dark pencil skirt. "He is a very stubborn man, though!"

I dropped my fork. It clattered against my plate. "Did he tell you that *I* showed him that house? And convinced him to buy it?"

Mom stopped adjusting her wardrobe to give me a skeptical look. "No, he did not mention that, and I very much doubt that it happened."

"It did." Mom clearly didn't believe me, and I appealed to Piper. "Tell her that I showed Jonathan the house!"

Piper also pushed her half-finished meal to the center of the table. "I told you, I have given up trying to figure out if you're a pet sitter, Realtor, detective—

not to mention friend, foe, or more than either of those things to Jonathan Black. And as for your relationship with Dylan . . ." My sister leaned back in the booth, rolled her eyes, and raised both her hands. "Please, just leave me out of this."

Piper's opinions, or lack thereof, didn't matter. Mom was sliding the strap of her bag up over her shoulder, clearly done with the discussion. And I felt less inclined to claim credit for the sale when she told our server, who'd approached the table, "Please, put this all on my professional tab."

Moxie wasn't afraid to risk losing a free meal. "How was this 'professional'?" she asked Mom. "All we talked about was murder and Piper's disastrous love life!"

"I took a *business* call," my mother explained, somewhat impatiently. She didn't like to have her sometimes dubious tax-related maneuvers called into question. "Hence, the meal was 'professional.'"

Then my mother swept off, presumably to celebrate with Jonathan, while I ordered some plain beef tips for the dogs waiting at home. They had earned a special treat for helping to solve the mystery—and trying to save me—and Mom hadn't said we couldn't add to the tab. In fact, Moxie set aside her concerns about the legitimacy of the future write-off and ordered tiramisu *and* a crème brûlée topped with fresh raspberries.

When we were all finished and my doggie bag was in hand, Piper, Moxie, and I walked out into the humid summer night and parted ways on Sylvan Creek's main street.

Although it was nearly nine o'clock, Piper, not surprisingly, returned to her practice to balance her own books, which I knew would stand up to the closest IRS scrutiny. Moxie, meanwhile, adjusted a pillbox hat on her spiked hair and headed to the restored 1920s Bijoux Theater, where the glowing art deco marquee that jutted out over Market Street advertised a late showing of Moxie's absolute favorite film, the 1959 Doris Day–Rock Hudson comedy *Pillow Talk.*

Although Moxie'd invited me to tag along, I'd declined on the grounds that I needed to get the beef tips home, and because she'd forced me to watch that film at least a dozen times. Plus, I was starting to get tired after a day of solving crime—and nearly getting killed.

Hauling open the squeaky driver's side door of my VW, which was parked just across the street from where Steve Beamus had helped me corral the rotties a few hours before his death, I paused to look around the town, which was peaceful that evening. A soft breeze rustled the leaves on the trees that lined the street; Sylvan Creek's distinctive streetlamps glowed against a hazy sky; and cicadas trilled softly, heralding the imminent end of summer. It was hard to believe that anything bad had happened that day, and I finally realized just how fortunate I was to be alive. The reality hadn't quite sunk in until that moment, when I was alone with time to think.

"I believe that I am done solving crimes," I said quietly, to no one in particular. "I think I've learned my lesson about 'meddling' in Detective Black's, or anyone else's, cases."

And yet as I hopped up behind the steering wheel, bouncing on the seat's sprung springs, I couldn't help feeling a lingering sense of accomplishment to have helped solve the puzzle of Steve and Virginia's murders.

Then I stuck the key in the ignition, twisted it, and

heard the welcome sound of an old engine sputtering to life.

Backing out of the parking spot and driving toward Winding Hill, I felt fairly confident that two dollars' worth of gas, and some good karma, would get me home.

Recipes

Making your own meals and treats for your four-legged friends is actually very easy, and it's a good way to make sure the food you're giving them is nutritious and healthy. Best of all, dogs are easy to please. They seldom turn up their noses when offered something tasty.

Well, Socrates sometimes turns up his nose. He is especially particular about dairy products and will eat only a locally made Greek yogurt available Wednesdays at Sylvan Creek's farmers' market. But he's the exception.

Bone Appetit Ham-and-Cheese Muffins

These are good for breakfast. Or if you bake them in cute cupcake liners, they are perfect for a favorite furry pal's birthday party, too. Also, feel free to substitute your pup's favorite cheese for the cheddar. And add a little more, if you're inclined. Never enough cheese, right?

Ingredients

    12 liners for a muffin tin
    2 strips uncooked bacon
    5 cups rolled oats
    2 slices deli ham, finely chopped
    ¼ cup (or a bit more!) shredded cheddar
        cheese
    ¼ cup honey

1. Preheat your oven to 375°F and place the liners in the wells of a muffin tin.

2. Cook the bacon until crispy, using your preferred method. I like to use a skillet, but if you have one of those microwave trays, that would work, too. Drain the bacon, and then chop it or break it into small pieces.

3. Combine the oats, bacon pieces, ham, cheese, and honey in a large bowl and mix thoroughly. (If the mixture isn't holding together well, you can add a tiny bit more honey.)

4. Scoop the mixture into the liners in the prepared muffin tin, filling each one almost to the top.

5. Bake the muffins for about 20 minutes. You'll know they're done when the tops get a little crispy.

6. Make sure to cool the muffins thoroughly before serving them to the dogs, who will probably be eagerly sniffing around you. Nobody likes a burnt tongue!

Makes 12 muffins

Banana-Apple Pupcakes

Have you ever felt guilty about whipping up a stack of pancakes while your dog sits at your feet, drooling hopefully? Because who doesn't love pancakes? Unfortunately, dogs don't need extra sugar in their diets and usually get shut out of the feast. This sweet but sugar-free recipe is Socrates's absolute favorite. He likes the tang the buttermilk adds, but if you don't have any on hand—and let's face it, most people probably don't—just double the amount of regular milk.

Ingredients

  2 large eggs
  ½ cup whole milk
  ½ cup buttermilk
  1 tablespoon honey
  1 cup whole-wheat flour
  ½ cup all-purpose flour
  1 teaspoon baking powder
  ½ cup mashed bananas, plus ½ cup for topping
    (optional)
  ½ cup diced apples, plus ½ cup for topping
    (optional)
  Cooking spray, for greasing the griddle
  ½ cup plain yogurt (optional)

1. Heat up a griddle or a large skillet.

2. Whisk together the eggs, milk, buttermilk, and honey in a medium bowl.

3. Carefully add the whole-wheat flour, the all-purpose flour, and the baking powder to the egg-milk mixture, doing your best not to make a mess.

4. Take a moment to clean up the mess.

5. Fold the bananas and apples into the egg-flour mixture.

6. Spritz your skillet or griddle with the cooking spray. Next, spoon 2 to 3 tablespoons of the batter at a time onto the hot surface, forming pupcakes.*

7. Cook until the tops of your pupcakes get bubbly, and then flip and cook them another 2 minutes or so, being careful not to burn them. When both sides are light golden brown, they're done.

8. Allow the pupcakes to cool. Then serve them topped with extra diced apples and mashed bananas, if desired. A dollop of yogurt is nice, too.

Makes about 10 pupcakes, depending upon size

*If you are a perfectionist like Piper, you can make cute bone shapes by pouring the batter into cookie cutters placed on the griddle or skillet. And if you're *really* clever, you can form the bones freehand with a piping bag. Although she didn't do a great job painting my van, artistic Moxie is pretty good at free-forming pupcake batter.

PowerPup Breakfast

I'm calling this a breakfast, but it's great to serve at any meal. It's full of nutrients. If you have the time or inclination, make the chicken stock yourself. It's even healthier that way. You can also adjust this recipe to make bigger quantities and freeze portions in plastic bags. It really makes sense. If you're going to the trouble of cooking chicken, beef, and barley, you might as well make a lot.

Ingredients

2 chicken thighs
1 cup barley
½ pound lean ground beef
2 large carrots, peeled
2 apples, unpeeled
1 small head broccoli
1 cup chopped fresh spinach
One 15-ounce can pumpkin puree
1 cup chicken stock

1. Arrange the chicken in a medium-size pot, and cover with water. Bring the chicken to a boil over medium heat, and then lower the heat and simmer until cooked through, about 25 minutes. Remove the chicken from the pot and set it aside to cool.

2. Meanwhile, in a separate medium-size pot, combine the barley and 3 cups water, and bring to a boil over medium heat. Reduce the heat, cover, and simmer for approximately 40 minutes, or until the grains are soft but chewy. (Make sure to check the barley as it's cooking. You may need to add more water if the pot gets dry.) Drain, if necessary, and allow to cool.

3. While the barley is cooking, fry the ground beef in a small pan over medium heat until it is fully cooked and crumbly, about 12 minutes. Drain off any fat and allow the meat to cool.

4. Slice up the carrots, apples, broccoli, and spinach enough to fit in a food processor. Process everything together until the mixture is roughly chopped.

5. Next, take the meat off the bones of the cooled chicken and chop it up. Discard the bones.

6. Mix together the chicken, beef, barley, and veggies in a large bowl. Using a ¼ cup measuring cup, slowly and alternately add the pumpkin and the stock to the chicken mixture, being careful not to make a mush. The mixture should be moist but have texture. You can freeze any extra pumpkin and stock for the next time. The proportions do vary sometimes, based upon things like how well the barley is cooked, how big the apples were, and so on. Use your judgment.

7. Place your dog's usual portion size of the mixture in a bowl, set that on the floor, and give your favorite pup the go-ahead to dig in. Save any leftovers in the fridge for up to four days or freeze unused portions.

Makes about 8 cups

Sweet Potato Puppy Crunchers and Tuxedo Popcorn

Once each summer, the folks who organize the Pettigrew Park outdoor film series show a pet-friendly flick. This year's movie was—happily—*Beverly Hills Chihuahua*. Of course, I had to take Artie—and Socrates and Moxie tagged along, too, although Socrates prefers film noir. Needless to say, Artie loved the movie. And both dogs and people enjoyed their respective snacks. (Don't let dogs try the popcorn. Chocolate is toxic to them!)

Sweet Potato Puppy Crunchers

Ingredients

    Parchment paper for lining 2 baking sheets
    ¾ cup mashed sweet potatoes
    3 tablespoons chicken broth
    2 cups whole wheat flour
    ½ cup cornmeal
    ½ cup dried cranberries

1. Preheat your oven to 325°F and line two baking sheets with the parchment paper.

2. Mix together the sweet potatoes and the broth in a large bowl. Then add the flour, cornmeal, and cranberries, and stir until everything is well combined and a dough has formed. (At some point, you'll probably want to squish everything together with your hands to form the dough.)

3. Turn the dough out onto a floured surface and roll it out until it's about ¼ inch thick. Either cut it into small squares with a knife or use decorative cookie cutters to form shapes.

4. Arrange the dough squares or shapes on the prepared baking sheets. Bake for about 40 minutes, or until the treats are golden brown on the bottom. Then turn off the oven, leave the oven door open just slightly, and allow the treats to dry out and cool for about 2 hours. Be patient, because that's when they get the crunch.

Tuxedo Popcorn

Ingredients

1 cup pecan halves
10 cups popped popcorn (aka "a big bowlful")
¼ cup salted butter
¾ cup dark chocolate chips
¾ cup white chocolate chips

1. Heat a small nonstick pan over medium heat, add the pecans, and carefully toast them, stirring frequently so they don't burn.

2. In a large bowl, mix together the popcorn and the toasted pecans.

3. Melt the butter in the microwave, drizzle it over the popcorn mixture, and stir everything around with a large spoon. Spread the mixture out on a cookie sheet.

4. Place the dark chocolate chips in a small microwave-safe bowl. Melt the chocolate chips in the micro-

wave. Start at 70 percent power for 1 minute, and then stir the melting chocolate. Repeat this procedure, but at 15-second intervals, until the chocolate is smooth.

5. Drizzle the chocolate over the popcorn mixture.

6. Repeat steps 4 and 5 with the white chocolate chips.

7. Try to allow the Tuxedo Popcorn to cool long enough for the chocolate to harden before returning it to a bowl and serving. But, let's face it, you're going to try some right away, and most of it will be gone before the movie even starts.

Makes 11½ cups

Keep reading for a preview of the next
Lucky Paws Pet-sitting Mystery,
starring Daphne Templeton, Ph.D.,
and Socrates, her long-suffering basset hound . . .

DIAL MEOW FOR MURDER
by
Bethany Blake

"When murder is unleashed in the idyllic town of
Sylvan Creek, it's up to spunky pet sitter Daphne and
her darling duo of misfit mutts to catch the killer.
A doggone charming read from start to finish!"

—Cleo Coyle, *New York Times* bestselling author

For more information about *Dial Meow for Murder*
by Bethany Blake go to
http://www.kensingtonbooks.com

Chapter 1

The Flynt Mansion sat high upon a hill just outside Sylvan Creek, Pennsylvania, its twin turrets stabbing at a huge October moon that was obscured, now and then, by passing dark clouds. Local legend said the sprawling Victorian house, which overlooked Lake Wallapawakee, was haunted, but the evening of the Fur-ever Friends Pet Rescue gala fund-raiser, the place was spirited in a different way.

"This is so cool," my best friend Moxie Bloom said, as we passed through tall iron gates that had concealed most of the property from the road. The gates clanged shut behind us, and I jumped, nearly dropping a big, plastic tub full of pet treats I'd cooked up for the party, which would support my favorite local charity. "Wow," Moxie added. "It's spooky gorgeous."

I had to agree. The curving stone pathway that led to the house was lined with at least fifty glowing jack o'lanterns, their flickering faces carved into leering grins, grimaces of agony, and threatening scowls. The twisted branches of the property's many crabapple trees were strung with twinkle lights, while three ornate, black-iron chandeliers—each holding at least

twenty candles—were suspended from the sturdier
oaks, so the grounds were bathed in a soft, mysterious
light. More grim-faced jack o'lanterns were propped
on the railing that surrounded the house's wrap-
around porch. It looked like the pumpkins were
guarding the mansion, which was dark inside, with the
exception of single, lit candles that burned in each of
the many tall, narrow windows.

The estate was already movie-set eerie, but the Fur-
ever Friends decorating committee—chaired by my
perfectionist sister, Piper Templeton—wasn't finished
yet. A few people still bustled around the grounds,
setting up chairs and lighting even more candles.

Standing just inside the fence with Moxie and my
canine sidekick, Socrates, I took a moment to drink in
the scene. Then I frowned and turned to Moxie.
"Umm . . . Why are we the only people in costumes?"

"I'm not wearing a costume," Moxie said, sounding confused. She looked uncharacteristically demure
in a vintage, mint-green wool suit with a high-collared
jacket and a pencil skirt that hit mid-calf. A string of
pearls circled her neck, and she'd dyed her hair from
flame-red to a soft blond. "Why would you think *that*?"

"I thought you were Tippi Hedren, from *The Birds*."
I resumed watching the volunteers, most of whom
wore sweaters and sweatshirts, then I adjusted a tall,
pointed hat that kept slipping off my long, unruly,
dirty-blond curls. I didn't see one other witch, not to
mention any ghosts or ghouls, and I started getting a
little sweaty under my polyester cape. "I'm the only
person who dressed up!" I glanced down at Socrates,
taking some comfort in the fact that he was also in
costume—only to discover that he looked like he always

did: like a contemplative, sometimes morose, basset hound. "Where is your wizard hat?"

"Didn't you see that fly out the window of the van, halfway up the hill?" Moxie asked, answering on behalf of Socrates, who was pretending he hadn't heard me. He was staring straight ahead. However, I noticed that the very tip of his tail was twitching the way it did when he felt guilty. "I assumed you noticed," Moxie continued, "and just didn't want to turn around, because we were running late."

I'd heard Socrates shuffling around in the backseat of my distinctive 1970s, pink VW bus, which advertised my business, Lucky Paws Pet Sitting—and featured a large, hand-painted dog that was often mistaken for a misshapen pony. I'd thought he was cranky about losing the front seat to Moxie, and I'd ignored him.

"I should've known you'd never really wear the hat," I complained to Socrates, who had started snuffling. The sound was very reminiscent of a snicker. "You were far too agreeable about putting it on. I should've known something was up."

Socrates finally looked up at me and blinked his droopy, brown eyes, as if to say, *"Indeed, you should have known that I would never deign to don a costume."*

"Maybe I should go home and change," I said, starting to turn around.

"You're not going anywhere," my sister called, hurrying across the lawn. She took the tub of snacks from me, like she couldn't wait one more minute to get her hands on it. "You're a half-hour late! There's no time for you to return to Winding Hill, change clothes, and come back before the gala starts."

Of course, she was right. It would take me at least twenty minutes to drive to Winding Hill Farm, where

Piper—a successful veterinarian—let me live rent-free in her gorgeous, restored, 1860s farmhouse. Well, actually, I was moving into a cottage on the property. The adorable, tiny house had recently become available when the former tenant, Winding Hill's caretaker, was arrested for the murder of Piper's ex-boyfriend. I'd solved the crime—not that anyone would give me credit.

"This is Fur-ever Friends's biggest fund-raiser of the year," Piper added. "People—and pets—will start arriving in less than an hour. You need to set up the snack table for the dogs . . ." She finally looked me up and down. "No matter how silly you look." Then she turned to Moxie and knitted her brows. "And who are you supposed to be? Tippi Hedren?"

Moxie's cheeks flushed, just slightly. "It's more of an *homage* than a costume," she said, lifting her chin high. "The woman was Hitchcock's muse. An icon!"

She *was* in costume. I'd known it.

"What happened to *you*?" I asked, thinking Piper was being a little judgmental for someone whose blouse was soaking wet.

My sister brushed ineffectually at a dark stain on her sleeve. "Pastor Kishbaugh and I were trying to move the apple bobbing tub. Water sloshed everywhere."

I located Pastor Pete Kishbaugh, who was across the lawn, attaching fake ravens to the branches of a crabapple. If he was also soggy, his black shirt hid the problem.

"All three of you, come with me now," Piper added, leading the way down the path. Temporary stain aside, she was dressed appropriately in dark slacks and a rust-colored top that hinted at fall, but didn't scream

"Halloween," like my getup. Her straight, shiny brown hair—the polar opposite of the chaos on my head—was smoothed back and held in place with a pretty peach-and-brown patterned headband. "There's still plenty to do before the guests show up," she informed Moxie and me, over her shoulder. "Let's go."

We all followed Piper, who lugged the plastic bin, while I tried to keep a grip on the billowing fabric of my cape, which kept getting perilously close to the gauntlet of jack o'lanterns. The last thing I needed was to make a bigger spectacle of myself by *catching on fire*. The tag on the cape had warned that the fabric wasn't flame retardant.

"This is where you'll set up," Piper said, stopping in front of a table with a placard that advertised *Howling Good Dog Treats*, in a spooky, drippy script. The tabletop was already decorated with two life-size ceramic black cats, their backs arched high and their tails sticking straight up. Cute orange-and-black platters featured similar hissing felines, in a vintage design. The table was also scattered with dog-appropriate bones, all real and available for the munching. Piper set the bin on the grass. "As you can see, I did most of the work, in your absence."

"Why are you so cranky?" I asked, because Piper—always Type A—was even more tense than usual. "This is supposed to be fun."

All at once, my sister's shoulders slumped. "I'm sorry. I'm just worried because Lillian Flynt, who is supposed to be hosting this event, is nowhere to be found. I've somehow ended up in charge of the whole thing. And to make matters worse, the power is out in the house, for some reason. These candles aren't all just for show."

"Miss Flynt isn't here?" Moxie asked, looking around, like she might locate the older woman who was semi-affectionately known as Sylvan Creek's "professional volunteer."

Gray-haired, never-married heiress Lillian didn't lack for money, so she'd made charity her life's work. The local *Weekly Gazette*'s "About Town" society column almost always featured at least one photo of Miss Flynt in her signature knit cardigan, doing good things for others. One day, she'd be pictured delivering meals to folks even more elderly than she was, and the next, she'd be accepting an oversize grant check on behalf of the public library or ladling stew at a church soup kitchen. But while Lillian might have appeared kind and grandmotherly, she had a spine of steel. I'd worked with her quite a bit, on behalf of Fur-ever Friends, and she always acted like she was my boss, and I was an intern.

As I bent to open the bin, I flashed back to the day she'd approached me about "volunteering" for the gala.

"You are aware of the upcoming Fur-ever Friends party, correct, Daphne?" Miss Flynt had said, stopping me on Sylvan Creek's main street by slamming a cane in my path. She couldn't have been more than sixty-five, and she was probably in better shape than me, so I didn't think she needed the stick for support. I was pretty sure it was a tool to keep others in line.

"Yeah, I know about it," I'd told her. Then I'd cut right to the chase. *"What do you need?"*

"Treats for at least twenty dogs. From your pet bakery."

She always acted like I had a storefront, and I always corrected her. *"Um, I just cook for fun, at home. I don't really have a bakery. . . ."*

Miss Flynt had answered the way she always did. *"Well, get to it, Daphne! What are you waiting for?"* Then she'd nodded briskly to Socrates, nearly dislodging her wiry, gray hair from its bun. *"Good day to you, wise Socrates!"*

A few moments later, Miss Flynt had moved on down the street, and I'd stood there with Socrates, both of us needing a second, as usual, to recover from the very direct, almost curt, exchange. Yet, I admired Miss Flynt. She had a different approach from me, but she was a big supporter of Fur-ever Friends.

"It is odd that she's not here micromanaging," I told Piper, as I removed containers of homemade goodies from the bin. Prying the lid off one tub, I began to place Tricky Treats on a platter. The snacks were "tricky" because they looked and tasted like peanut butter cups, but I'd substituted dog-friendly carob for the chocolate, which could be lethal to canines. "Where do you think she is?"

"I have no idea," Piper said. "And, as if things aren't bad enough, when Tamara Fox went into the house to get some matches, she accidentally let Lillian's prized Persian cat, Tinkleston, run out the door. Now we can't find him."

Moxie and I shared a look, then we both started snickering.

"What is so funny about a missing cat?" Piper demanded. "Especially since I'm sure I'll get blamed for his disappearance."

"I'm sorry," I said, slipping Socrates a Tricky Treat. He feigned disdain for a few moments, then accepted the sweet from my fingers. "But what kind of name is 'Tinkleston'?"

"It's a horrible name for a horrible cat."

We all turned to realize that we'd been joined by none other than Tamara Fox, who made a mock shudder, so I got the impression that she wasn't upset about the feline's disappearance.

Tamara—whom we'd all known since high school—didn't bother to really greet us. Kind of like she'd snubbed us back in school, too. Tossing her long, dark hair over her shoulder, she gave Moxie and me a skeptical once-over, then didn't ask about the costumes, either. It was almost like she assumed we'd misread—or lost—our invitations, like I had done.

In my defense, though, who *wouldn't* assume that a "gala" held in late October at a *haunted mansion* would at least be costume optional?

"Have you seen the cat?" Piper asked Tamara. "I'm dreading telling Lillian that he's gone."

"I hope I never see that beast again," Tamara said. She adjusted a large tote that was slung over her shoulder, and her adorable little Maltese, Buttons, poked her beribboned head out just long enough to blink. Then she disappeared back into the bag, like something was spooking her. "I swear that cat was stalking Buttons and me, the whole time we were inside."

"Most people think cats are aloof, but they actually like company," I told Tamara. I felt like I had some authority on the subject, since I was a professional pet care expert. "He was probably just lonely in that big, dark house and wanted to be friends."

Tamara shot me a dark look that said she wasn't interested in my credentials or my opinions. "There's nothing friendly about that animal. It's evil."

Giving her hair one more dramatic toss with a hand smothered under heavy rings, Tamara took her leave of us without another word. We all watched her sashay off with the same hip-swaying stride she'd had back in her cheerleading days. Soon after graduation, she'd surprised all of Sylvan Creek by marrying much, much older—and very, very wealthy—attorney Larry Fox. Tamara hadn't worked a day in her life and was considered heiress-apparent to Lillian's informal title of "professional volunteer." On days Lillian wasn't in the *Gazette*, Tamara could usually be found smiling for the camera.

"What does she have against cats?" asked Moxie, who had a wide-eyed kitten tattooed on her wrist. "They're adorable!"

"Actually, Tinkleston—nee Budgely's Sir Peridot Tinkleston—is a difficult animal, to put it mildly," Piper informed us. "I've had to give him shots, and I have the scars to prove it."

I didn't think it was fair to judge a cat based upon his behavior while getting stuck with a needle, but I didn't mention that to Piper.

"We'll keep an eye out for the runaway—and finish setting up the table," I promised, waving my fingers to dismiss my sister. "You go oversee everybody else."

"Okay, thanks," Piper said. "I actually need to track down an old CD player Miss Flynt promised we could use to play spooky music. That thing's missing, too." My sister eyed the table warily as she backed away. "You two do a nice job, okay?"

I didn't dignify that with a response. I just started arranging Batty-for-Pumpkin Cookies on a plate—a task that absorbed me until Moxie tapped my shoulder.

"Hey, look," she said. "Somebody else dressed up, as a priest!"

"That's not a costume," I corrected Moxie. "That's Pastor Pete Kishbaugh, the guy Piper was just talking about. He always wears a black shirt and a clerical collar. Don't you know him?"

"No," she said. "He's completely bald. How would I know him?"

Moxie was the owner of Spa and Paw, Sylvan Creek's unique salon, which catered to people and pets. She seldom met anyone who didn't have hair. Or fur.

"He's kind of cute," Moxie noted. "Some guys can pull off the shaved head."

"He's also involved in a scandal right now," I whispered. "You've probably heard the rumors about his church, Lighthouse Fellowship." Moxie might not have recognized Pastor Pete, but she was the motor that turned Sylvan Creek's busy gossip mill, and I knew she'd at least be familiar with the *stories* surrounding him. "I don't know the details, but I heard something about embezzlement, or misappropriated funds."

"Oh, he's *that* minister?" Moxie mused, just as Pastor Pete—thirty-something, with a gleaming white smile and kind eyes—noticed me and waved. I sometimes watched his golden retriever mix, Blessing, while Pete was on mission trips. He was a very peripatetic man of the cloth. "Yeah, I've heard about that mess," Moxie added. "That's probably going to be fall's big story. I can just tell."

Feeling guilty, because the subject of our discussion was still smiling at us, I told Moxie, "You know, Socrates—the logician, not the dog . . ." I often quoted the ancient Greek scholar, who'd been central to my doctoral dissertation, so I was always making that clarification. ". . . Socrates once said, 'Strong minds discuss ideas'—not people. I kind of wish I hadn't even brought up the rumors."

Moxie waved off my concerns with a gloved hand.

Why had I believed, for a minute, that she wasn't in costume?

"I've seen pictures of that old philosopher," she informed me. "He could've used a haircut. And I bet he would've dished on Plato for hours, if he sat in my chair."

At my side, the canine Socrates was rolling his baleful eyes, like he disagreed. At least, it appeared that way. Or maybe he was just sniffing the air, which smelled wonderful. The night was crisp and the breeze off the lake was fresh, but tinged with the bittersweet aroma of falling leaves. Somewhere inside the mansion, a fire was burning in a fireplace, too. The smoke, coiling from the chimney, gave the air a distinctly autumnal tang. Raising my slightly upturned nose, I sniffed, too, and I was pretty sure I could also identify the scents of apple cider, cinnamon, and pumpkin.

"Do you think we could take a little break and wander over to the table with the people food?" I asked Moxie. I glanced at my bin of treats, which was still pretty full, while the waiting trays were mostly empty. "We wouldn't be gone long."

"I could go for something sweet," Moxie agreed. She was already heading across the lawn. Passing under a crabapple tree, she ducked and placed a protective hand on her blond bouffant while warily eyeing one of the ravens Pastor Pete had wired to a branch. Then she called back to me, "I'm pretty sure I see cookies for humans."

What could I do but follow, with Socrates in my wake?

"You know, I'm actually surprised Lillian threw this shindig," I said, when we reached another table that was completely stocked with an array of very clever treats, including meringue ghosts, chocolate cookie "spiders" with licorice legs, and cheese sticks decorated to look like severed fingers, with almond-sliver fingernails and marinara-sauce blood. That was sort of

gross, but I took one, anyhow, adding, "I know Miss
Flynt loves animals, but I can't recall her ever opening
her house up for a party."

"She doesn't love all animals!"

Both Moxie and I started at the sound of an indig-
nant, almost angry, voice, right behind us.

"Hey, Mrs. Baumgartner," I said, taking a step backward and greeting the head of the local cats-only
shelter, Whiskered Away Home. Bea was also active
with Fur-ever Friends, and carried a plastic-wrapped
plate. "We didn't see you there."

Now that Beatrice Baumgartner was upwind, I
could *smell* her. She carried the faint odor of a litter
box that needed emptied. I didn't understand that. I'd
worked in lots of homes with multiple cats, and that
smell was avoidable. It kind of put me off my cheese
finger, and I had no intention of trying one of the
chocolate-chip cookies she was unveiling from under
a crinkled sheet of plastic, either.

Moxie's nose was wrinkling, too, but she wasn't dis-
suaded from eating the meringue ghost she'd chosen.
"Miss Flynt loves stray dogs, and she must love cats,
too," she said, pausing to bite off the specter's head.
"We were just talking about Tinkleston, who is supposedly on the loose."

For a woman dedicated to saving felines, Bea didn't
seem overly concerned about a missing prize Persian.

"Lilllian is no friend to cats—except *purebred* show
animals," she said, crossing her arms over an ample
bosom. She had to be in her late sixties, and, while I
was definitely the least appropriately dressed person at
that party, Bea wasn't exactly up-to-code, either. She
wore stained khaki pants that I was pretty sure came
from the men's department and a frayed sweatshirt
that featured an applique of a black kitten sitting

inside a pumpkin. I supposed I could at least give her credit for making an effort to honor the holiday. The expression on her deeply lined face was also suitably scary. "I am positive that Lillian only agreed to host this fund-raiser to get herself noticed by the media— again."

I wasn't sure I'd call the *Weekly Gazette* "media." It was delivered free, whether anyone wanted it or not, and it only reached about two hundred homes. As I made my pet-sitting rounds, I found a lot of copies on floors in houses where dogs were being house trained. However, I didn't argue that point with Bea, who was excusing herself, anyway. She nodded at me, Moxie, and Socrates. "Enjoy the party."

"Well, that was awkward," Moxie observed, when Bea was out of earshot. All at once, her eyes gleamed. "And while we're on the subject of uncomfortable situations, what are you going to do if Dylan and Detective Black *both* show up tonight?"

She was referring to one guy I sometimes dated— and another I hadn't seen since I'd *solved a murder* for him, after numerous clashes.

I really didn't want to discuss either of those men.

I was also suddenly distracted by something I could see inside the mansion, over Moxie's shoulder.

A shadowy figure, who stood at one of the tall windows, observing the party preparations from behind a curtain.

I blinked twice to make sure my eyes weren't playing tricks on me, then I got a funny, nervous feeling in the pit of my stomach.

What was that person doing *there?*

Grab These Cozy Mysteries
from
Kensington Books